Apex Familiar

Book Six of Freelance Familiars

Daniel Potter

FALLEN KITTEN PRODUCTIONS

For everyone who's joined me in the Familiar Freehold.
This one's for you.

I

THE MAN RESTED HIS elbow on the bar and scryed into the tarry amber of his fifteen-dollar whiskey with the intensity of a seer. While he peered into the past, I beheld the future of House Khatt: him and others like him. After stalking him for two hours I knew this was the moment, balanced on that edge of drunkenness where you felt sadness even more strongly than when sober. He had no idea that a mountain lion had singled him out from a herd of other gamblers as prey, watching him through the mirrored glass that paneled the back wall of the bar. The only thing saving him thus far had been the apex predator's cold paws.

"Go on, get on with it. Or you want me to do it?" spoke the high-pitched voice of Rudy, the squirrel, perched on top of the array of cameras that also watched this distant corner of the MGM Grand, a dark alcove furnished with rich wood and a sparsity of neon that offered at least the illusion of solace from the flashing lights of the casino floor.

I rumbled, but didn't give an articulate response. My friend was right; it was now or never with this one. I'd already let the last one slip. Lifting my forepaw, a thin band of force extended out from a thin chain that encircled my wrist. It curled around the doorknob to the right of the mirror and pushed it open. The bartender, a young spell dog, sucked in a breath through clenched teeth when he saw me step through the doorway to his stockroom. He nearly leapt at a patron, who was slurping at the ice in his glass through a stir straw. "Hey can I get you another drink?"

The lake of guilt I carried burbled at the spell dog's condition. One problem at a time, I told myself. Mountain lions, and hence I, work better with a single target in mind. Slinking around the bartender's legs without touching them, I made my way to the end of the bar where the man and his whiskey perched. Pawing a milk crate over, I stepped up onto it. Conversations with humans sitting at bars is always awkward as a 200-pound cat. When I sit on my haunches, my head doesn't quite reach the bar, but if I perch on a barstool, I'm towering over the humans next to me. A stack of two plastic milk crates, which had never touched a dairy product, worked as a happy medium so long as they didn't break under my weight. In the last eight months, I'd broken enough that it was happening less often. This pair creaked a bit, which led the man to look up from his drink and freeze.

Giving him a tight-lipped smile, my talking spell allowed for the easy mimicry of human expressions that feline facial muscles don't normally do. I greeted him. "Hello Jason, are you enjoying your stay?"

Jason glanced back down into his drink and scowled at me for not disappearing. The way his thick lips twisted in the blackness of his full beard made him a good scowler. When he realized that an expression wouldn't banish me, he spoke, "Iz fine. What do you want? Arn't talking cats are supposed to be bad news?"

"Oh? Who told you that?" I asked casually, although I heard a chitter from behind me. According to his records, Jason had been in the MGM five days now, long enough to comprehend that not everything in Vegas was a special effect and you stay out of the way of anyone with an unleashed pet. He might have even seen me before. I'm not very subtle. I wear a black harness with the word BOSS embroidered on either side in gold thread.

"Uuuh," He hesitated.

"Never mind. It's not important." I waved at the air with the back of my paw while chiding myself to stick to the script. "I represent an opportunity, a way to do what you came here for."

His laugh was more like a dry heave. "If this is some ploy to get me back at the blackjack tables, I've gotta tell you right now, I'm done."

"Come on, Jason. You're not drinking over the loss of a few grand. I want to buy your hurt." I placed a paw on the bar and groomed between the digits, listening to Jason shift uncomfortably.

"What do you mean? Buy my hurt. How do you know about Lilly?" The scent of his anxiety flooded the space between us.

"Facebook," I said, failing to conceal all my teeth with my smile as Jason swallowed. "I believe the post was, 'Fuck this. Fuck Lilly. I'm going to Vegas. I'm going to bury myself in booze and bitches. Gunna forget all about her!" I paused, watching his lips pucker with sourness. "How's that going for you?" Jason put both hands on the bar and gathered himself while I swallowed down a curse. The movies made this Faustian bargain bit look easy. Quickly, I grabbed a poker chip from a harness pocket and shoved it beneath my paw.

He opened his mouth to tell me off as I tilted my paw up to reveal the red poker chip studded with blue, five grand. The highest denomination Jason had likely seen during his brief flirtation with the higher stake blackjack table. His body paused.

I pushed it between us. "Just finish hearing me out."

That grade A scowl came back as he reached for the chip. I let him take it, turn it in his fingers. "I want to buy your connection to your ex-wife. You don't want it. Why not make a significant amount of money off it?"

He clutched the chip in his fist. If this were a movie that would indicate I had him, but people were more fickle than any narrative would have you think. I'd lost two other fish at this stage. "What do you mean, connection?" He croaked.

"There is a strand between you and your ex-wife. It is severed, pulsing and unrequited. Causing you intense pain. I am in need of such strands." I watched him carefully as I floated a few higher value chips up out of my pocket.

"What's the catch? What will happen to me?" He choked a little, whispering, "to her?"

"Not much. You'll remember it like a lecture in middle school. It happened, but there will be zero emotion, no pain. You will have moved on. That's what you're here for, right?" I inhaled and waited. Two others had walked away at this point. Although the last one was totally Rudy's fault. I resisted the urge to check behind me, afraid to see him pressed against the glass.

Jason looked down into his drink as if it were a magic eight ball. "How much?" He asked.

Had I real thumbs, this would have been the perfect moment to flip a high value poker chip. Instead, I floated up a stack of those five grand chips, twenty of them, and set them on the bar with that signature weighty clack. "You will wake up tomorrow, having had a wonderful day at the tables."

"I won't remember making this deal?" Jason's eyes locked on the chips.

"You will until you leave. What happens in Vegas stays in Vegas. That rule is way above even my pay grade. Your mind will fill in the hole with a suitable wild story like everybody else." From another pocket I pulled out a black leather folder about the size of an iPad, placed it in front of him and opened it. Therein lay a heavily textured piece of parchment with the contract laid out on it. A large red ebony pen lay next to it. The physical contract and pen had been Riona's idea, to make them feel important.

Jason made a show of reading the nearly incomprehensible swooping, cursive script before signing his name with a dramatic flourish.

"Yeah! Got him!" Rudy cheered from behind me. "Finally!"

Jason jolted, dropping the pen onto the bar. "What?!"

"And so the deal is sealed." I pronounced and closed the folder, narrowly pulling it back to myself before Rudy jumped up on the bar.

"So, on the scale of one to ten, how would you rate the conduction of your Deal of a Lifetime experience?" Rudy pulled off the iPhone from his back and braced it on the table. "At which point did you almost run screaming from the experience?"

"Rudy! Lay off. That's not funny," I growled.

"Hey, if this works, you're going to have to get much better at this; your success ratio is terrible. We should get feedback while it's fresh in his head." Rudy chittered with laughter.

I attempted to back-paw him off the bar, but I only got the phone. It tumbled back behind the bar. "Hey, watch it, nut brain! That's brand new." Rudy dived for his precious hardware.

Jason's face was the dictionary entry of regret. Fortunately, backup with more tact approached him from behind and tapped him on the shoulder. He spun and froze as the woman turned on a gigawatt smile, pearly whites framed by black lips.

"Hi! I'm Riona." She said with forceful cheer and swiftly captured Jason's hand while his brain was still trying to process her brightly colored fashion choices. The punky magus was deep in the eighties today, her long hair rocking multicolored jags and her body clad in black denim decorated with chrome spikes. Magi could be divided into two camps: those who were thrilled that magic could apply hours' worth of hair stylings and make up in minutes, and those who thought even that was way too much effort. Riona took a particular joy in playing with her appearance. "Pleased to meet you, Jason." She filled in the blanks for him as his brain attempted a reboot.

"Uhhhh. Yeah." He stuttered.

Eagerness shone in her eyes, and unfortunately for Jason, it had very little to do with him. She'd proven brilliant by proposing the theoretical possibilities of harvesting a powerful relationship, and tonight we'd find out if she'd been right. "Won't you please follow me and we'll get all those sads right out of you." Her voice went sickly sweet before turning to lead Jason away into the floor.

"See! I bet Riona would be much better than you at this," Rudy commented once Jason passed out of earshot. "Two cans of cashews say that she'd have gotten him to sign for five grand or less."

"It's my responsibility Rudy. If... harvesting things like this is something we have to do regularly, then we need to make sure it's at least somewhat fair."

"Oooooh, Serious Kitty is Seriously Serious," Rudy snickered.

With a huff I turned away from the bar, "I gotta go grab O'Meara; you going to come watch?"

"That depends; on a scale of one to ten, how likely is this going to result in pyrotechnics?" He jumped down onto my back.

"Hopefully zero?" I ventured as I walked behind the bartender with a nod and set off for my personal elevator near the casino's front entrance.

"That sounds like a ten to me!" Rudy said.

2

"HEY O-" I STOPPED my calling out to my magus, spotting her red-clad form as the door to my apartment slid open. While roughly in the same location I had left her in when I'd left to recruit Jason, on my black leather couch, her position had become decidedly horizontal. She snored lightly, head cradled on a plush white pillow; a thick leather-bound tome lay open on the coffee table.

My tail lashed with annoyance as I padded into the room. I hated it when she fell asleep on my couch. Without a mental link between us, waking her up was like poking the offspring of a grizzly bear and a porcupine with a stick: extremely hazardous. Usually, I'd let her finish her nap, but everyone would be waiting for us in the lab. I slunk around the coffee table to get a good look at her eyes. No movement beneath her eyelids. Good, no dreams. Careful to be gentle, I nuzzled the underside of her chin.

Her snoring stopped, and with a rumble midway between a grumble and a growl she brushed my muzzle away with the back of her hand.

I countered by delivering a little lap to the hand. "Come on, O'Meara, time to get this done. We're almost there."

Two thick arms snaked around my neck and crushed me to her soft bosom. "Do you know how long you have been saying that?" she asked into the top of my head.

"Uuuuh." I hesitated, providing any answer at this point would probably get me noogied. Her grip tightened, and she kissed my head. Good thing she fell asleep on the couch and not the bed. Her next move would usually be to drag me onto the mattress for enforced cuddles, but the couch barely had enough room for her, let alone an additional mountain lion. Instead, she rubbed her face in the fur between my ears, the sensation drawing a purr from my throat as I leaned into her.

She savored that little gesture of surrender a few moments longer. Confirmation that despite the lack of a mental link between us at that precise moment, I remained hers. Every time I lecture magi and familiars about the importance of choice in choosing their bond, I always feel a bit hypocritical because I feel so... owned in O'Meara's arms. To be sure, it's mutual ownership and to everyone else it's a partnership, but when we're alone it's always her hands around me or threading through my fur. A level of protective possession that says, *I love you and you are mine.* As more people address me first in public over O'Meara, I have to let her possess me a little more in private. Doubly so when I ask her to share me, like this day.

It's not a deal I have many complaints about except it has a tendency to make us less punctual than I would like.

"O'Meara... Everyone's going to be waiting for us;" I protested as soon as her grip loosened enough for me to twist out of it.

"Just giving Her Loudness a chance to set up her toys." O'Meara yawned before reaching for the tome on the coffee table and flipping it closed. It was one of Dominicus' journals that had been delivered to us on the night of his death. O'Meara had been trying to glean some insight as to how the Archmagus wove spells in a minute that took most magi hours, but the only thing miraculous about them so far were the speed at which they'd put one to sleep. Written in a blend of German, Latin, and sloppy handwriting, they made less sense to me than the graffiti tags on the Vegas bus system.

I tugged at the sleeve of her shirt. "O'Meara, shake off the grogginess. This is the big one, we have a connection. If this works-"

She reached out and closed my muzzle with her hand. "Then we are going to be very busy, Thomas. So let me take this last unhurried moment before we have every magus with an apprentice banging on our front door."

With a sigh, I settled back to wait. O'Meara rose from the couch and went through her usual "getting ready for other people" routine, splashing water on her face and forcing her wild mane of red hair into a frizzy braid. She attempted to brush the wrinkles out of her red button-down shirt before picking up the thin black jacket from the back of a chair. Together, we headed to the elevator and proceeded to the spell lab we'd built in the basement.

Jason had been prepped. His eyes stared at the door, pupils wide and unfocused. He stood at the dead center of a room half the size of a basketball court. Around him stretched a silver pentagram, with circles at each of the points. They had placed a small circlet over his head that glowed blue in my magical sight: a mind stiller. Nobody really wanted to know what the previous owner of the casino, a magus named Death, had used it for, but in our hands it functioned as a mental anesthetic.

Two other magi-familiar pairs waited for us on either side of the pentagram. Riona stood with Tack, a formerly human, ex-military German Shepherd. His tail gave a half wag although it remained tucked between his legs. While he broadcasted uncertainty, his multicolored magus brimmed with confidence as she fingered the acoustic guitar she held. Its strings glowed with the gray magical aura of tass.

The other pair both broadcast a more guarded attitude. Willow, tall and lithe as her name implied, with skin the light brown of tree bark which made the orange-reddish hair and green eyes shocking. While O'Meara's eyes and hair could be described with the same colors, Willow's colors were not of the Irish variety, rather the green of leaves and the hair so paradoxically thick and fine you'd think it to be fur. At her feet sat Reynard, a fox so foxy that you'd think him a fugitive from a children's story book.

Rudy stood on a desk against the wall. He had a small bag of popcorn next to him.

Ignoring the rodent, I cracked a smile at Riona. "Sorry we're late, somebody was taking a nap." I bumped my shoulder against O'Meara's hip.

Riona put her fists on her hips. "Hots, I thought it was the cat that needed eighteen hours of sleep, not you."

"Oh, Bloody ashes," O'Meara chuckled and thumped my side, "I'm lucky to get eight being bonded to this slave driver."

"I hope we're all... adequately rested for this one," Willow said, fingering a set of beads that hung on the fringes of her leather jacket. "Unless O'Meara's wrestled some insight from those journals, we're going to be at this for a while."

O'Meara shook her head. "I'm beginning to think the only reason he willed them to me is he thought I was sleep deprived."

Everyone laughed lightly, treading softly on the memory of the Archmagus' haunting last visit to the MGM, a body of frost and ice except for his eyes. I shook the image away. "Enough about the past. Today's about the future. Are we all ready?" I asked Riona.

"Should be," she answered. "Double check for me."

I obliged by walking a circuit around the pentagram, inspecting it with my magical sight. Truth be told, there wasn't much prep work to do. The pentagram and the surrounding circles were silver inlays. Each point of the star had a small pile of tass in easy reach, and a bottle or bowl of water.

Inspection complete, I stepped into the center of the pentagram with Jason. Each of the magi and familiars swiftly claimed their own point. The pop of Riona cracking her knuckles echoed through the room as a rectangle in the floor beside me rose into a pillar. It opened to reveal three silver chains hanging on hooks, each with a collar at either end. They wriggled as if excited. I took a deep breath and looked up at Jason as he stared over my head. My pulse climbed into my ears. I really hoped this worked.

"Okay, just like we practiced on those minor threads." I lifted my voice. "We're about to do something no magus has done since the age of Atlantis."

"No pressure!" Rudy called out. Nobody laughed, just nervous glances.

I continued. "Even if it doesn't work, we'll be much closer than we were. Riona, Tack and I will extract the silver thread. Next, O'Meara will stabilize it. Finally, Willow and Reynard's task is to reel in its length while the rest of us build the housing. If something goes wrong, Rudy will trigger the panic ward."

"What?! You mean I have to pay attention now?" Rudy quipped back. That got a bit of mirth from everyone except Tack and Willow.

"Thank you, Rudy, for watching our backs. Now, everyone sound off with your affirmations."

"Fire," O'Meara answered.

"Earth," Tack.

"Air," Riona strummed one note.

"Water," Reynard yipped.

"Spirit," Willow.

"All are one." I closed my eyes and reached out to the chains beside me. They sprang upon me like a trio of snakes, their collars snapping around my neck. I pictured the three human magi in the circle, the focused sparkle of Willow's eyes, the movements of Riona's lips to a song within her head and O'Meara's warm grip around me. With each thought, a chain whipped out to secure itself around the magus's neck. The moment it snapped closed, a connection opened between us. While Riona and Willow held themselves back, O'Meara flowed into me, a near giddy excitement washing through me that made my teeth chatter with eagerness. I pushed her back playfully. It was important to balance these connections to keep track of which sensations were coming from whom. Then I opened my eyes to the task at hand. Jason's dead-eyed stare did not see any of this. Dark to my Sight, which registered the energies of other existences and bends of ours as a spectrum of light, he had no magic other than the circlet's gentle pulse of blue around his head. But this is a false impression. While the soul of a mundane lacks a strand attached to different dimensions, they're not without connections. Riona plucked the strings of her guitar, sending a soft melody drifting through the room. I stared into the blackness of Jason's face, blocking out my mundane sight, searching for something.

There: a glimmer of silver in the darkness as Riona's notes lengthened, becoming mournful, shaky. Through Willow, I watched Jason's lower lip quiver. My sight squirmed with the false colors of the visions you see when you squeeze your eyes shut in the dark. In that, the barest shadows of strings. Mentally, I pounced, my awareness homing in on that movement, and the darkness fell away. An array of silver threads came into focus around Jason's head which had taken on a white glow of its own. These were not a dense web, but there were still over a hundred, each a connection to someone who had touched Jason's life.

In our tests, with small strands that no one would miss, it had always been difficult to find the one we were targeting. Here, one strand shone like a strand of spider silk sparkling in sunlight as it vibrated to Riona's mournful song. Shadows moved above me, weaving a gold and silver finger that curled out and gave the single strand a pluck.

"Lilly!" Jason gasped. Willow and Reynard spun a force cage, to prevent him from toppling; this added a glare of yellow that intruded on my vision. Riona and Tack continued to weave, the finger lengthening into a snake that slowly spiraled down the thread. Time for me to do what only I could do. With a prod, Mr. Bitey uncoiled from that odd place within my mind where he rested. Rearing into my vision as a cobra composed of the finest silver jewelry chains, he regarded me with his ruby eyes. Mr. Bitey, crafted by the Dragon from a broken Fey chain and anchored in my very soul, had given me my freedom from being under the control of magi, allowing me to forge a mental connection to anyone and break it at will. The snake struck at Jason, breaking up into a tangle of chains that wrapped around his neck. He mutely assented to the connection.

I experienced a brief impression of speed and a tunnel, before tumbling into a mindscape awash in sticky grief. In the center of it a colossal Jason knelt, holding the corpse of an angel in his arms. Perfection radiated from her face, while the skin of her dangling limbs bore great cracks and fissures. I hissed through my teeth, removing her would not be a simple task, even without him fighting me.

Find something else for him to focus on. O'Meara suggested.

Gotta understand what I'm working with first. I floated toward the angel. Several years of married bliss replayed in her eyes and smile. Scenes of the pair dancing, in a house, at a club, in a park. They were both dance instructors that loved to dance together, tango, swing, and many more I had no names for. If it was a dance for two, they had done it. Between the dances, things were great, through the haze of memory. They decided they wanted to buy a house. Jason took up trucking, and then it was all downhill from there. They strayed away from one another, covered it up, patched it up, and ignored it. But Jason knew how to fix it. Just had to get that house, quit trucking, and it would snap back together. So, he plowed on with hope in his heart.

Hope that she dashed, totally and utterly, just as he had reached that goal. She'd found another dance partner and left him. Now the grief had swollen the memories, so they filled his mind, everything about her and losing her blotting out almost every other thought.

Nothing for it. I crawled into the angel of memories and got to work. Using my mental claws, I snapped the emotional strings that held onto each memory. The love and devotion were easy. The harder ones to find were the slow suspicious anger that had built between them; those threads liked to hide. Then there were memories which overlapped with other people. Carving her out without damaging those other connections was a bit like defusing a bomb by tugging on the wires to see where they went. Through Riona's perceptions, I slowly felt the thread loosen as Jason's grip on the angel grew slack. Finally, after hours and hours of mental surgery, he let her go and she rose into the gray sky of Jason's mindscape.

I prodded O'Meara. *Here she comes.*

She braced against my soul, reached out along her anchor to pull forth a crystalline light. *Ready,* she replied.

I waited until the last bit of the angel disappeared into the gray. *Now!*

Above Jason, back in the web of threads, a thin beam of light struck the gleaming silver thread between the coils as Riona and Tack pulled the thread free. It stopped dead in its tracks as if freeze-framed in the midst of snapping up into the void. O'Meara held it captive in stasis. At its very tip, it branched into grasping roots. Tack and Reynard focused on these. To me they were indistinguishable, but Tack's nose was more sensitive to subtle variations than my sight and he quickly mapped out the branches. Reynard and Willow forged fine hooks of pure tass, which Riona anchored to the end of each branch and then spun fine chains along the roots. O'Meara relaxed the stasis as the spell along the thread's length compressed, pulling it from the ether beyond our spell circle. O'Meara and I captured it in the cage of stasis, while Willow and Reynard broke off half of the roots from one end and grafted them to the other. Finally, we all cinched our spells tight. The spell compressed; a silver cylinder capped by golden chain roots at either end. Suddenly real, it fell directly on Jason's noggin and rolled off. I reached out and caught it on the pads of my paw, holding it there with my telekinetic thumb.

We did it! Jubilation flowed through the links, even Jason smiled dreamily. Tack let out a long howl. It looked little like the fey chain we modeled it after, but this strange little contraption would replicate the ease with which I made and broke my bonds. Now that we could make them, familiars of the future would truly have choices. Fingers found my ears, and I looked up to find O'Meara kneeling down beside me.

"Well done," she whispered.

"Couldn't have done it without you," I murmured back in a low purr as I leaned against her. Letting my gratitude flow through the links. *All of you.*

"Let's get Jason back to his room and then let's all have some drinks. We deserve that."

We totally did. Little did we know, the relative peace of these last eight months was about to be unraveled.

3

RUDY HAD APPARENTLY WANDERED off sometime during the seven-hour casting session. The six of us celebrated in the magic-only bar on the 13th floor of the Casino. Back when Death had owned it, the MGM had been the place to be for magi in a gambling mood, as it had been one of the few places where you could bet tass instead of mundane money. While we hadn't continued that practice, we'd opened a mages' bar, called the Skulking Cat: its mascot, a black cat with a skull head stretched across the sign. So far, it was hardly as popular as Death's tables, but it was rarely deserted. We crowded into a circular booth, the magi drinking, the familiars savoring the buzz second hand. I'd broken the links to all but O'Meara, and after six fingers of whiskey our decorum had disintegrated. I sprawled across her lap, belly up, babbling about the testing of our new linker.

Riona though, she bubbled as she inhaled pink cocktails, "You don't get it, Thomas! This is Archmagus-level stuff! Think about it, for a single magus to do what we did today, they'd have to figure out how to manipulate silver strands, find a stasis plane, and then be able to bend space, too!"

"Ha!" O'Meara grabbed my belly fluff and shook me. "You have no idea how much work Thomas did inside that poor fellow's head." I huffed at the abuse.

"And serious mind magics," Riona added. "Point stands. That's a combo that's tough for any magus and familiar to master. Nobody's brave enough to bond six minds together like we did."

Reynard gulped down a meatball from a silver bowl. "And Thomas shares our senses between us nearly instinctively now. Bravo!"

If I purred any harder, the staff might report an earthquake. Still, the compliment made me try to hide in the crook of O'Meara's elbow.

"Oh right, now you're modest," she chided me. "Mr. 'Let's survive by the skin of our teeth and then claim an entire casino.' I don't buy it for a moment."

Riona tipped back her mostly empty glass to catch a piece of ice and crunched it thoughtfully.

"Does this mean I can get back to work?" A fresh voice intruded on our circle, belonging to a tabby cat perched on the edge of the circular booth, behind Riona's shoulder.

"Why hello Midnight who stalks at... Midnight?" Riona slurred, twisting in her seat to sweep her hand across his back.

"The Shadow who Strikes at Midnight!" the cat huffed as he endured the petting, his tail twitching with annoyance. "And I wasn't talking to you Madam Be-bop. I'm addressing the one who's shamefully displaying his belly rub addiction for all the world to see. Have you no pride at all, Thomas?"

"I have a pride! Shina's prrrr" My protest faded as O'Meara's nails found the spot, right under my ribs and it made words slip out of reach. My front paws kneaded the air.

"Sorry, Midnight." O'Meara chuckled, "Thomas is out of order, try again later."

Distantly, I watched Midnight shudder and stalk out onto the table. "I am the only freelancer left and I haven't had an assignment in over a month due to lack of available Fey chains."

The petting stopped and O'Meara sighed before draining the dregs of her drink. "I'm sorry, Midnight but at least we have a new Fey chain now. I know it's been less fun for you without Tilly-"

"I don't care that the stupid mutt got himself bonded permanently just because the magus offered him roasted mutton!" Midnight hissed, his tail going puffy. "It's perfectly logical that *he* would choose food over everything else."

The outburst was loud enough to pull me from my purrific stupor and lift my head to peer at the tabby. A few months ago, Tilly had asked to be bonded to a Picitrix magus whose anchor was the concept of roasting, because in his words, "Best treats ever!" We'd all been sad to see him go, but the pair seemed very happy together. Midnight had not attended the farewell party.

With a huff, I righted myself enough so I could rest my muzzle on the table. "Familiars are going to come and go, Midnight. Not everyone's going to want to be a free agent forever, like you do. Tilly found a good match."

"How do you know that?" He gazed sullenly at the pepper shaker in the middle of the table.

"You could go visit him. He's still in the city, unlike Melissa," I said.

Midnight swatted the pepper shaker over. "I thought you weren't keeping track of Melissa?"

"Oh, Bloody Ashes," O'Meara swore suddenly, both saving me from answering Midnight's question and flushing away my borrowed drunkenness, spotting one of our security personnel hurrying towards us. Together we banished the eavesdropping ward we had surrounded our little party with. "Yes, Simmons? What is it?" O'Meara addressed him with the merest trace of a drunken slur. The other magi, who had been sitting with their backs toward the door, rounded on him slowly.

"Sorry to interrupt Lady O'Meara and Sir Thomas." He bowed his head respectfully. "But there is a... thing from house

Erebus who is claiming it has a message for you from Michael the 2nd."

O'Meara's broad smile didn't waver, but she winced internally. "We will be down in a moment. Please thank it for its patience."

"Damn," I swore as the security man retreated. "Looks like we're going to need that security detail from Morganna now."

"Let's not jump to conclusions yet," O'Meara counseled, although I didn't need the mind link to know she placed little hope in an alternative. "Finish your drinks," she urged Willow and Riona. "Might be the last ones we have time for." She edged herself around the table and pulled herself out of the booth. I walked along the cushions and placed myself at her side.

How do you want to play this? I asked her. *Sober up and keep him waiting, or just go on down?*

Let's get it over with, O'Meara responded. *If it's what we think it is, something must have shifted without us noticing.*

I nodded as we walked back toward the elevators. We'd had eight months of uneasy peace after the Council of Merlins had dissolved because the actual building up and left Vegas. As soon as we'd all filed out of the last Council Meeting, the entire tower had simply vanished in a great burst of the purple of bending space. Everyone still in it, including the Archmagi, were scattered all over North America. Rumor was that Michael the 2nd, who had forced the Council to dissolve, had found himself in the middle of a New Jersey landfill without his familiar. The building had taken all the enchantments that Magi society had relied on for centuries to communicate with it. The war had been placed on pause, because suddenly the hundred-year-old magi in charge of things had to figure out how cell phones worked, and they completely cut the major houses off from their pocket dimensions.

The blitz that Erebus had planned to take over Vegas with that very night had never happened. By the time they reorganized, House Picitrix had called nearly every single magus they had to the city, and we'd cemented a very expensive deal with House Morganna for protection.

We stepped off the elevator and spotted the thing from House Erebus. I had expected to see a shambling mass of bones and skulls, but they'd opted for creepy animated statuary instead. A humanoid figure composed of chalk white stone waited for us, holding a small white square of fabric with two fingers. Its limbs and chest were carved to give an impression of plate armor, decorated with skulls, small and large. Its head broke the motif, a featureless wedge of stone that presented not even the impression of eyes. Curiously, I saw not a glimmer of magic at the thing's core. Had to be a damping ward, but usually they're pretty obvious up close. That smooth plane of a face immediately oriented on O'Meara and me. It straightened as O'Meara and I approached.

"Greetings to House Khatt from the High Merlin, first of the New Council of Magi," it called out to us when we were within fifty feet of it. "I bear a message from him to you." Moving with a dancer's imitation of a robot, one joint at a time, it pulled a scroll from the palm of one hand.

I had half-expected a dozen titles to be thrown on top of High Merlin, but apparently Michael the 2nd had realized that his name was clumsy enough without adding to it. More self-awareness than I had previously given him credit for. Maybe he had a smidgen of shame for setting up a council that consisted of only his own house and a few minor houses that he'd bullied into joining. I'd been waiting for this moment to come for so long, gaming it out in my head. Now I seemed to watch myself from afar, a member of the audience and not one of the actors. I watched the arrogant roll of my eyes and the sneer pull up one side of my mouth to display the tips of my fangs. "House Khatt does not recognize this Council's claim to authority, but we will humor their entreaties and hear-"

O'Meara reached into my head and plucked the word I had been about to say, "mewling" from my thoughts. I sputtered briefly before concluding, "the message." And sneaking a glare up at my magus.

Stay polite! She chided me back.

The courtier's eyeless gaze shifted from O'Meara to me and back. "Allowing your familiar to leash you always leads to tragedy." It told her.

O'Meara's eyes narrowed as her anchor lit. "We thought you were here to deliver a message, not offer unwelcome advice. Rock is more resistant than bone to heat, but at eight thousand degrees you wouldn't perceive a noticeable difference in the speed they vaporize at."

So much for polite. I noted.

If this thing wants to go home molten, I can arrange that.

"Bravado is useless." The messenger flicked the seal that closed the scroll, and unrolled the missive, text facing us. "The High Merlin declares that since House Khatt has declined to present their case for their claim to the MGM casino, it is null and void. House Khatt has twenty-four hours to vacate the premises and turn over all tass, artifacts and surviving spell work to its rightful owner, House Erebus. Failure to do so will be met with a forceful eviction and the declaration of all House Khatt members as renegade magi." It finished lowering the paper so I could see the scratched signature of Michael the 2nd.

There it was, the threat that I had bought off once, but I had nothing to offer this time. They hadn't told us about any such hearing, they were just words that hid the sword House Erebus wanted to stab into our collective guts for claiming what had been theirs.

"No right?" I growled. "The only reason Michael the 2nd and your entire house isn't in the maw of a hunger demon right now is because of O'Meara and me. Surely a single casino compared to your dozen is a fair reward for that."

"A reward is given; it is not claimed. Death's legacy, no matter how obtained, belongs to House Erebus. We will not allow you or anyone else to possess it." The statue's voice answered in an authoritative monotone.

I bared my teeth. "This casino is under the protection of House Morganna. To attack us is to declare war on them, exposing yourself to war against both of the remaining great Houses."

"Your faith in the carrion crows is misplaced. They will not aid you. Not today." It stated, its lack of face not hiding the smile in its voice.

Not today? A chill of fear bounced between both O'Meara and me, setting my tail lashing. What happened to House Morganna? I groomed my paw to cover my sudden uncertainty. "If after you leave, House Erebus sets one foot on this property, then I will end Michael the 2nd's existence. We possess the Spear of Remus and we will use it if forced."

"So did House Hermes, but it did them no good in the end. I will convey your message, cat. Twenty-four hours." With that the statue floated about three inches off the ground, using no magic I could detect. It turned smoothly and glided out the casino doors and into the brightness of the Vegas night. O'Meara and I stared after it, exchanging mental expletives. Twenty-four hours of warning was better than none, at least. Time to call in favors.

Rudy waited for us by the elevator and jumped up between my shoulder blades as we entered. "I can't believe you let that rocks-for-brains messenger walk out of here. Could have at least shoved a firecracker down its pants or something," he grumbled.

"Flag of truce, Rudy," I sighed. "You have to respect those."

"You send somebody with a 'flag of truce' to House Erebus and only their bones are walking back," he responded, and was probably right.

Once we were all safely in my office, we called Morrian, who had been the Archmagus of House Morganna.

To my surprise, the video panel flashed to life after the first ring, revealing Morrian's hunched, frog-like figure, her heavy eyelids nearly obscuring her eyes entirely. "You have been threatened by House Erebus."

She hadn't phrased it as a question but I answered it anyway. "Yes, they gave us twenty-four hours to surrender the Casino or they will repossess it. We request your promised assistance."

That wide mouth of hers pursed as her gaze drifted off camera. "Blast. We cannot provide the aid you need now, Thomas."

I growled. "That's what they said. What is going on?"

"We... are on fire from within, I'm afraid. I will not give any more detail than that."

"Surely you can spare us a few magi, Morrian. Why else would I be shipping your house nearly a third of the tass we produce?"

She answered me with chilling calmness, "Thomas, wars consist of many battles, and House Morganna cannot respond in force at this time for reasons that are surely not coincidental. If I could spare you a single cabal I wouldn't; I will not waste the lives of my sisters. If Erebus attacks, then House Morganna will declare war; we will honor that agreement."

"That doesn't help me, Morrian. I thought we were allies."

"We are, cat, but I'm afraid you might be the unlucky first pawn to be taken in this game."

"I will not be anyone's cat's paw," I hissed. "Anyone who has taken me for one has regretted it."

She crackled, "Poor choice of words perhaps. I still can't help you until we put our own fires out. Three days. You prove yourself a very tough nut to swallow, and the whole of House Morganna will arrive to shatter the bones of those who threaten you. Good luck, House Khatt."

The call blinked out and I let out a sawing hiss of frustration. "You have to give us something! An artifact or even all the tass we gave you! Something!" I raged at the call-disconnected display.

O'Meara put a soothing hand on my back and I shrugged it off. I turned on her; no anger could be found in her face, and the fire magus's thoughts were running cold, calculating.

"Feh!" Rudy huffed, his tail buffeting my desk behind him. "We don't need that flock of vultures. I'll drag Stompy out of storage and pound those dead heads so hard, the next time they crawl out of their graves, they'll be in China."

O'Meara spoke. "It won't be like fighting Hermes mages, element against element. House Erebus wields a combination of negative energy and dark conceptual planes. Difficult to ward against unless you know the particular magus gunning for you. To last against multiple cabals, we'll have to be aggressive. We'll need shock troops. Hire some Shaman Mercs." In her head she'd already ringed the MGM with multiple layers of defenses, armed with all the spell dogs.

This wasn't how it was supposed to go. House Morganna didn't have many casinos, Houses Picitrix and Erebus had snapped up the majority of them when House Hermes fell apart. Picitrix and Erebus were the ones who had been squaring off for months. The deal with House Morganna had been to keep us out of the war. The specter of fighting two houses at once should have deterred House Erebus from moving against us.

What the hell did we have that House Erebus wanted so badly?

One person in the casino might know something of the distraction Morrian had been talking about. Leaving O'Meara and Rudy devising defense plans, I shot out of the room towards the elevators. Hopefully Morrian kept her spy in the loop.

4

THE OTHER MAGI OF House Khatt, our so far nameless cabal, occupy a cluster of suites in the middle of the MGM's hotel tower. Willow, Reynard and Farah all lived together in a suite, while Naomi and Riona lived in adjacent units with their familiars. There were plans to build a common space for all of them, but they hadn't amounted to anything yet. The cabal had some lopsided dynamics thus far. Riona and Tack hung out with O'Meara and the rest of the magi. Farah familiared up with Smiley when we had a Fey chain available to hunt, err find, new intelligent animals that we could interest in being familiars. Naomi and Morie often joined them on those expeditions. Willow and Reynard generally assisted us with the research projects.

It was Naomi and Morie's door I scratched on, hoping the bird magus was home. A surprised chirp sounded from inside and a muffled "Hang on!" through the door. It opened to reveal Naomi, her long gangly legs sticking out from the bottom of a robe that was too short for her. Her somewhat bulbous eyes blinked at me, and a pink tongue moistened her lips before speaking, "Thomas, what... uh, can I do for you?"

"We need to talk," I said. "May I come in?"

I watched the tendons in her narrow neck flex as she glanced off to the side. It's the height of rudeness to invite yourself into a magi's home, but I needed to get what information she had. My voice shifted low as my tail moved with my annoyance. "Naomi, you can either let me in or come with me. Either way we need to talk. Now."

She swallowed and stepped back into the apartment. "Come in, Magus Thomas. Apologies about the mess." I padded in warily, concerned by Naomi's guilty expression. My consciousness slid through the link, peeking through O'Meara's eyes. She and Rudy already had a map of the MGM in front of them, budgeting time and tass for defenses, I left her to it and focused on Naomi.

Her apartment stank of poultry, not in a bad unclean way, but in the same way the rest of the building reeked of humanity. Her anchor was the concept of birds, and judging from the scent, she spent most of her time in the apartment as one. While there was a single couch and a coffee table, most of the furnishings were perches of various sizes. Most flat surfaces were covered with books: thick leather tomes festooned with sticky notes. Morie the wolf slept on the floor, his nose laying in a casting circle burnt into the carpet. "I suppose you want to know what we've been up to all these months? What I've got to show for all that tass I've been burning?" Naomi followed me in, fingers fluttering nervously.

"Uh... Not really," I admitted, feeling off balanced by the question. I did the books and Naomi got as much tass for personal use as the rest of the Cabal did. What they did with it was up to them. "That's not why-"

"I'm doing my best to broaden my horizons, Thomas, but I'm finding it difficult." She blustered over me. "I felt really bad that I couldn't help Melissa. You'd think shapeshifting into a human wouldn't be that hard. My entire thing is turning anything and anyone into a bird. I spent two months looking for a plane of humanity for her and the closest I got was a plane of six-legged monkeys. When she left, I switched gears, tried my hand at warding. I got the basics of that, probably couldn't stop a fireball, but if you need a good pigeon repellent..."

"Naomi this isn't a performance review! Not at all," I said, popping up on my hindlegs to put my face into the field of her far-off stare.

She shook, her short hair briefly standing up like a crest before falling back to lie against her head. "It's not? Then why are you here?"

If she didn't have an inkling why I came, then it didn't bode well for her being much help. *How to do this delicately*, I pondered as I stepped up onto the offered couch and lay down. Naomi herself fetched a folding chair and sat in it across from me. I watched her for a moment. "I'm hoping you still have some contacts in House Morganna, because I have received some disturbing news that I need to verify." As delicate as a brick through a window, that's me.

"What news?" Her brows slid closer together.

Damn, she didn't know off-hand, did she? I was wasting my time here. I huffed, "Something has forced all the House Morganna magi out of the city. Preventing them from helping us against an Erebus attack. I need to know if this thing is real or an excuse to watch us get trampled."

Her face fell. "Thomas, I'm not a House Morganna magus anymore, despite what Riona thinks. I'm not Morrian's spy." She sighed. "Not like the movies, anyway. She promised tutoring and I promised gossip. So far neither of us has done much of either."

"Can you find out? Make some calls? Morrian refused to tell me anything other than the Morganna house is on fire and she can't send troops when we need it most." Clearly Naomi had been feeling a bit neglected, but I couldn't do much about that now.

"Send troops? Wait," she squawked and Morie's head jerked up from the floor. "Erebus are going to attack us? When? But we have the spear!"

"They gave us twenty-four hours to pack our bags before they attempt to evict us. Morrian literally told us to look to the east on the dawn of the 3rd day or whatever."

Naomi stared at me blankly, "Look to the east?"

I flinched, realizing that not everyone spoke Tolkien. "House Morganna isn't coming to help for a long time."

She swallowed hard, "So we're going to fight House Erebus? All of them?"

"I don't know precisely what we'll do yet. Still counting allies, and if House Morganna's proving less solid than advertised, it changes things. I'll call a general meeting soon." I looked her over; fear shone in her eyes, and I wondered if she'd show for that meeting, if I'd see her again after I walked out her door. "Thanks," I said, turning back to the door.

"Okay, I'll find out what I can." She said as I hooked a paw around the L shaped handle and pulled open the door.

And froze.

There, exiting the door on the opposite side of the hallway was a tall dark-skinned man whom I had met twice before. Once on the steps of House Morganna's tower, and the second time in Shangra-la. Both encounters had been cryptic and confusing, but this time I knew who he was.

"Archibald," I growled as his eyes widened in panic.

"Shit, bad path." He broke away from the door and lunged into a sprint.

I launched myself, claws snagging his hoodie. My weight yanking him back and down to the ground, he yelped as his butt impacted the floor.

"I surrender! Don't hurt me." He flung his hands up in the air.

My teeth clicked closed less than an inch from the back of his neck. It took effort as anger roiled up inside of me. "You better start talking then, Archibald. We have a lot to catch up on." Something about his very scent conjured the agony of my extremities being slowly sliced away in that pit of suffering. My very bones ached to complete the dragon's vengeance.

"Listen, man, you got the wrong guy. Name's Nick." He tried to twist around but I cuffed the back of his head with a paw.

"Don't move! You've been screwing around with my future and I don't appreciate that." My voice sounded full of gravel as I strained against the urge to grab O'Meara's power and reduce him to ash.

"You have to let me go! I can't stay here long. There's a demon after me!" He pleaded as a pair of glowing eyes opened in the shadow of a fire door farther down the hallway.

"A demon, eeeh?" A rich Scottish accent rolled through the air. "Wat, you don't recognize your old familiar, Archie? I sat on your lap for fookin ninety years!" The eyes narrowed as a vaguely cat-shaped glob of shadow oozed into the light.

The man shivered. "You're not Scrags," he whispered, "Scrags believes in the work."

"The werk? Pff. You're nuthing but a ghost. I'm tired of being ded. It's your turn. Lenshie sends their best." A pair of dark tendrils flowed up from his back as he spoke, curving like snakes about to strike.

"Scrags," I growled, "We need to find out what he's been doing."

"You let him move even an inch, Laddie and he'll slip through the gaps of your teeth." The tips of Scrags' tendrils took on the sheen of blades.

"Mercy, please!" Archibald shouted as the tendrils struck forward.

A bolt of energy sprang from the wall and exploded. On instinct, I threw myself into the space between realities, the sideways space, as a concussive BANG! ripped through the hallway. There, sheltered from the explosion, I watched it blow the tentacles back the way they came. Freed of my claws, Archibald tossed himself forward and reached out to grab something. The air around his hand surged with a color I have no word for other than time as I shifted back into reality. The magic flared out into a crack the width of his shoulders and sucked him in. I lunged forward but only caught the heel of his shoe with my teeth. Better than nothing. I hauled back. My paws slipped on the carpet and that color without a name surrounded me.

5

FRIGID COLD SLICED THROUGH my fur as the light faded to black. The heel of Archibald's unbitten boot slammed into my nose; pain rammed through my skull and I released his other one. He scrambled to his feet as I shook away the sparks in my vision. "Shit shit shit!" He swore with every step.

"Come back here!" I growled as I tore after him, my paws slipping on the rubbery ground beneath me. He had gotten maybe twenty feet away, not far, when it's four versus two legs. I bounded toward him and leapt. My paws only found empty air as he dived to the side with perfect timing. The tip of one claw snagging and tearing the elbow of his suit coat. My tail and hips swung out, pivoting me so I landed on my side, rolled and sprang back onto my feet. Above us stretched a starless void, but Archibald ran towards a light on the horizon.

Thomas! O'Meara's panicked shout was a burbled thought in my head as if she were underwater. *Where are you?*

Dunno! Worry about it after I bite this arsehole! I dashed out after Archibald, digging claws into the rubbery ground. He threw out his hand, casting out a thin whip of power that arched into the horizon's light as a fisherman's line. I could see it through him as it pulled taut. I pounced forward for a second time but aimed low, spreading my forelegs wide.

"No!" He screamed as my teeth bit into the meat of his thigh and my forelegs clamped around his knees. My surroundings whipped by me as if I'd just been flung into the air. Instinctively I reached for O'Meara's heat, but reached further and further without finding her. All the gods be damned, it was like the far void! My shock at being beyond O'Meara caused me to let go more than the force of Archibald's fist pounding on my skull.

I found myself in the heated glare of a Vegas afternoon, Archibald hurrying away from me at a desperate limp down the crowded sidewalk. Standing, the entire world wavered; that color of time lay over everything, shining through the ground, the people were dimmer, an uncertain flicker in them. Archibald had a silver shine to his aura as he lurched through a crowd who barely reacted to the bleeding man, parting only when he got within arms' reach.

Following after him earned me a kick in the ribs from a pedestrian who tripped right over me. They couldn't see me at all, forcing me to weave through the dense forest of legs, tracking Archibald by the bloody footsteps he left in his wake. "You're bleeding out, Archibald!" I hollered through the crowd. "Give it up!"

"Get away from me! You're too connected; they'll find us both!" I heard him shout.

Trying to avoid a phalanx of long-legged women walking down the street, I tried shifting sideways and was shocked when it worked. Instead of viewing the real world through dark sunglasses, my vision fragmented, like those nature shows where they try to give you an idea of how a bee sees, in each cell I saw the same but different view of the seven women walking toward me. Each with their own time brightness: in a dim one the center one stumbled; in another, brighter pair, she turned her head left instead of right. Hundreds of minor possibilities, playing out as they walked through my position. I flung myself back into the simpler reality with a gasp, my mind fizzing from the overload. Legs dodged, I stumbled forward to where the crowd thinned, and recognized the MGM fountain stretching out before me. A wall of water jets behind a waist-high concrete fence, but in the middle there was a statue of a cougar: me, with a squirrel perched on his head. The plaque read, "In Memoriam, Magus Thomas Khatt, Founder of the High House." The water jets died away, revealing Archibald standing right next to it.

"You were never supposed to live this long!" He raised a pistol.

Archibald didn't split into thousands of possibilities, he stayed whole. A meshwork of time and silver covered his chest and arms. That had to be how he was doing this. I slipped sideways as the muzzle flashed. Hurdling the fence, I leapt at him, rematerializing my head past the barrel of the pistol, both paws slamming into his chest and bowling him over. The gun fired in my left ear as his back impacted the pavement. The momentum carried my teeth toward his throat but his palm snapped my muzzle closed. Instead, I bludgeoned his windpipe with my nose. Both of his hands grabbed my head, pushing against me with desperate strength. I drove my head down on him, teeth snapping for his flesh. A thumb found my eye and pressed hard; the pain forced me to spring back.

He rolled for the gun, but it had gone transparent and his hand passed right through it. Swearing, he rolled up onto his knees, curled fists set into a fighting stance.

A low threatening hiss rattled up my throat as I started to circle him. "Give up." In the distance I heard a high-pitched buzz, the ringing of my ears, a growl and a mosquito.

"You hear that?" he asked. "That's death coming for both of us."

"Do that line thing then and take us back; then you can beg O'Meara not to kill you before you explain what the hell you're doing," I growled back, not taking my eyes off him.

"That doesn't work in the strands. I need a significant branch point to exit." He kept glancing over his shoulder. "Closest one is two blocks away."

"Best get walking, limpy gimpy," I responded. Something silver shone from far behind us. "They're coming."

He ground his teeth together and wrenched himself up to his feet. Grunting with pain, he started staggering down the street. I moved right behind him so his butt was in biting range. To keep him motivated I could snap to it!

"You're not helping anyone now," he spat as he hurried, the buzzing growing louder. "You've only gotten this far because of me, and now your time is up."

"My time is up? You're the ghost in a stolen body." I snarled back.

He didn't seem to have an immediate comeback for that, and we made it to the crosswalk without any more wit. The buzzing was growing loud enough to drown the sounds of the traffic and tourists.

"Whatever you do, do not look at the Keepers. If you see them, they see you. They'll render us both worse than dead," he said before lurching into the traffic. Abandoning the use of his injured leg entirely, he did a one-legged hop across the street. I followed in his wake, smelling the fear in his sweat.

"I liked you better as a senile old man with the tiny cat." I raised my voice to be heard as the buzzing grew into a vibration I could feel on my whiskers.

He gave a one note laugh, "You were a pathetic shell of a man so desperate for affection that you tolerated dating a werewolf despite the Veil. My experiments could only improve your life, even if they had ended it."

I growled, hard to be snappy with a comeback when what sounded like a giant mosquito from hell was about to land on your back.

"There's the split." He directed my attention forward, towards a man staring down into his cell phone. The flickering time essence within him had separated within him like two cells getting ready to divide. My perception peeked sideways, my fragmented sight again showed me hundreds of possible actions, but two swelled to prominence. He started texting or slipped the phone back into his pocket. Archibald limped towards the man, first slapping his own chest. The magic on his chest pulsed, wreathing his hand in time's color. This he shoved directly into the hapless decision maker. Light flashed out between the man's time essence and beyond him.

I hopped up on Archibald's back as he threw himself forward into the light. The world split apart and we fell through a dark chasm that yawned open everywhere around us. Colors and fantastic light streamed through my peripheral vision but I kept my gaze centered on the back of his neck. "Now take us back or I'll hole punch your neck." I shouted in his ear.

Without answering, he cast out that line of time again. A sensation of speed came, and we were zipping through the space. I held him tightly, jaws poised to crush his spine. Then I made the mistake of glancing up to where we were heading. We flew through a universe of dancing strands stretching across the void. Thick and thin, they wound together and occasionally broke apart, pulsating and writhing. Things of flashing silver swarmed over the thicker bundles while gargantuan spiders skittered among the more delicate strands. Everything glowed with time's color, but here there were colors within that nameless color, an entire spectrum I had no words for. We were heading for another strand, a thick one. Then I suddenly wasn't. Archibald twisted out of my jaws with a hard jerk and a kick to my stomach. I spun through the space, the strands spinning around me, a blur of colors.

I flung out my legs, extended my claws, trying to latch on to anything at all to stop my tumble. Nothing in reach, as it seemed to go faster and faster. I cursed Archibald's name, the fucker. My mind flipped through all the desperate maneuvers that had saved me before. I coated my teeth and claws with tass to tear at space itself, nothing caught. I remembered the strange scales that had protected me in the void and found them again, pulling them from the parts of me usually hidden sideways, they coated my body, forming an etheric second skin. Still, I spun. Closing my eyes, I visualized the network of silver strands that tied me to my friends and enemies, but each strand fanned out in almost all directions at once. Mind fumbling, I found the impossible thing that is the name of the Dragon I freed and called it out, screamed it with my mind like a child calling for mother.

And finally, to this I received an answer, but it was not the dragon.

"My, my, you are a noisy fly." A thin, almost forgotten strand vibrated with words. Dread seized me even as I answered.

"Weaver! Help me please!" I cried into the thread, having no other option. I hadn't seen the spider spirit since I left Grantsville, when she had offered me a respite from death, in exchange for releasing her on earth in a proper body.

"Desperation is my favorite flavor. I am not allowed where you are but I have family nearby provided..."

"I'll let you back into the world."

"For starters. This time I will not settle for a body of metal or stone. You will carry me to that body your wolf friend made for me. Agreed?" The spider's voice purred in my head.

"Agreed!" I responded immediately with relief that was all she wanted.

Simple enough, my mind spun with contingency plans. She hadn't specified where I released her exactly, so Noise and I could drive the body deep into a forest. Hopefully that would keep her away from people for a few days. If that didn't work, a rumor of a tass-laced spider monster would have magi scrambling to hunt her. Pitting the Weaver against House Erebus, that would be fun. Maybe I could turn this to my advantage.

6

THE SPINNING STOPPED ABRUPTLY. A grip of steel clamped around my torso and I yipped with the force of the impact. I found myself in the grip of a massive crablike claw, but the pincers curved, as if made for plucking. The claw was attached to a long leg as thick as it was, and extended an almost unimaginable distance, through many joints, before joining with what watched me with eight mirrored eyes that depicted the vast distance between us, reflected my own and the fear within them. "Hi?" I said, fervently hoping that this was the family Weaver had referred to.

Two of the eyes grew small black spots that focused on me. Hissing static slithered through my ears. Prickles erupted all over my body and my mouth convulsed as it attempted to say every single word I knew at the same time. The static formed into words, too many at once. *Larva-Dragon-Cat-Thinone! Out bounds-Forbidden-NOW-Back. Break-You-What? HOW HERE? Break Strand?! Punishment! End Strand Yours.*

It was like talking to the dragon, but worse. Blasted with a dozen jumbled demands. *I didn't mean to come here. I was trying to-* And it pulled the entire sequence of events from my mind. Felt like a beaded string yanked through my nose.

Slippery fish. Infested. Collapsed strand. WASTE. The static buzzed with anger and its head tilted away from me. *Thin One-Back NOW.*

It tossed me aside all the care of a slot machine junky flicking a spent cigarette butt on his way into the casino. I cried out in protest as I flew away from the massive spider thing. It had thrown me with very little rotation, and I spent what felt like minutes watching the eight legs reach out to the other strand and start to heave its body up into the thinner branches. As I flew, or fell, the strands seemed to all coil together, creating thicker and thicker stands. I witnessed one spider wrapping them together with a silver thread. Occasionally a foot would snare a squished-out piece and shove it into its mouth. And then I turned enough to see where I was heading.

A creature, flying through the void with two gentle undulating wings, it dwarfed the spider that had thrown me as a planet does a mountain. New York and London could ride on its back without straying onto the wings. The closest animal I had for it was a manta ray; that held for the shape of his body, but at its center, the mouth, the comparison failed. Circular, surrounded by twisting tendrils, all the strands spiraled down into it as if it were a black hole. Within its depths, the light of time shone like a raging sun. And I was heading straight for it. Was that it? Was that where I was supposed to go? Into that light? It was so bright it couldn't be healthy, could it?

I had no choice but watch it loom larger and larger as I flew along the strands, which swarmed with silver beings like ants nesting in a tree. A chorus of buzzing, but they didn't seem to notice me. Still too distant, in fact, as I neared the massive being, the strands were getting further and further away. I wasn't heading for the mouth at all. Somewhere to the side of it would be my impact crater. I considered trying to construct a shell of tass around myself when I noticed a shine heading directly for me. Unable to dodge a football sized glob of something that smacked into my thigh and stuck there. The impact sent me spinning again but only briefly before the glob tugged hard, pulling on a wide patch of fur and skin. The goo had splattered all over my left flank, and from its transparent mass extended a single transparent thread as thick as a thumb.

"Weaver?" I direct the thought outwards.

Laughter echoed through my head. "Been a long time since I caught a fly in this way. Hang on, the line is long."

Minutes passed until I saw her, first a black speck on the back of the consumer of strands. Then a dot with eight legs, four of them reeling me in like a boatman pulls their ship to dock but far faster. She resolved further, black carapace shining and for the first time I saw that her bulbous abdomen wasn't entirely black; it had a marking, three red interlocked triangles. Better than a red hourglass, I hoped. As I approached, she stopped reeling and instead spun the line into a net stretched out between her four front legs. The webbing enveloped me and she croaked with glee, throwing me to the gray, rubbery ground. "Haha! Got you, little fly!"

"Weaver!" I shouted in protest, struggling against the sticky fibers. "We had a deal!"

"Did we now?" She asked, picking me up, tumbling me over and over without effort, the web constricting around me. "What deal was that, little fly? I might have forgotten. Hunger does that to me sometimes."

"I can take you back with me! To the body you requested," I squeaked out, nausea from the way she turned me pressing bile into the back of my mouth.

"And?" she hissed, the webbing suddenly constricting around me, painfully crushing my limbs against my body.

"Three days?" My voice little more than a wheeze. Attempting to slip sideways did nothing, that part of me was as bound by her thread as the rest of me. Still, I extended my struggling into that space, but the webbing had no more give to it there.

"I do vaguely remember that deal." She dropped me and I hit the ground with the grace of a sack of potatoes. Cocooned up to neck, she rolled me over and her terrifying face loomed over me. Mounted in the chitinous skull of a spider were eight human eyes, each a slightly different color. A cluster of four of them in the center stared down at me, while the others were mounted at the edges of her "face." Beneath it two bulbous mouthparts jutted, each ending in a curved fang as long as my paw. From the sides extended two segment arms that ended in slender human hands, one of which gripped my chin and kept me from looking away. I panted through clenched teeth. "You misremember, fly. A piece of you is what I desired, but now you can offer so much more. You've grown, fly. It's impressive how you hide so much of yourself away. Even here in a place where dragons hold no power."

"What is it you want, then? The dragon scales?" I asked, mentally cataloging all the hidden parts of myself: Mr. Bitey, my storage stomach, whatever strange limb I used to pull myself into and out of the sideways space. All of them, except Mr. Bitey, I'd give her eagerly in exchange for getting back to O'Meara. Mr. Bitey I would miss.

"Had your wings grown in, I would have taken those." She laughed with a different voice, high and beautiful. "You will carry my mark and once you transport me to that body, you will grant me your hospitality."

"What?" I gasped.

"Earth is a dangerous place even for me. No matter where you make your home you invite me into it. Hide me if I am hunted, defend me if necessary." The four eyes on me fluttered their long lashes.

I swallowed hard. "On a few conditions."

Fingers clamped my jaw shut. "Never fear, I am a good house guest and I will not harm those within your household, but beyond it, you do not get to dictate my behavior. I live by my rules, not yours. The choice is, you give me freedom on earth and we return to it together. Or you are a fly and I consume you right here." A bit of liquid dribbled from a fang.

I wish I could say it was a hard choice. That I carefully weighed the amount of harm the Weaver could inflict on the world versus the amount of good I could do. Truthfully, she could have asked for more and I would have done it to avoid those fangs from piercing my hide and dissolving my internal organs. She let go of my mouth and the first thing out of it was, "I agree to your terms."

"Good!" The creepy spider-human arms clapped once and my bindings fell away. I immediately got my feet beneath me and backed away from her. My heart thundered as my meat brain screamed at me to run away from Weaver. Her head cocked slightly and those human eyes watched me with curiosity. Gods damnit, I wanted to go home. I'm not usually afraid of spiders, but Weaver invoked an urge to yowl in terror. Legs and all, she took up the space of a large SUV. She stayed still as a statue, watching me as I argued with my body. She wasn't going to kill me. I was okay. We had struck the deal. Yet I shook with adrenaline, as my tail lashed in great sweeping motions behind me and every single follicle of hair I possess stood straight up from my skin.

I forced myself to sit and groom a trembling paw, claws fully extended. Only once I set it down did I manage to take my eyes off Weaver to scan the landscape. It was the same place that Archibald had first pulled me. The back of the titanic manta ray, the Now apparently? I took a deep breath, "Where are we? And how do we get home?"

She animated, waving one leg across the landscape. "This is the NOW. It feeds on the collapse of potential to a single solitary moment, defecates the past." The limb pointed behind her; the NOW's long tail extended into a dark void and further behind it, a dim line extended into the infinite distance.

"So, the past is this thing's poop?" I asked.

"Yes," she confirmed, "Our planes share a NOW and hence I am able to come to your aid, Kitty."

Kitty was definitely an upgrade from fly. "I was pulled here by a magus. How do you get here?"

"More pressing is finding our way back inside and rejoining the causality." With that she moved, not with her legs, but her form billowed like flag lifted by a sudden wind. Two pin pricks jabbed either side of my neck. All my legs locked instantly as her shadow settled over me. "Now hold still."

"What are you doing?" I gasped, struggling to move, but absolutely nothing happened.

Twin pinches on my back and with a gentle pull, I felt myself open. "I need somebody to use until we reach the one that is intended for me. What other choice is there?"

I could only wheeze in protest as she stepped down into me. The first leg threaded up through my shoulder and down my foreleg. Muscle and bone seemed to part to make room. The small claws at the end of the leg dug into the underside of my paw pad. Then she repeated the process until each of my legs was filled with two of hers. Hands gripped the edges of the seam she had opened in my back. "This will be a bit of a squeeze." She said before yanking hard and forcing her head down into me. Fingers closed around my ribs as she hauled herself up into my chest. Her bloated abdomen followed and a strangled gasp escaped me as my rear stretched around her. A sharpness lanced through my skin where she had opened, swiftly followed by another on the opposite side, the pattern had repeated halfway up the opening when I finally realized she was stitching up my back with herself inside me. She drew me closed and control of my body returned to me suddenly. I staggered to the side, gasping with relief. I still felt her presence inside, her limbs were the bones of my legs and rest of her resided in the space my internal organs usually were. Only my tail and head felt free of her. I glanced at myself, expecting to see my body distended and distorted, but to my shock, my body appeared completely normal. The only evidence of her within me were the red interlocking triangles that now branded my rump.

And most won't even see those. Her voice hissed from within my chest. *Relax, Thomas, we are made of different stuffs. Overlapping like this is not comfortable for either of us, but I haven't eaten your sweet organ meat yet.*

"That's so comforting," I said, grimacing at the crawling sensation of my skin. "What's next? How do I get home?"

Walk between the past and the future. Do not look at either. Eventually, we will find a hole, a sinus. From there, I suspect you will know your own way.

I walked, eager to be done with carrying Weaver as soon as possible. Keeping my eyes on the gray ground. Weaver stayed quiet, although I could feel her presence using my vision. My own perceptions drifted, examining my silver threads; in that I saw thick binding that now connected me to the spider spirit. A leash that could be pulled.

There. Weaver drew me back to my normal vision, if that's what I actually used in this place. An eight-foot wide, puckered slit in the fleshy ground confronted us. *Pry it open.*

I lifted my wrist and attempted to call forth my telekinetic hand, but nothing happened.

The spider laughed with what had to be a stolen woman's voice. *No thread transmission works here.*

Had been worth a shot. Cautiously I turned my paws outward as far as I could, digging claws into either side of the split.

It opened with the speed of a blink. Gravity itself seemed stunned as I hung midair, staring down into the dark chasm for a breath before it sucked me down. "I have had enough of falling today!" I screamed out, finishing the phrase just before my paws slapped down onto something solid. While my eyes detected nothing in the blackness that surrounded me, my magical vision churned with madness. Whirling images and objects collided all around me, morphing and disintegrating.

I whirled around, trying to make heads or tails over where to go, when a faint voice burst into my head. O'Meara's voice, etched with worry, "Thomas! Where are you?!"

Hope and happiness flooded my being as I grabbed hold of our link and tugged. It had a direction! I ran for it, heedless of the wild magics around me. My silver threads had all regained their directionality, and I followed them. Only my whiskers saved me from running into several walls; the corridors within the now were full of turns, but I worked myself closer and closer. The images surrounding me became recognizable. Flashes of O'Meara, Rudy, and Riona, among others. I didn't pay much attention, just hurtled through until the ground beneath me ran out and I leapt. Reaching out, I wrapped those hidden pieces of myself around our bond and pulled? Pushed? Neither of those precisely but the sensation of sliding down rope, but it was a rope that I was also connected to.

Space and time tore as I reached the end of the bond. O'Meara appeared in the center of the flash. She caught me as I slammed into her chest. Arms clamped around me even as we both fell to the ground. Her relief flooded into me as I licked her face and tasted tears. *Thought I lost you for good this time.*

It was a bit touch and go there for a few moments, I thought back, the warmth of our love flowing freely between our minds as she squeezed me.

If this is an attempt to drive me out, it will not work. Weaver sounded amused as O'Meara recoiled, her presence whirling in my head.

*Blood and Burning Ashes. What in the nine hells is that?!*O'Meara's body lit with a city-block-burning power.

*Aaah...*My thoughts churned with uncertainty. *That's the Weaver. She was my ticket home. The only one I had.*

We have an arrangement. Weaver's laugh was mocking.

O'Meara's fingers dug into my fur. *You get out of him right now. This instant.*

Thomas is in my debt. Once he completes the task, I will take my leave. Not before. Weaver hissed and used that musical laugh at the same time. Equaling amusement in threat.

My familiar is residence for no one. Final warning, whatever you are, O'Meara growled; my mind's eye filled with the image of a flaming sword.

O'Meara please don't... I thought whispered, imagining a stone wall between the two. *It's a simple favor. Just need to find Noise and the body she built.* I had never explained my previous encounter with Weaver to her.

Thomas! We have less than 24 hours to prep for a siege. We do not have time to hunt down your ex-girlfriend! She seethed, and I felt a sharp crack inside my skull. A strike on the wall? *If you do anything more to him, you will answer for it.* She called out in my head. In the real world, she grabbed my ears and forced me to look into her burning green eyes. "And you! You are not to break this bond with me while she's in there, not for a single second. Do you understand me, Thomas?"

"Yes," I whispered.

She hugged me tight, any tighter and my neck would have snapped.

Weaver laughed and settled back into my body. At least she didn't comment.

"It will be okay," I wheezed.

"Okay does not happen when dealing with spirits like that." She kissed the top of my head and relaxed, but as she did an errant prayer slipped through the link: *Please, almighty whatever, do not force me to kill him.*

She froze, realizing she'd slipped; neither of us was good at guarding our thoughts from the other. "Hopefully it doesn't get that bad."

7

THE FIRST THING O'MEARA did was call Noise's number, but it didn't pick up. It was the waxing moon now; most werewolves gave up on cell phones at this point. Immediately she switched into investigative mode, trying old contacts to figure out if Noise's family pack was still in the Grantville area and if she was still with them.

She left it to me to let everyone know that I'd returned.

Not that everyone had been aware that I had even been gone. It had been less than an hour, and O'Meara had told no one who hadn't been in the hallway except Rudy.

He pounced on my back as soon as I left O'Meara's quarters. "So, you been through time eh?"

"Yeah, it's not a place I want to go again," I said, pawing the elevator button.

"Welcome to time club. First rule of time club is-"

"You don't talk about time club?" I guessed.

"Got it in one!" Rudy chittered. "Whatever futures you saw were possibilities. Possibilities that could be altered by the fact you've even seen them. So forget about it."

"What happened to you?" I asked.

"Nuthing, and I was lucky. Got punted there some time in the 1800's. Don't remember much, but it was two decades later when I got back. And that's all I'm gonna say."

The elevator dinged in front of us.

Not going to tell him I came back with you? Weaver asked as we stepped into the elevator.

No, I thought back at her. *If we're lucky, we can find Noise and the body within an hour and then nobody has to know.*

That would be ideal. A hint of sarcasm buzzed along with her hiss but I didn't call her on it.

We found that the hallway that led to the Magus apartments stinking of smoke and the carpet charred away. *O'Meara what happened after I got pulled after Archibald?*

Bit of a mess, she responded with a flush of embarrassment. *I had to stop Riona from going after Scrags and I was... rather rough with everyone. Once your head guest is gone, I will have some apologizing to do.*

Uh oh. I started treading a bit carefully up to Riona's door. It was closed, but there was an O'Meara-sized hole in the wall next to it. I heard Riona's voice, full of indignation. "I don't see why I should believe a word you say. My Dad can't be Archmagus Archibald. And why should I care about some dragon's vendetta against him?"

I peered around the edge of the hole to see everyone who'd seen the attack. Naomi, Morie, and Tack sat on a couch facing Scrags, who sat on the coffee table. Riona stood leaning against the wall, a cold pack pressed against her cheek. "Well," I spoke loud enough for everyone in the room to jump, "he's officially trying to kill me for one, second he's attempting to manipulate the future of House Khatt. For that, he's 'kill on sight.' We make our own way, no matter how we bungle it."

"Thomas." Riona blinked at me. "You're back."

Scrags' eyes and mouth floated around to face me without his ears turning. "There ya are ladd, talking sense."

Rudy jumped up onto a counter. "I already gave him the time club spiel."

"I didn't see much. Too busy trying to get my teeth into Archibald. He ditched me in the void and," I took a deep breath, feeling Weaver's weight inside me. She was keeping her own counsel, but the spider spirit probably had a bucket of popcorn stashed with her. "I got out. It wasn't cheap." I stepped into the apartment and Scrags' form flickered to stand on all fours, back arched defensively.

"I see that, ladd." He said, his tail flicking warily.

Another little dragon, Weaver commented. *This one even has wings. You have interesting friends.*

Riona had lowered the ice pack, revealing a bubbled burn on the side of her face, roughly the size and shape of O'Meara's hand. She squished the gel back and forth in the plastic packet. I circled around the coffee table, ignoring the way Scrags slid away from me to sit at Riona's feet. "Why haven't you healed that?" I asked softly.

"If Tack and I do it, I'm afraid it will scar. Don't need to remember Hots slapping me off my feet every time I look in the mirror." She kept her eyes on the cold pack. "I don't understand; he had just stopped by to chat. He goes on a bit long about the importance of making the most of a bad situation but," her eyes pleading, "He's my dad. The one I remember."

"Instead of the one who appeared in his place on your ninth birthday, not recognizing his little girlie." Scrags hmpfed.

Riona's eyes teared up and she sucked in her lips to try to hold it all in.

"He was awakening!" Tack growled, jumping from the couch as he shoved himself between me and Riona. I didn't back away so he bared his teeth inches away from my face. "It wasn't his fault!"

"Awakening takes mebbe a month at most. Where was he when Riona finished her apprenticeship laddie? Think about it." Scrags said.

Tack growled back.

This wasn't the conversation to have in public. "Everyone out!" I ordered. Naomi and Morie practically ran for the door.

"Yuuup." Rudy declared, "I think ol' Stompy needs some looking to. Ya gots this, Thomas." He leapt up to the hole and scurried up into the wall.

Scrags didn't move.

"Scrags..." I said as a nudge.

"I won't be far." His liquid form collapsed into a black puddle that flowed down into the carpet, streamed over to the wall, and disappeared into the electrical outlet. It was all probably for show. If I checked under the reality's rug he'd probably be hiding there, listening. That's where he lived.

Riona took a deep breath and patted Tack's side. That got him to stop baring his teeth, but he remained alert, full of tension.

"Thomas, you've done so much for me, for us, and I kinda believe you... But it's been so nice to have my dad back." Riona said, slumping back onto the couch. "Remember that bad fight I got into with Dorothy while you were bonded to Veronica?"

"Yeah," I nodded. I had spent six months as Veronica's familiar after Grantsville had been destroyed. The Blackwings had emerged from their imprisonment with a vow to forgive each other for their sins. A vow that had started fraying between Dorothy and Riona almost immediately. Veronica had managed their spats even handedly while I had been there. That had changed once I left. Still, there were a couple occasions both Dorothy and Riona had been told to leave and cool off.

"Even Tack was mad at me for that one. So, I went to my usual bar alone, and he was there. Sat down next to me. Said, hey pumpkin, it's been awhile." She sniffed. "And that was it, he gave me a story about a rough awakening and a terrible apprenticeship."

"And you let it slide."

She nodded and sniffed hard. "I didn't care, really. He was someone not in the cabal to talk to. He came by every few months. Recommended a few books and gave helpful suggestions. And now that cat-thing says he's mucking with time? And you're trying to kill him? That makes zero sense. He encouraged me to go to you two for help when things got bad with Veronica."

"I think he is trying to help you. In his sociopathic way," I said very quietly. "Have you thought about what happens if I die?"

Her sculpted eyebrows furrowed, eyes searching the space between us. "O'Meara would..." Tack put his paw on her thigh and she trailed off. Their eyes met for a moment. I felt O'Meara's attention flicker to me briefly, glare at Weaver and give me a wordless squeeze.

"She wouldn't take another familiar," Riona said after a bit. "So... As the second magus to join..."

"Leadership would fall to you by default And then I bet all sorts of things would happen to let you hang onto the house's resources."

"You can't let tragedy stop you," she muttered, sounded like a quote, before giving me a calculated gaze. "The answer is clear, then. Tack and I have to leave until I can convince him to stop whatever he's doing."

"I thought about that. I almost asked you to leave several months ago, would have told you all this," I said, "And then you came up with how to isolate and harvest a silver thread."

She sucked in her lower lip and shook her head before answering, "That came from him. Said something that made me have a brainwave."

"Making more links is this House's future if we have one and that means I need you to be part of it. Nobody else can do that part of the ritual, not without months of instruction from you at least. You've been experimenting with the silver threads since before you joined us. I remember that song you played for us." I paused and paced around the room. "I think Archibald set it up so it's very likely that O'Meara and I will die during this siege but in dying, give you and the others some opening for the house to continue." It was all adding up as I spoke, and it seemed right. It totally clarified what we actually needed to do.

"Unfortunately for us, for me at least, he's fucked it up. I almost caught him and I injured him. Hopefully that throws a few wrenches in his predictions and I'm going to throw what I hope to be a big one into his plans."

"What do you mean?" she asked.

"We're not going to fight house Erebus. We're running."

She swallowed, nodded. "I think... that's wise."

"Find Rudy and tell him begin Operation Exploding Porcupine," I said, distantly hearing O'Meara talking on the phone about the Grantsville pack and where they ran.

"Me? Why can't you tell him?" Riona asked, wiping at her eyes.

"O'Meara and I have to fulfill a debt I incurred coming back home," I said, mentally referring to the timetable of that particular plan. We would have to be back in ten hours to do to some heavy drilling. Hopefully it wouldn't take us more than half that to find Noise and Weaver's body.

Riona tossed the ice pack onto the table. "Sounds like Tack and I have more important things to do than worry about a scar."

"S-show time?" Tack asked, his tail giving a nervous wag.

"Good luck," I told them and started for the hallway. Several floors above, O'Meara hung up her phone. *Got anything?* I asked her.

Nothing. It's too late in the lunar cycle for werewolves to use phones. I can't get any firsthand info. I know Noise left the Grantsville pack couple months after you moved to Vegas. Walter boasted his little pup had joined one of the largest packs in Pennsylvania. If we go out there, can you find her? Do you have a strong enough silver thread?

Weaver answered before I did. *I can always find those I have deals with.*

That made things easier. Tracking someone by their silver thread only works if they want to be found. Learned that trying to find Oric six months ago. That had been a waste of time. The damn owl was keeping to his word about lying low. *I'll go find Willow and Reynard; we're going to need a portal we can drive through.*

I'll meet you in the garage. Going to throw a few things in a bag first, she said, heading for her weapons rack.

Grab my gun harness, will you? I asked her.

She stopped, *you won't need that because we're not breaking this bond.*

In the place Archibald pulled me, all I had were claws and teeth; they weren't enough. If I had been wearing that harness, he might not have gotten away.

Do you want your warded one too?

No, the werewolves won't be flinging spells, and I think we'll need to approach as politely as possible.

Meet you there in 5 minutes.

Pity, Operation Exploding Porcupine seems like a very pretty web. I might like to see it. Weaver laughed in my chest, as I mentally pushed her away from the memories of it.

8

THE VEIL DOESN'T LIKE portals to be open for any length of time, but you can get away with them so long as you open them in unoccupied areas. O'Meara's old Grantsville residence definitely counted. It was all that remained of the town. The rest of it had been deleted from the map and mundane world. The swirling purple portal deposited the two of us and O'Meara's Porsche onto a driveway blocked by a gnarled tree half the width of the pavement. While the two-story box of a house sat lonely and glum, looking surrounded by vegetation that, after over two years of abandonment, had crept across the yard and were in the midst of devouring the brick walkway.

"Doesn't look like anyone's been using the house." That had been a hope, that the pack had decided to use the house after O'Meara had moved to Vegas. But without even a forest path leading to it, nor any utilities hooked up it was bit rustic for even a werewolf. Would have been convenient to ask Noise's parents about her whereabouts and situation but we didn't have time to go looking for them.

Did you miss your target? Weaver asked, plucking at something with her hands. *She is quite distant still. It will take us hours, if you had a road.*

"Guess I forgot about the lack of roads. Oh, well." O'Meara laughed to herself, as I dug my claws into the seat. "Give me a direction."

A tug, and thread of silver snapped into focus in my magical sight. *She lies to the east. Why is the kitty so nervous?*

O'Meara touched her anchor and placed her hand on the crystal in the center console of the car. Flame roared beneath us. With a small rattle, the car swiftly lifted from the ground. I felt the tingling warning of the Veil for the first time in nearly a year as the treetops fell away but also a tensing in my legs. We slowly rotated until the little bubble compass mounted on the dashboard pointed due east. I took the opportunity to double the straps of my harness and make sure the impending acceleration wouldn't kink my tail.

What is she doing? Weaver hissed, her fingers drumming nervously on inside of my ribs. *Why are you so concerned?*

With a thunderous boom the forest below became a blur as we shot forward, the acceleration pressing my butt into the webbed seat cover. I heard a startled scream and it wasn't mine. *Too Fast! Too Fast!* Weaver's hissing voice became an anxious buzz.

I gave a tight little laugh.

"Does our passenger not appreciate my driving? A spider who's afraid of heights?" O'Meara asked as innocently as a battle-hardened magus can, which is not very. "Let me lower the altitude then."

It not the height! It's the speeeeeeeeeEEEEE! Weaver shrieked in terror as O'Meara banked us into a double barrel roll. For the first time since the spider spirit boarded my body, I became aware of my own stomach as it lurched toward my heart. We crashed through the foliage and down onto a nominal paved road. Hovering over it with about a foot of clearance, O'Meara maintained the ludicrous, eye watering speed along its twisting curves, the tree trunks passing by so rapidly that they resembled a solid bark colored wall. Weaver jerked at my forelegs, trying to cover my eyes but I fought her, digging in my claws.

If you bruise my delicate abdomen, you will pay! Do you hear me, Ashbringer! I will feast upon your children! Weaver screamed inside my head.

"Good thing I don't have any!" O'Meara laughed and flung us back into the sky. "Tell me when I'm getting close."

Weaver's response amounted to little more than a primordial squeal of terror. The car shook as we pressed against the sound barrier. The night clouds raced over head as the landscape below dwindled to a gray blur broken by an occasional streak of light.

The silver thread Weaver held onto suddenly changed its angle.

Here! I thought.

O'Meara threw the car into a sharp turn and my vision swam from the force shoving me down into the seat. We inverted entirely as O'Meara picked out a road then dived onto it like a peregrine falcon targeting a mouse. The thread pointed due north as we raced over the road. I wonder how many tales of UFOs we seeded as we hurtled over the few poor souls who were driving through the forest at three AM.

Close, Weaver hissed after a time. *Stop or you're going to pass it.*

O'Meara took her hand away from the crystal and the car fell down onto the road. Weaver screamed anew as O'Meara stomped on the brakes, and the momentum threw me against my harness. She turned onto a narrow logging road and pulled to a stop. "See, you're fine and so is Thomas," O'Meara said as she set the parking brake. "I'm merely trying to accomplish your request as fast as possible."

I tried and failed not to chuckle as Weaver sputtered incoherently inside of me. *If you mock me host, you will regret it,* she finally hissed.

No mocking, simply enjoying the fact that O'Meara's driving inspires terror even in gods. It's the closest thing I've found to be a universal constant.

O'Meara lightly thwapped my shoulder as she undid her seat belt. "Watch it, you."

Weaver settled back, perhaps mollified, perhaps plotting her revenge. *She is still some miles distant.*

"How many?" I asked.

Weaver pulled at the strand. *A man could walk the distance in a few hours.*

If a man can do it in three hours, then I can do it in one. Close enough, then. I responded. Flying a flaming car into the middle of a werewolf pack could spawn more drama than it was worth. I slapped the button to release my harness.

"We could try to get a little closer," O'Meara gestured up the logging road.

I shook my head. "Noise didn't tell me much about werewolf politics, but many view any association with magi as corrupt and unclean. Hopefully I can get in, ask her where the body is, and then leave without anyone realizing I was there."

O'Meara nodded. "I'll move on down the road. I'll be watching though; we can't afford to get bogged down here. If you're in trouble, I'm not going to wait for you to ask for me to come get you."

"Understood."

I received a good ear scratching before slipping both sideways and out of the car. The entire forest smelled of lupines. I didn't need my body's hackle-raising instincts to remind me to tread lightly. After five minutes' walking, the Veil started to make staying sideways uncomfortable; its cold pins and needles occasionally jabbing me with a sharp poke. I relented, resuming my journey in reality and wincing at the thunderous crunch of the leaf litter underfoot.

Straining my ears and nearly jumping when shadows shifted in the breeze, I nearly stepped on the first werewolf I encountered. In the grey palette of night, the huge werewolf resembled nothing more than a pool of darkest shadow nestled in a gully. A small huff was all the warning I got before a great lupine head snapped into the air. I stepped sideways before his eyes shone in my direction.

His ears roamed as he peered through the night, sniffing. Slowly the pool of shadow unfolded and stood up on two legs using a tree to steady himself. Hunched, his long lupine neck extended forward from his torso. A strap across his back held a long gun across his belly. He held his arms out in front of him, forced by shoulders that had gone flush against his sides but he still had thumbs on those paws.

Hoping he wouldn't smell my magic, I trotted around him as he moved up the hill in my direction. As I walked away, I heard the hiss of a walkie talkie and the werewolf spoke in a surprisingly clear voice, "Rudolfo here. I smell a cat and there are tracks. They're too big for a lost bobcat."

"I'll get Aldrich; stay put." The radio hissed back.

Comb me backwards, I mentally swore. *Why the hell is the scent of a cat worth even getting up?*

Cats mean high ranking magi, O'Meara answered. *Stay sideways until you find Noise. Most can't pull a disappearing act like you can so hopefully they'll be busy peering up into the trees for awhile. I'll see if I can circle around so you don't have to come back this way.*

Good idea, I thought back and continued on. When the prickling of the Veil climbed into pinching me with crab claws, I rested in a gully of my own in reality until I felt its attention wane, then continued on.

On my second rest I heard something crashing through the forest, coming vaguely in the direction that the thread indicated. A werewolf with a mottled gray coat emerged from the trees, this one even larger than the sentry I'd tripped over. He moved with an awkward quadrupedal shuffle hop. I wasn't in his direct path so I stayed still and hoped he wouldn't notice me nestled among the trees. He barreled on past without a glance in my direction.

I continued in the shelter of the sideways space. The strength of that lupine scent grew with every step. Of course,

Noise would be in the most densely populated part of the woods. Couldn't be out on patrol or something.

With them at this awkward stage of their transition I don't think they'd do much of anything if they can help it, O'Meara commented. *Just find her.*

Among thinning trees, I spotted werewolves curled up on the ground, some in pairs and others by their lonesome. As a group, they were more wolfish than Noise's family, but most sported some sign of domestication, whether that be a blunter muzzle, long wavy fur, or markings foreign to wild wolves. They rested but most were not asleep. Their gazes drifted in the direction I had come. Waiting for something.

I heard a bark, well more of yap, followed a scolding whisper, "Wiget! Shush." The voice had a deep register, but it triggered a flare of recognition: Noise.

"Oh, you can throw it," another voice counseled. "It's probably nothing. Rudolfo seeing shadows."

My ears led me through a dense thicket of brush into a clearing where a small cottage stood in the center, its roof decorated with solar panels. On its porch lounged at least four werewolves, Noise among them. She lay on the very edge, looking down at three wiggling shapes on the ground below her, one of which gave another playful yap. With a huff of resignation, Noise tossed a round object out over the pups' heads. It bounced and rolled halfway to the bramble line. They gave chase with an enthusiasm that their awkward little bodies couldn't match, taking tumbles, falls, and in one case a full-on somersault before they even reached the ball. The cuteness escalated when the lead pup, sporting the black and russet colorings of Noise herself, attempted to claim the ball. Her two gray siblings objected strongly, resulting in a full-scale puppy brawl of wagging tails and tumbling bodies. The biggest of the three emerged victorious, holding the ball up proudly in jaws that were much more blunt than his siblings', like a bulldog's.

They were Noise's pups, and suddenly all my certainty about doing this soured. The werewolves were all encircling Noise's children, and here I was. Charging into the middle of it.

Promises are rarely a convenient thing for mortals, Weaver chided me.

A radio crackled. One of the other werewolves on the porch lay in front of a small stack of equipment. He pawed a foot pedal and acknowledged the broadcast with a light wuff.

"Definite mountain lion tracks, a large male, but I don't smell magic. Not yet anyway. The tracks end abruptly, might be in a tree. Stay alert. If Noise scents any magic at all, then grab the pups and howl." The voice wasn't Rudolfo so it must be the wolf who passed me in the forest.

"A large cougar, huh?" Noise's eyes scanned the clearing as she herded the pups onto the porch with a paw. "This one sure knows how to stir up drama."

"Cats where they don't belong mean magi. Magi are evil things sweetie," an older werewolf said. "Best to be cautious."

9

HOW THE HELL WAS I going to get to her without every single other werewolf jumping down my throat? Or rather at my throat.

Maybe pull the fiery messenger of doom act after all? Might be faster, O'Meara wondered. *Back off, announce our presence, and ask to talk to her.*

Gimmie a moment, I told her. That wolf said he didn't smell magic and then specifically referred to Noise smelling magic. Then perhaps not all of them could. Question was then, would she raise the alarm? Only one way to determine that. If they were cats, they'd probably see a subtle purple-tinted ripple as I approached if they were paying attention. In Vegas with the magical background, it's almost impossible to see unless you're watching for it. Dog familiars can detect me almost without effort within ten feet or so, but did not know precisely where I stood in that radius.

Noise's nostrils flared when I got close and she pulled the pups close to her stomach protectively, holding them there with her knees and paws. She didn't howl; her eyes bounced around the clearing. I growled in frustration. She smelled me, well the subtle bend of space I hid behind but she didn't know what it meant. With a huff I took a step back and noticed a gap between the ground and the porch, big enough for me to slip through. Beneath I found a rather cozy den furnished with old couch pillows and occupied by four older pups, each the size of a German shepherd piled up in the far corner. Plenty of space for me. I looked around for something, anything I could scratch a message into.

Don't you even think about breaking this bond, Thomas, O'Meara warned me. *That gun you have isn't even loaded with silver bullets.*

I didn't really want to know what was going through Noise's head, anyway. Probably fantasizing about cutting off my tail now. Fortunately, I found a bit of scrap lumber that looked left over from building the porch. Flickering out to reality I snatched it in my teeth and dragged it back into the sideways space. There it felt slippery, like a bar of wet soap. Risking Noise's alarm, I channeled tiny amount of O'Meara's heat into a claw tip and wrote: NEED TALK. NOW. On it.

Praying the pups wouldn't wake up, I slipped back to reality and tossed it lightly out of the gap.

Noise's pups exploded into a chorus of yaps and leapt down onto the block of wood. "No!" Noise scolded as her own paw slapped down on the wood. "Pocket, could you give me a hand?" she asked as she snatched the bull-faced pup with her teeth. The other female swiftly grabbed the other two, and Noise flicked the wood back under the deck. Guess she'd seen it.

The other female, Pocket, chuckled. "They don't know the meaning of danger yet."

Noise huffed in agreement. "Keep them on the porch for me? I gotta take a stretch."

"I'll try. Be quick."

The floorboard groaned as Noise stepped off the porch and staggered around the side of the cottage. Once out of line of sight she hurried for the tree line. "Thomas? Where are you?" Her voice so soft I strained to hear it right next to her.

"Botching the stealth level of life, apparently." I said, stepping into view. "It's been awhile. Looks like you're doing alright for yourself."

She stared at me a moment, before her eyes closed as if she'd been struck by a sudden migraine. "You did not just sneak into the middle of my pack's territory on a rest day just to catch up. And if you did, then you better run." Her teeth flashed at me.

"Yeah... Sorry. I really am. Unfortunately, something's come up that won't wait," I told her, backing off a little from the fangs.

"Then why couldn't you have told me in a text two days ago when I had thumbs?" She glanced back over her shoulder at the cottage. "You know what, it doesn't matter. Tell me what you want and get out of here."

My teeth clicked together in a nervous chatter. "I need to know where you stashed the body you built for Weaver."

"Weaver?" The entire left side of her face twitched hard. "The spider spirit that accosted us in Grantsville?"

Weaver reached her hand up into my mouth and moved it like a puppet. "The very same, girl. Where is it? I felt you make it those years ago. It's rather tight in here and I'm eager to stretch my own legs."

"You're in Thomas?" she whispered, her eyes widening.

I shook my head, hard, pulling my jaw out of Weaver's grasp. "Ach!" I sputtered and moved my jaw side to side. Once I was sure I had reclaimed my tongue, I said, "I had what you could definitely consider a 'game over' situation a couple hours ago. Weaver, uh, kindly fished me out. I have to deliver her to that body. Please tell us where it is. O'Meara and I can just get into any storage facility no prob if you can't think of the combo or we need a key."

Anxiety flooded over Noise's face as I talked, pointed ears slowly sagging as she started to pant. "I-it." Mouth closed, tongue licked her nose and then swallowed hard. The six-foot wolf, who was clearly still nursing, looked on the edge of a panic attack. "I was gonna fix it. I got so busy. I moved and then

I got pregnant and well... when I have hands, they're juggling three infants."

Oh Gods, she didn't have it. Weaver laughed her sweet musical laugh and reached up for my mouth again. *May I?* she asked this time.

I assented and once again her voice rolled off my tongue. "You were charged with the body's care and maintenance until I came for it. You are in default of our deal."

"Heh," she laughed nervously. "Look, I still have all the pieces; you can use those. You were an entire toolset last time. Maybe you don't need all of the connective bits?"

"Maybe you don't need to be a wolf anymore." Weaver hissed back and I felt her rear up out of me; green light flared over me as Weaver poked out into the world sans body. She stabbed into Noise's chest with two legs and tugged on something within it. Weaver ducked back inside of me as Noise clasped two paws over her chest.

"No! Not again. I can feel it..." She clenched her mouth closed, as if holding her breath. Her struggle lasted a few seconds before bursting forth a low moaning, "Mooooo!" Already two white horns were forcing themselves from the sides of her skull. "I'll fix it! I'll fix it."

I tried to speak but Weaver had a last word, "If I am forced out of Thomas before my body is presented to me in a suitable condition, then your connection to the meadow will spread to your children." Then she settled back into my chest, radiating an awful smugness.

You had to do that to her now!? I internally shouted at Weaver.

Obligations are to be honored. We will both suffer for her lack.

"What's going on?" Someone called out from the cottage and the very forest seemed to stir.

Noise stopped pawing at her horns and hung her head in abject misery. "I'll have to come with you. Can you use that invisibility spell on me?" She asked.

I shook my head. "No. It's a personal trick. I could maybe grab a pup. Beyond that I can only light things on fire. I'm so sorry, Noise. I wasn't planning on an extraction. O'Meara can be here in about five minutes, but it will be messy."

"Call her." Noise gave a laugh that dripped with bitterness. "I thought I'd have mooooo-" she bit off the sound and continued, "-time. I'm going to get my kids. You might as well let them see you. Might be easier that way." She lifted her head and her voice. "It's alright, Pocket. He's an old friend."

She walked back toward the cottage and I followed in her wake.

Bloody Ashes, Thomas, O'Meara groused as she lifted the car into the air. *I don't know precisely where you are. I'll need you to flare.*

A chorus of growls accompanied my stepping into view. The two other werewolves who'd been on the porch blocked our way, their muzzles displaying sharp teeth and grey fur. Pocket peeked out from the porch, a struggling pup in each arm.

"There's no need for that Sasha, Grisam. This is Thomas; he's actually an ex of mine if you can believe it." She laughed without humor. "It's a long story, really. He's uh, brought me some news. I have to go away for a bit. So, uh." Kneeling down, she gave a deep but soft bark and the unheld pup shot off the porch and raced up between the two elderly werewolves. He leapt into Noise's open arms and lathered the underside of Noise's jaw with puppy kisses. The remaining two struggled and whined in Pocket's grip. "Let them go Pocket. Please. I'm still nursing!"

The werewolf squeezed the pups tighter and lowered her ears. "You've got horns, I dunno what you are. We can feed them by gullet; they're almost old enough. You can take that little mongrel to the magi. That's probably where he'd wind up anyway, but Sprocket and Gear stay here. They're my brothers, too."

"Course you'll let Wickett go. No surprises there. And say I left Sprocket and Gear with you, how often you going to tell them that their mooother is some sort of magi-tainted demon? Just daily? Every mooooing minute?" As she spoke, her body filled with green energy, pulling on the meadow Weaver had reconnected to her as if were an anchor. Noise's muscles swelled as the small horns grew into wickedly pointed weapons. "They won't grow up like that."

One of the elderly werewolves leapt forward to attack. Noise dodged back, caught him with her horns and with a heave of her head, launched him behind her. Widget still clutched to her chest, she charged forward, clipping the second one so hard she spun into the cottage wall. Pocket turned to run but tripped, letting go of the pups as she fell to all fours. They bounced, legs and arms scrambling over the deck to run toward their mother. Pocket managed to snatch one up in her mouth and booked it. Noise skidded to pick up the black and russet pup as she barked my name, "Thomas! Please!"

At the same time O'Meara asked for my location.

I sprinted forward, diving sideways to overtake the she-wolf's unbalanced run, grabbed the heat, and reappeared with the force of a fireball. Pocket yipped in surprise, skidding to stop. I snatched the pup from her surprised jaws and fled back sideways. I felt a twinge in those hidden parts of me as I dragged the puppy with me.

A blaze lit in the sky. The rocket powered Porche swooped down onto the clearing between Pocket and me, the columns of flame it rode on scorching the grass. Staggered gunshots rang out as O'Meara circled once before landing the car in the middle of the clearing. The car's ward glowed as bullets pinged uselessly off it.

O'Meara threw open her door and stepped out, battle wards ablaze. "Get in!

I ran to her, popping back to reality to toss the pup into the car. The pup landed with a soft yip. Turning swiftly, I saw Noise lumbering toward us, her back and neck curled protectively over the two pups she cradled in her arms. O'Meara and I knitted a fence of bullet vaporizing heat around her path to the car. Noise hesitated only a second before placing the pups into O'Meara's outstretched hands.

"I can't fit in that," Noise said, looking over the tiny car.

"Then you'll ride on top. I'll open the sunroof; use that to hang on," O'Meara said as she slung the other two werewolf pups into the back seat.

She closed her eyes and nodded, squeezing tears out of her eyes. I smelled blood; she'd been hit. "I'll hang on."

This all felt awful and wrong, but I had no way to stop this at this point. "I'm sorry," I mumbled at her before dashing into the car. The grey pup I'd tossed stared up at me curiously from the floor of the passenger seat.

"Noise!" The grey werewolf who'd passed me earlier charged out from the wood. O'Meara and I slammed a kinetic barrier down in front of him. He hit it like a dog running into a sliding glass door. Clutching his head and nose he wobbled back from the barrier. "What?!" He shook himself out. "What is going on?"

"Aldrich," Noise called out over the crackling heat of the barrier. "I lied. My family had nothing to do with the disappearance of Grantsville but I did. I was smack dab in the center of it. Fighting with and against the magi involved."

"You're, you're a spell dog?!" Aldrich nearly lost his footing as this appeared to hit him harder than the barrier.

"No!" Noise growled so deeply it shook the car. "Do I look like a flea-ridden spell dog to you?! Do spell dogs have moooooooing horns? You wouldn't understand. You call your own son a mongrel behind my back, Aldrich!"

The mention of his children prompted Aldrich's expression to flip from that of a kicked dog to teeth-filled menace. "Bitch! Whatever you are, give me my children back. I demand it. They belong to this pack. They belong to me."

"So you can raise them as outcasts? So you can grind them into the dirt after you find a new mate? I trust magi more than you with our children, so stick that up your tail hole and spin it!" Noise bellowed back at him, gripping the edge of the sunroof so hard that parts of it started to snap.

I'm ending this conversation before my car looks like their relationship, O'Meara dropped the heat fencing and channeled into the console crystal. Carefully she lifted us into the air.

Words seemed to fail Aldrich; instead of retorting, he threw back his head and let loose a howl loud enough to bully the roar of our flame. The pack answered him as we turned south toward the nearest town. I don't speak wolf howls, but they all sounded pretty angry.

Noise collapsed, the roof denting, softly whimpering to herself. The pups answered with tiny howls of their own outrage.

"Hey, hey, hey." I tried my paw at calming the pup in the front seat. "Your mum's okay. It's all going to be alright... maybe."

The pup shot me a big-eyed look of absolute skepticism and lifted his nose to howl again; his brother and sister joined in from the back seat. The car filled with small off-key awoos.

"What a bloody mess," O'Meara laughed and sighed once the pups had howled themselves out. "Where am I going, Noise?"

She gave an address. "It's my human home. Or was."

10

O'MEARA SETTLED ON THE road and drove slower than I'd ever experienced, so as not to fling our despondent passenger off the car. Nobody spoke, although the pups whined as Noise let her muzzle hang through the sunroof. Twenty minutes later we arrived at a small house set far back from the road. Even in the dim pre-dawn light I could see the chipped and flaking paint from its siding. We shut the pups in the car and Noise rolled off the roof. She lay there on the ground long enough for O'Meara and I to grow concerned.

"Noise?" I asked, lifting a paw, then hesitating whether to touch her with it.

A deep low of distress came from her. "Let me wallow for a moment. This is a total 'game over' for Noise the pack mother. It's a shitty game, Thomas. A real shitty game."

I had to chuckle at that. "That one never made it onto my wish list, but I'll take your word for it."

She pushed herself up. "It was so well-rated I decided I had to give it a shot. Couldn't be as bad as I thought it sounded. Thought I'd grow up, ya know?" She laughed and then sighed. "Turns out it's better in some ways, and also way worse than I imagined."

"What happened?" I asked.

"Nothing was left in Grantsville for a werewolf who prefers four walls no matter how many feet she has. That means joining another pack. I let Pa present me at the next gathering.

He let it be known that I can smell magic." She got to her feet and began leading us towards the house.

"How rare is that?" I asked.

"Unless the moon is full, it's pretty rare. Since Grantsville, I smell the colors of magic." She said, flipping one of several rocks strewn in an unkept flower bed, revealing a sliding door on its bottom. O'Meara picked it up, extracted a key and Noise continued, "Soon as that got out, I had pack leaders from all over the east wanting to meet the mutt with the magic nose. Among them was Aldrich, full of promises and offering himself instead of a son. He had an enormous pack, and that was exciting, too. With his own magical talents and mine, our children could be true seers of the moon."

O'Meara unlocked the door and Noise led us inside. "Plus, his pack wasn't too far from Ma and Pa's territory.. So I took his offer, stupidly thinking it was the best way to play the hand I'd been dealt. If I had to be a momma wolf, why not do it with the alpha of a large pack. But I had no idea how larger packs work. Turns out being the mate of the big cheese doesn't get you as much pull as I thought. I tried to throw around clout I didn't have, and stepped on some large toes." She sighed. "This pack is very focused on wolfish things, nobody's impressed that I can work a game pad without a thumb or query a database. They called me Aldrich's dog behind my back, and I had to endure remedial "wolf lessons" until I was seven months pregnant with the litter." She paused her talking to grab a door knob with her mouth and twist the door open. Flicking a switch with her nose, a single bulb lit a stairway down into the basement.

She laughed again, "Things were getting better though, once the pups came, I didn't have time for anything but them. Apparently full-time childcare is wolfish behavior. Motherhood was letting me have a little bit of a reset. The pack loves Gear and Sprocket. While they look at Widget and hint that I shouldn't get attached."

"There are of plenty of wolves in this pack that are not perfectly wolfish," I commented and she rounded on me. Shoving glistening fangs into my vision.

"Familiars who live in Vegas and sleep in penthouses don't get to judge, Thomas." She snarled, her muzzle had started to broaden, the teeth thicker but no less sharp.

"Sssorry!" I said, meaning it.

She snorted hard, and I felt moisture catch in my whiskers. With a shake of her head, she led us down into the basement where there were rows of metal shelves stacked with cardboard boxes and old wooden crates. They were marked with black marker in different hands. "Baby Clothes, Toys YR 2-5, Canning stuff, Blankets." Noise came to a stop in front of several newer boxes marked "Halloween decor."

"Here it is. I had it in a storage unit. Aldrich frowned on me doing coding work. Pack provides for the mothers and all that. I didn't pay the bill because I didn't want to explain what really happened to Grantsville to Aldrich. If he'd known how contaminated I am by magic he never would have taken me as a mate. Anyway, I came back from the woods three months ago to a notice that they'd disposed of the contents of my locker. I got there to find it in their dumpster, smashed."

Defiled. Weaver hissed in my head.

Noise looked at my chest, as if she could see the spider god inside me. "Yes, just like my life. They both need to be rebuilt."

"Let's get it all outside." O'Meara walked forward and placed a hand on my head; I curled my tail around to touch her ankle. We quickly knitted together a small force spell that grabbed hold of the boxes and floated them off the shelf. "Grab anything else you need, Noise, try to keep it limited to one bag that you can carry, no matter your form. Next few days we could be moving around a lot."

"Moooo?" Noise shook her head, "I mean what? Pa said you two owned a casino! And it had to be you, because there was something about a squirrel piloting a robot."

I laughed, but it collapsed into a sigh. "War's coming to magus town and its starting on our doorstep in about nineteen hours now. We'll try to get you somewhere safe before the fighting starts. I'm hoping a friend in Reno will put you up."

Her ears, which had been somewhat wilted, folded tight against her skull. "Try? Thomas, you really know how to spike a difficulty curve on my life. Now I'm taking my pups into a magical war zone?"

I bit back an answer to that, instead following O'Meara and the floating boxes back up the stairs. "Pack first, explain later."

"You're back!" Rudy chittered as soon as I stepped through the return portal, bounding across the roofs of several vans and a few hard hats to land on my harness. "Right on schedule, too. Death's Vault is almost ready to get moved. I was just telling Riona that if you didn't get back soon, she and Tack would have to make a tunnel for it. Made that dog choke on his treat."

Noise walked through behind me before I had a chance to open my mouth.

"Smashed cashew brittle salted with licorice! Is that Noise?" He squeaked and I heard the click of him checking the chamber my harness's gun.

Noise hadn't heard him though; she'd immediately sat back on her haunches staring at her surroundings with wide amber eyes. Over all the company vans and security sedans loomed a huge red eighteen-wheeler and the skeleton of a trailer. On which several hundred rodents labored. A crew of rats operated two cranes which were lowering a gatling gun and a missile launcher onto the trailer's frame. Waiting beneath them were a team of beavers wearing toddler-sized welding masks. The hood sat open with Naomi attacking something in the engine compartment with a wrench, a crow flapping to maintain his balance on her shoulder. Riona and Tack sat in a casting circle nearby, concentrating on an engine part that had sprouted crystals.

Alarm flowed from O'Meara when she spotted the grease-streaked magi. *Bloody hell. They started on the engine refit without me. Hang on, I'll be right back.* She hurried towards Riona.

"Be cool." I told Rudy and turned to Noise. "Pretend you don't see the rodents; they're not supposed to be here."

But Noise wasn't even looking at the truck, she was staring up at the ceiling, which thanks to a little space bending, stretched a good seventy feet above our heads. "This smells..." Her nostrils flared, "twisted."

"Good nose!" Rudy leapt up to the roof the car, "All of Vegas is in a shallowing, but we had to add some more headroom for the truck refit. Too bad we're about to run out of here, Fury Road style! You coming along? Cab's gunna be pretty full but we could strap you to the roof and have O'Meara rig ya up a fire-spitting guitar."

Noise simply looked at the squirrel's four-tooth grin and blinked.

I had to laugh. "She's not taking the truck; she's got some cargo that's rather precious." I pointed at the window of the Porsche. All three pups jostled for a position at the passenger side window.

"Oh... tiny wulfs. Right! I'll page Geoffrey." Rudy unslung his phone and poked at the screen.

When the pups saw Noise, they started yipping excitedly, and the black one gave a tiny howl. Noise nosed them, "Yes, yes. I know you're hungry, soon. Little bit longer. Ssshhh."

The black one, Sprocket, tossed back its head with an even more insistent, "Aaaawwwwooo!" while her siblings were distracted by the whirring approach of a goat-driven electric cart.

"May I take your baaaaaggs?" Geoffrey the goat asked.

After a telekinetic assist loading the cart, I pried O'Meara away from supervising the engine work, and after a couple of elevator rides, we all arrived in the portal room. A simple doorway that could take you anywhere on the continent provided it wasn't warded, and the Veil wasn't too pissed off.

"So what now?" She gestured at the door. "What corner of the world you going to stick me in? While I try to put a spider together with paws?"

"Like I said, Reno." I smiled tightly. "Hopefully you get along with lions."

"Oof," Rudy commented, "Making your ex stay with your current girlfriend? This will end well."

"Current girlfriend?" Noise's tail fled down between her legs. "Lions?"

O'Meara suppressed a laugh. *Probably not what Shina meant when she offered to store our baggage.*

Its either this or renting her a room somewhere random, I thought back as we re-targeted the portal to the parking lot of the Cat's Meow Casino. The heat of the rapidly approaching desert noon flowed into the room as the scene beyond the doorway became a parking lot that shimmered with heat. The closet vehicle to the portal was a cargo van with its back doors open. In it, a young lioness lounged, grooming her elbow.

"Aaah, cracked claws and tough hides," she grumbled softly. "I thought we were done for a bit?" The ridge of her ears bore a collection of golden rings that jangled softly when they flicked.

"Sorry, Kia," I told the lioness. "I've got some very precious cargo for you to haul down to the Savannah."

At the sound of my voice, Kia flinched and sprang to her feet only to bow her head. "Oh! Giver! It is you! You honor me. I will call the God Mother."

"Kia, that's not necessary," I said, annoyance flicking my tail. It could take Shina a half hour or longer to come up from the underground.

But the lioness lifted her head and roared, "GOD MOTH-ER! GIVER IS HERE!" out into the parking lot. Which meant this she was already above ground and stomach-clenching introductions were in order.

"You're in trouble now," Rudy whispered from my back. One of these days I was going to get a harness with an ejector seat.

Shina ran out between two parked cars a moment later, her muscles rippling beneath her short golden fur. The sight of her made me smile despite the situation. Slowing to a more dignified pace, she padded up to the portal and delivered an affectionate but harder than usual headbutt. "Hello, Little Lion," she purred.

"Hi, Mount Cuddlins," I purred right back as we rubbed cheeks to exchange scents.

"Give me one good reason I shouldn't grab you by your scruff and drag you downstairs." The purr gained an edge of a growl, although she kept the words quiet. "You can't fight an entire house with a single cabal."

"I can bloody their nose a bit. Hopefully that will attract some larger sharks," I said back.

"Why fight at all if that's all you can do?" she asked to my ear. "I do not want this to be our last meeting."

"It won't be." I hoped. "But I can't let them take the MGM for free. I've thumbed my nose at the actual Council; I can't roll over for this one. I have a rep to uphold."

"Fine, after you give Michael the 2nd his bloody nose, I want you to come here." Shina grabbed the side of my neck with her teeth, reminding me that my entire head fits in her jaws.

"I'm not leading all of Erebus to your doorstep. You barely have any wards at all on the casino."

"You are not a solitary male anymore, Thomas," she huffed. "You are part of my pride. If Death comes for us here then they'll face us all. We're better defended than you think we are."

I rolled my neck and hissed. Pulling back first and then thrusting my head forward, our foreheads touched and my world was swallowed by her golden eyes. "We'll consider our options when the time comes, Shina. I won't put the pride in danger of being slaughtered."

She made a sound like she had trapped rolling thunder in her throat. "I will be waiting for you tomorrow morning. You better show, Thomas."

With that we separated, both our chests heaving as we watched each other out of the corner of our eyes.

"True luv cat style," Rudy giggled.

"Shut up Rudy." Both Shina and I said in unison.

O'Meara laughed. "Be safe or I will kill you. Tends to have good results when it comes to Thomas. And don't worry, Shina. I'm not letting my familiar get offed tonight because he's going to be good and stay bonded." Stepping into the lioness's view, she hip-checked me. "Why don't you introduce the reason we're holding this portal open?"

"Right." I quickly stepped aside, clearing the way for Shina and Noise to see each other. "This is Noise, a friend from way back. She and her cubs need a place to stay and do some work. Away from this chaos."

Tentatively Noise stepped up to Shina and put a sack full of pups down at her feet. Widget growled fiercely at the lioness as his siblings ducked back into the sack. Shina's stern expression melted immediately, "Awww. I can't say no to a face like that." She turned to the young lioness, "Kia, get Noise and her children set up with a room in the hotel, a suite."

"Yes, God Mother." Kia bowed.

Noise made a step toward the portal and I stepped in front of her, mentally asking O'Meara for a bit of help. "One moment." O'Meara knelt, and after a moment of fiddling detached a thin chain from my right wrist and presented it to the were-wolf. Noise sniffed it.

"What's it do?"

"I call it my magic thumb, but really it's an entire hand," I said.

With a nod, Noise raised her paw to accept it. "I'll get settled, feed my pups and get right to work. In the meantime, stay alive, Thomas." She looked down at Weaver, who laughed softly. "For several reasons."

"Don't worry, Moof!" Rudy chittered. "They'll have to go through me first, and I got lots and lots of booms!"

With a shake of her head, Noise grabbed her kids and headed through the portal, Geoffery following, driving her bags. He nervously explained to Kia how to drive the cart and came back through. The portal closed and O'Meara clapped her hands.

"Alright then." She looked at me and Rudy. "Let's see what we can do about keeping those promises."

II

FIVE MINUTES BEFORE TIME ran out on House Erebus' demands, Rudy perched in a squirrel sized replica of the captain's chair from the original Star Trek. He'd bolted it to the dash of the truck, along with a mounted tray that held his phone flat in front of him. It displayed a grid of green buttons labeled with tiny text that O'Meara couldn't read from the driver's seat. Her eyes glanced at her hands, clad in fingerless leather gloves, gripping the large steering wheel. Around her, mostly behind, were the core of House Khatt. Farah, Smiley, Willow and Reynard sat poised around a casting circle in the back of the truck's cab, which was equipped like a camper. The married magi had bonded each other with a Fey chain. Riona and Tack were strapped into a couch off to the side, both staring at a shared laptop that displayed the casino's mundane security systems. Naomi and Morie sat up in the bunk above the cab, waiting to deploy their talents in phase three of the plan.

O'Meara flirted with the nuclear furnace that was her anchor, as one might play with a lighter. Both of us wished I was in that cab with her, but the cats of House Khatt were out prowling. I stood fifteen stories above them, five of them above ground, on the top level of the MGM's parking garage toward the rear of the complex, yet no wind flirted with my whiskers as I held myself just out of step with reality. The most eagle-eyed of familiars might be able to spot me against the purple tint of Vegas, but with the added glare of the building's many encapsulating wards, I didn't think it likely.

For as bright as the magic blaze was, to a mundane eye, it would appear that this corner of Vegas was suffering from a power failure. The MGM's great neon-powered signs and LED announcement billboards had gone dark, and yellow police tape danced in the comparatively cool desert breeze.

Our neighboring casinos to the west and south, the New York-New York, and the Tropicana, had gone still, their own more selective wards shimmering. At their highest vantage points, the auras of the magi of house Picitrix shimmered. Gathered for the same reason I still lurked here, to learn how House Erebus would make war. The Picitrix had been happy to donate tass to our frantic ward making, but like House Morganna, wouldn't put forward a single one of their number to the fight. Everyone knew how this was going to go. House Erebus seemed to know this. Their casino, the Excalibur, kitty-corner to the MGM, had gone completely dark; the seething, roiling darkness cloaked everything within that city block. Conceptual darkness, the dark of the mind that hid even magics from the eyes of the awakened. Like a panic ward, it worked both ways. To attack, they'd have to lift their curtain.

Nothing moved on the streets: not a car, not a single tourist. Everyone in Vegas knew to steer clear. Quiet *here*, I commented, but not only to O'Meara.

The humans and their familiars are tense here, The Shadow that Strikes at Midnight responded, *the magi sip warily at their drinks while their familiars stare at our home as if waiting for a mouse to emerge. Ceres and Doug are not pretending this is a party; they have battle wards up.* The domestic feline - never call him a housecat - had snuck into the private balcony on the top floors of Tropicana where Ceres' faction of House Picitrix gathered. How had he managed to do that? Nobody knew. That was the thing about magic. As soon as you figure out a rule, you find the exception for it. Midnight broke several.

"Four minutes!" Rudy called out. "Operation Exploding Porcupine is a go! Deploying quills." The squirrel tapped a button, setting off a tiny charge deep within the MGM, starting a fiendishly complex spell Farah had woven. A golden ring of power rippled outwards from the top of the residential tower. From it, hundreds of golden triangles formed in its wake, assembling into a protective geodesic dome: a giant panic ward. It shielded the main building from both magic and conventional attacks, and even when they did manage to crack the barrier, it had a surprise in store. The golden glow made it hard to see the gray tass bombs that hid in each junction of the magical panels. Precisely the thing you'd need to hold out for days against elemental magi. We were less sure about what death magi could do about it. "Quills deployed!" Rudy declared as the last triangle settled into place. "Thirty seconds left."

Through Midnight I heard the magi of House Picitrix oooh appreciatively, although he noted that Doug was shaking his head. Weaver too, seemed unimpressed and tsked impatiently. *It is pretty, dear, but they only need a single crack to turn your shell into a trap.*

I smirked. She'd see.

Something stirred in the north, a formation of lights.

Wait, Midnight thought. *Doug's ears are twitching, he's looking toward the northeast.*

Tracking, I responded, hearing the growl of a motorcycle pack, as I ran over to the rear inner corner of the parking garage. Five lights guided a wedge of darkness down the street. Then from the east, a blue spark caught my attention; it originated from between two lead headlights higher than the cars that made up the majority of the sparse traffic: a truck.

Gargantua just walked out of the Excalibur, Midnight reported, *and there's a bus loaded with tass coming in from the north.*

Weaver tapped on my rib. *Your pitiful mundane sight is too limited. Since you have put us in harm's way here, I will assist.* The spirit reached up into my head before I could protest, and her fingers touched the interior of my skull.

I blinked as if something had touched my eyelids and forced them far more open than I was used to. My mundane sight had expanded. Suddenly the breadth of my vision nearly matched my all-encompassing magical sight. Only the area directly behind my skull remained outside my vision.

Weaver! O'Meara seethed into my mind. *What did you do to him?*

No need to set your webs on fire, magus. I'm helping. Nothing major, just hanging some drapes in here, Weaver said in a pleasant tone before hissing. *I could stretch him out, make him much more roomy.*

Please don't, I pleaded to Weaver, watching both the motorcycles and the truck approach the MGM at the same time. It caused a queasy sensation, as if I were crossing my eyes.

She settled back. *I will be content for now. Your magus is fun to tease.*

O'Meara's anger curled in on itself, a mental curling, and a physical curling of her fists and shoving them in her pockets. In the real world, she glared at Rudy and said, "Go to phase one!"

Rudy flinched at her expression. "Okay, uh right. Go phase one." He smacked his phone. "Let there be light!"

The top of the dome lit with the brilliant white of burning phosphorus. Conceptual Light turned the midnight dark into bright noon. The wedge of darkness being shepherded towards me evaporated, revealing five low-slung choppers and between them a swarm of dark purplish worms. Their auras black voids in my vision. The riders each held glowing leashes attached to a half dozen of the creatures. They stopped at the T intersection that would have led past my position and right up to the edge of the ward. At the same time a black big-rig truck barreled on down Tropicana Avenue, its cab lighting up with an array of defensive wards as I counted at least three magi worth of auras inside. The blue of their magic blazed as a black disk of energy swirled over the cab, heedless of the light. Regardless of Weaver's modification, I had to choose between watching the motorcycles or the truck unless Weaver wanted to render the concrete transparent. Running across the parking lot as they passed the building, the black disk burst out toward it in a wave of black miasma. I expected it to do something to the ward, but it passed through it as if it weren't there. The crackling of glass echoed. Reaching the edge, I put my paws on the concrete barrier and peered down. The mist swirled around the glass-covered pillars that held up the massive canopy that shielded the valet parking operation of the casino from the heat of the sun. Cracks spread through the structure like rapidly growing vines and chunks broke away to crash onto the pavement.

O'Meara swore. *Has to be a pure entropic force. It shouldn't go through that ward.*

But it is. I watched as their own defensive wards increased their brilliance. *And they're expecting a counterattack.*

Wouldn't want to disappoint them. O'Meara turned to shout, "Rudy! Hit Tropicana from Audrie street to Koval lane!"

"Stones away!" High above, a line of purple magic flared over the street. Followed by a chorus of high-pitched whistling as a barrage of five-ton granite stones rained down. The familiars in the truck no doubt saw the portals open, but only figured out what came through when the first stone shattered on their wards, and threw the truck in reverse. Tires squealed as they deftly weaved around the stone rain.

Midnight chimed in, *the bus has ignited: large tass bomb.*

Planned for that; should hold, O'Meara thought back. *This time.*

My ears heard a hissing scream, and I looked away from the truck to see the hunger worms swarm up from the street like a cloud of long-tailed insects. They landed on the ward's surface and their teeth sang like a chorus of buzz saws. *Bugs are on the ward!*

"Pulse the bug zapper!" O'Meara shouted out to the bunker interior. The points of tass flashed and lightning danced across its surface, striking each worm with the amount of electricity the casino usually consumed in an hour's span. They didn't fry, they popped.

The next moment, an explosion rocked the front of the building. My magical sense flashed white and the garage trembled beneath me.

Ward's holding, Midnight reported, *but cracked. Gargantua is heading directly for it.*

"We got a breach and a golem heading for it. Make it dance! Barrage the strip!" O'Meara gave the order, and the sky over the road filled and rapidly emptied of stone. A barrage of purple spells lanced up from the Excalibur to the portals. Tracking spells, but they'd just find themselves at a quarry twenty miles outside Vegas.

"Ward should repair itself in like a minute!" Farah said.

New cabal's coming out of the Excalibur; Ceres' calling them the Hell Hounds. Four hooded humans, three dogs, and a really large cat. Gargantua's buried but digging itself out. Do you want me to get closer?

Stay where you are, Midnight. Looks like we made it to level two, I thought back. Below me the truck magi had reinforced their kinetic wards and were moving back into position for another pulse of whatever they were using.

And Morrian had asked us to hold out against this for two days? We'd be lucky to hold out for two hours at this rate.

"I'm losing cameras!" Riona announced. "They've got somebody inside. North tower, 17th floor. 16th floor too!"

"Walnuts in a woodchipper," Rudy cursed. "I thought we chased everybody out."

"Hots! I got a visual- damn, gone now. I don't think that pastiness was makeup!"

"We checked that tower!" Naomi called down.

"Doesn't matter now!" O'Meara shouted, cutting off the argument. "We're breached! Rudy go to phase two!"

"Already? We've barely been at this for ten minutes!" Rudy gestured at his iPhone control panel. "The ward's still got lots of tricks left!"

"And if those bloody things get downstairs and see that we've ripped out everything remotely magical, they'll know we're running! It's your plan, Rudy. Stick to it."

Rudy chittered, "Stupid zombies, ruining all my fun! Okay, phase two! Big kitty showtime!"

On a monitor next to Rudy, O'Meara watched a hastily carved statue of me come to life as tass flowed up into it. It stood on its hind legs and raised a paw as a length of pipe floated up from the roof next to it. In my magical vision I saw the gleam of my battle wards on the top of the west-facing tower before a spiraling shaft of dark and light washed them out. When it comes to magic, black can have a radiance all its own. This was an imitation spear of Remus. Our one-shot weapon that unmade reality. In the distant past, it had been used to erase entire cities. We didn't know how to get it to do that, but erasing a building would be point-and-click. This imitation had been crafted primarily for looks, but had enough punch to delete a magus or two.

"Enough!" My voice boomed out of every speaker in the area.

And fast as it began, the show ended. A thin line of black shot across my vision, piercing the giant ward and several smaller ones that had been set around the illusionary me's podium up on the roof. The spike's entry and exit point shone black and rapidly expanded, consuming the statue entirely. I heard Rudy shouting "oh, Nutsnutsnuts! Kill the speech! Kill the speech," as I followed the black line back to a figure hovering far above the strip. Too distant to make out any details more than a white sprinkle with black wings. Not a glimmer of magic radiating. On the monitors the pipe belatedly fell back to the ground, still blazing with magic.

"We agree on that, Thomas Khatt." The voice of the thing who had delivered Erebus's ultimatum boomed through the air. "Enough of your defiance. Enough of your house. By order of the High Merlin. All former members are considered renegades. Anything but absolute cooperation will be considered hostile."

Down in the bunker, O'Meara and the others scrambled to figure out what sort of spell had pierced all the wards. At least Rudy had been quick to silence the recording. The magi debated moving to Phase 3: the skedaddling.

Needing more info, I shoved myself into Midnight's head to borrow his eyes for a clearer view. He acknowledged me with a flicker of annoyance, as if I could give away his hiding place while I was in his head. He'd gotten himself beneath a catering cart and peered out from between the wheels. All around him were tense Picitrix magi. Ceres stood on the balcony, a long oval shield in one hand and a spear in the other. More telling as to the danger she felt was the way that the usually black stones around Doug's neck were sparking with power.

It was definitely the same animated statue. Chalk white and now supported by great black wings that remained completely still as he rotated toward Ceres and floated towards her. On its shoulder rested a massive raven with glowing red eyes, still and stone as its magus. Midnight squinted to scry at the pair, but I could see only the barest glimmer of magic in the figure and the bird, their workings concealed. It floated right up the edge of the New York-New York's wards, blank face fixed on Ceres from fifty feet away. The raven croaked, "We do not come for you today, Lady Ceres. There is no need to brandish your teeth at me. Stand down."

"You're Ahimoth the first, right?" Ceres asked, not lowering her shining weapons.

"The one and the only," Ahimoth said.

"The council executed you." Ceres took a deep breath.

"They ended my life but not my existence. Michael the 2nd called and so I have returned. I am told you are talented and shrewd. The High Merlin will offer you a seat at his table, otherwise..." His head swiveled almost a full hundred and eighty degrees back toward the MGM, his body and wings following afterward.

"All you did was kill a statue!" A voice shouted at his back. Midnight's attention flashed towards the voice to catch a man running back into the casino. The color of time clung to his clothing. Archibald.

And now the strands shift, Weaver whispered.

Ahimoth didn't react immediately, but the raven stretched up to give a half flap. "Is that so?" said the raven, and the pair started to drift towards the MGM.

12

WHO THE HELL IS Ahimoth? I asked.

"Ahimoth was, or is once again, Michael's primary enforcer within House Erebus." O'Meara spoke out loud so everyone could hear her. "The council executed him, sometime during the war for treason, but it was widely viewed as a power play by Archmagus Ghenna to wrest control of House Erebus away from Michael. The execution had been said to be very resurrection-proof."

Let's see about that. His back is turned, Midnight thought, *Give me the fire.*

No, you're too far away, O'Meara argued back through the whirlwind of my own spinning thoughts. Whatever Ahimoth was, his raven wasn't able to see through the glare produced by the fake spear of Remus. So long as he didn't know where everyone was, then the plan was intact.

O'Meara, wind down the ward. Make it look like we're cooperating.

She hesitated, riffling through a list of options other than a bluff of our last ace. The hope had been that House Erebus's minor league would have spent hours or even days chewing through the ward before they sent in the big guns. Clearly Michael the 2nd thought the opposite and sent in a bogeyman to crush us. "Bloody ashes," she huffed after finding no better options. "Prep the finale, Rudy."

"At least I get to show this doozy to the world!" Rudy crowed. "Setting the bear trap."

Outside in my magical vision, the triangular panels of the ward all tilted slightly, then slowly, starting at the top of the dome, slid over each other. It would take several minutes for it to fold completely into the ground. The Hell hounds approached under a bubble of defensive wards. Ahimoth waited for the ward to be completely down before drifting toward the MGM. And as soon as he crossed the threshold, the fake spear whirled up from the roof and projected a beam of twisting black and white energy at the dead magus. His silhouette shone black as it struck him and all that destructive force disappeared.

"Scattered cashews!" Rudy cursed. "That was like taking a tass bomb to the eyeball! What in the warren's name is that guy made of?!"

"We are not sticking around to find out!" O'Meara replied before directing a thought at me: *We are bugging out. Thomas, prepare for extraction. Midnight, last chance to come along.*

I'm staying; you'll need an eye on the city, Midnight thought at us, hunkering down in his hiding spot.

Rudy slapped two paws down on to his phone console. "Snapjaw!" The massive ward sprang up behind both Ahimoth and the Hell Hounds, trapping the invading Erebus magi inside. "Now everybody smile for the flash." A bright tass source lit within the bowels of the MGM. The largest tass bomb that Rudy had ever made, at least the largest that he's told me about.

The giant tass bomb exploded, converting the dome of the ward into a blazing white star on the strip. Against the roar of magical brightness, Willow, appearing in a whirl of purple two feet in front of me, was hard to see with either magic or mundane sight. As I stepped out from beneath reality, she threw her arms around me. In a blink, I stood within the casting circle in the rig.

"Heya dere, boss, Dat's a new trick," Smiley greeted me with his diamond studded crocodilian smile. As everyone else stared at me with a mixture of bewilderment and horror.

I blinked, suddenly reminded of the reason of my very wide field of vision.

"Yes, he's grown six extra eyes," O'Meara's voice startled us all back to motion. "Worry about it later. Thomas, get your tail up here now."

After a shake of my head, I rushed to obey. She thumped my side as I joined her in the cab. The race car harness strapped me in without assistance as she reached toward a crystal globe jutting out of the sloping dashboard. "Going to be a bumpy ride." In front of us stood a concrete wall.

Rudy squinted at my new ocular arrangement before shrugging and turning his chair forward.

With the inferno of the tass bomb still raging beside us, I could barely see O'Meara's plasma-hot magics sweep around the truck and its cargo. We rolled forward; the wall melted away. Wielding temperatures commonly found on the sun, O'Meara drove through solid rock and stone. The interior of the truck reverberated with the roar of a furnace. Although beneath the roar I could hear Rudy singing, "*Spider-cat, Spider-cat. He thinks he's all that.*"

"One mile," Willow announced after several long minutes; the space-bending mage kept track of our progress, counting off the distance as we tunneled. O'Meara's grip on the wheel tightened with every mile until the plastic squeaked in protest against her leather gloves. The manic grin that usually accompanied her driving contorted into a grimace of concentration. We'd done this before with O'Meara's Porche but the truck was twenty times its size, and we'd never tunneled this far. At mile ten, we both felt the smokey strain on her soul that was the prelude of a soul burn. A thing that neither of us want to go through again, "Bloody ashes, I'm not going to get us all the way outside the city," she announced. "Everyone get ready; we're going up."

With a grunt, she angled us up toward the surface, and we burst from the road like a breaching whale, O'Meara using the fiery energy as thrusters to land us softly.

Rudy whooped, "Well that's gunna be one ginormous pot-hole."

"On it," Farah and Willow answered, magic flaring between them. Behind us green magic shone as they summoned stone to fill in the collapsing tunnel we'd left.

O'Meara let out a breath and wiped sweat from her fore-head. Reached out to scruffle my head in response to my concerned thoughts. *I'll be fine. Just don't ask me to toss too many fireballs in the next twenty minutes. Do your job.*

With a nod I pawed myself out of my harness and peered back at the cab full of anxious magi and familiars, only Smiley seemed relaxed, his long body half encircling the casting circle. In the center, the four of them were building something between them.

"Good job, everyone," I said, carefully edging around the circle, brushing up against Riona's knees as I climbed beside Tack. "Hopefully we got away clean but-"

"N-not counting on it." Tack grinned doggedly at me as I reached up and hooked my paw around a lever on the ceiling. With a pop and a rush of air, the hatch beside it popped open. The entire trailer had what Farah termed a damping ward on it: a ward designed to hide its dazzling magical contents. It's not perfect up close, but it works well at long distances, but you can't see through it well, either. So we'd built a crow's nest of sorts behind the truck's rooftop air dam, that's the swoopy thing that redirects the airflow over the top of the trailer. I sunk my claws into its rough padded interior and climbed into the seat and faced backwards, peering at the sparse traffic. The city behind us glowed with a combination of casino lights and protective wards. Above them, large shapes fluttered, blacker than the night sky. Damn, us running had occurred to our opponents, and they'd posted lookouts.

I watched one of the flying things bank into a dive near to the spot where we'd surfaced. Its wings spread wide as it leveled off, skimming over the tops of the street lights. "We got company!" I shouted down into the cab.

"Something like that won't last outside the shallowing. We have two miles to the border," O'Meara called back as the rumble of the engine grew to a roar.

"I'll take them out!" Rudy added.

"Only if they attack first!" O'Meara argued. "Unless you want their entire house to know where we are."

I squinted, trying to get an idea of how the thing was warded. The thin membranes of its broad wings shimmered with the green of a summoned creature, and over that a spider-web-thin kinetic ward stretched. Just enough to shrug off a few rounds from a handgun. Farther above, a second creature flew a distance parallel. If we took out the low one, the higher magus would see it. We had to either take both out or pray that the damper ward was good enough. "Rudy!" I hollered down, "You got anything that can take both of them out at once?"

"Lemme see, lemme see." The squirrel scrabbled up beside me, followed my gaze and chittered with laughter. "I got just the thing." He set his phone down beside me and slapped a button with a paw. A panel on the far corner of the trailer's roof opened and a missile rack popped up. "Heat seekers. And the desert sky is awfully cold."

"Got anything less... explosive?" I asked. I had forgotten about how much ordinance the squirrel and his friends had welded into the top of the trailer.

"Nope! Not for this range. Been saving these for a special occasion. Moving day counts!" He slapped his paw on the phone and it made an audible beep. Two rockets took off with a *Sssshoooom!* One streaked directly into the closer bat and exploded with a thunderous clap, sending the wings in opposite directions. The other bent upwards; the magus lit with blue for a half second before both he and the bat disappeared in a fire ball.

"I now pronounce you Ex Bats!" Rudy sang as the missile launcher slid back inside and the traffic behind us corrected for the surprised swerves.

"Rudy!" O'Meara scolded from down below. "They know which direction we're going now."

"Yeah, but they don't know what truck we're in and they got no eyes on us!" Rudy shouted back. "Let's do the distance."

"Tack and I will craft the illusion," Riona said, unbuckling and pulling a loop of wire from her pocket. Her familiar was slower at undoing his seat belt.

"Willow and I, like, almost have something that, like, might work against that attack that went through the ward." Farah said, not looking up from their work.

A crow that I assumed was Naomi fluttered down to perch on O'Meara's seat. "We can help you go off-road."

O'Meara patted the channeling crystal. "I can fly this thing if I have to, it's less energy than tunneling."

"We will fly interference, then." Naomi hunched, clearly disappointed.

Nothing else pursued us as we raced across the border of the shallowing, spiders crawling on my spine as the Veil reminded us all major displays of magics would not be tolerated. Late-night traffic was sparse, but we weren't alone on the road, either.

Rudy had been right; killing the observers quickly had bought us some time and we were well outside Vegas, closing in on the intersection, when I spotted the glimmer of combat wards behind us.

A pack of five. The motorcycle magi that had herded those hunger worms to the battle were behind us. They were barreling around cars and trucks, making no use of any stealth spells. Outside of Vegas, in clear view of mortals, using their pets would be difficult, but the Veil had few objections to magical attacks that mortals couldn't see. If a car hesitated to move out of their way, there'd be a flash of black or blue energy and it would immediately swerve off to the shoulder. They swarmed up to the side of every truck they passed.

Riona and Tack had assembled a small illusionary truck between them, trying to duplicate the subtle shine of Farah's dampening wards.

"Drive casual, O'Meara. We've got bogeys. Everyone else: We've got to kill or disable this cabal before we hit the intersection. If anybody has info on these motorcycle magi, now's the time to share," I announced to cabin.

Willow answered, "They're called Rolling Entropy, two shamans and three channelers. Nice enough, wards are not their forte, though. They hired Farah to ward up a couple of bars they liked a few years ago."

"What is their forte?" I asked.

"It don't matter if their wards ain't good." Rudy laughed darkly. "Just gotta wait for them to get a bit closer. Really don't want to miss with this one."

"Illusion's ready." Riona announced as the pack of bikes swept near a truck a few hundred feet back. They rode in a single lane formation, one bike in front and the four other members two by two behind the first. The rear two had sidecars carrying large dogs, while the leader had something cat-sized perched between his handlebars. A lane-wide ward protected the entire pack from frontal assault. The front three also wore personal battle wards but the magi in the back were working without. Probably to maximize the sensitivity of their dog's noses to sniff out damper wards. I described this to Rudy, who nodded, head cocked to the side to stare into the iPhone with one beady black eye.

"Almost... come on. Little closer," Rudy said to it, his paw raised over the screen.

The motorcycles swept towards us in the passing lane, the heady buzz of their engines growing louder and louder. At my feet I had an inquisitor's sword and a few other magical nasties. Everyone in the cabin below went still in anticipation of the coming violence. O'Meara increased the speed of the rig, putting distance between us and the minivan attempting to ride our wake. The motorcycles kept coming, closing within two hundred, then a hundred feet.

"Gotcha now!" Rudy crowed. A panel opposite the missile launcher opened as a distinct whine cut through the wind and engine noise. A fully spun up mini gun lifted from the compartment and opened fire. The bullets ripped into the leader's shield.

"Mage killer!" He shouted the term for the one conventional firearm that shredded most personal wards and turned hard to the left before his shield gave out entirely. The gold of panic wards bloomed around each magus as they ditched off the road.

"Eat your uranium slugs, ya cowards!" Rudy shouted as the biker's lights rapidly grew distant.

In the distance, I caught a flare of purple and black. A second later, the mini gun exploded, pierced by a spike of darkness. Ahimoth!

13

GET DOWN! O'MEARA SHRIEKED in my head as I stared back at the origin of the spike. The desert moonlight clear enough to show a white figure in the distance hovering over the road. Dread seized my guts as I hunkered down in my lookout nest.

Step on it! I sent, but she didn't need the thought. Everyone yeeped as the truck swerved out into the passing lane and a horn blared as we picked up speed. The exhaust chimney next to my nest spat out a column of flame as O'Meara's magic coursed through the huge engine. Through O'Meara's eyes I watched the speedometer climb past a hundred and twenty miles an hour and bury itself at one forty.

I called down into the cab. "We need a new plan, because the bikers were decoys for that Ahimoth guy. I'm guessing getting slapped in the face with a tass bomb didn't improve his mood. Willow? Farah? How are we on warding against whatever that black spike is."

"Nowhere for a ward, but I might hold him off for a while if it comes down to it," Willow said. "I still don't know what it is. All those wards at the MGM were designed with negative energy and hunger planes in mind."

"It's negation," Rudy said with a chitter. "It's not negative energy or a hunger plane. It's the concept of negation, a universal 'no' button. That spike's got some space-bending in it. For the speed. Nasty combo." Rudy heard magic rather than saw it, which generally was a disadvantage, but it allowed him to get more detail about a spell's nature than I could from a glance.

"Then we'll need a conceptual... 'yes' plane to counter it?" Riona looked up from the circle.

"Ha!" Smiley thwapped his tail against the mattress. "Ain't nobody finding a new plane before he catches us. Since we not ded, den he don't wanna damage the cargo."

"Cargo..." Rudy muttered.

I dug my claws into the pad I sat on as the truck shook beneath us. "Then we don't bloody let him catch us," O'Meara snapped. "Hang on."

Another black flare and a thin spike of darkness streaked above us.

"Either something is throwing off his aim or that was a warning shot," I said.

"Intersection!" O'Meara warned as we blazed down the off-ramp at triple the recommended speed, jets of flame erupting along the side of the trailer to keep it upright. "We're ninety miles out of Crystal Springs. There's three ways out of that town; with that decoy we might shake him there. The veil has to ground him at some point."

Archibald is helping him. I reminded her.

Then we'll roll a bloody die for the route we choose. Let him predict that!

"Gonna have to get there first!" Rudy squeaked." He had popped his iPhone up over the edge of the nest. Sure enough, the white figure had grown and was raising himself higher into the sky and gaining speed. "Alright, buddy! Let's see how well you dance up there." The missile launcher sprang up from its hiding place and fired the two remaining missiles. One exploded, impaled on a black beam. The other rammed the distant figure head on, a wave of darkness covered the white body the instant before impact, and plowed through the explosion as if it had never happened. Hadn't even changed his pose, legs held together and toes pointed straight down, as if he was too important to worry about gravity.

"He shrugged off a huge tass explosion, Rudy," I said. "In what universe was that gonna work?"

"I don't see you doing nothing!" he snapped back. "He only hit one of them! Might be able to swarm him."

"How 'bout if we flock him instead?" Naomi cawed from below and I felt the rush of another cabin door opening.

"Naomi! If you use your anchor, you'll give him a target!" O'Meara shouted.

"I gotta see what I'm birding! We're already sitting ducks in a big red barrel!" She called back as the cabin pulsed with the blue light of her very odd anchor plane.

Thomas! Cover her. The statue me being consumed replayed in her mind.

On it. I grabbed the one stasis pearl I had up in my nest and crept to the side of the truck. Below me, Naomi stepped out onto the running board under the cab's back door. Morie in crow form, sheltered in the crook of her neck as she leaned out far enough to peer up at Ahimoth.

"Here goes!" She lit with the strange blue light of her anchor and cast it out onto the lane beside us.

Hundreds of gray wings fluttered from the pavement as the light struck it. The asphalt dissolved into a swarm of birds as it rose from the ground to meet Ahimoth. Again a wave of darkness sheathed his body, but this time it pushed outward, forming a shield. Naomi's magic winked out as soon as the flock collided with it, the stone birds tumbling off the shield like a stream of water striking an umbrella, but it slowed his flight.

The shield winked out, the wings snapped closed and Ahimoth plummeted from the path of the asphalt flock. His darkness pulsed back into his body and flowed into his outstretched hand. Below me, Naomi flinched back. The black spike caught her wrist instead of her shoulder.

I spat the stasis pearl. It hit the top of her head as the black spots the spike left expanded. The white energy raced through Naomi's body as the layer of blackness consumed her arm. The white and black energies clashed at the center of her bicep, stasis verses a consumptive '"no." They paused, sparked. The blackness won, slowly marching further up the arm as Riona grabbed Naomi and hauled her frozen body back inside the cab. There O'Meara whipped around in her seat, projecting a thin beam of heat from her finger. It sliced through her upper shoulder to down through her arm pit. The severed flesh disappeared before it hit the floor.

"Bloody fucking ashes!" O'Meara exclaimed as she grabbed the wheel, "Everyone stay down. Don't give him a target." 'Course, she immediately poured her power back into the truck. Glowing like a beacon.

"How long will the stasis last?" Riona asked, gently lowering the statufied Naomi down.

"Supposed to last an hour, but that spell might have drained the duration. Watch it, and if it fails, get ready to stop the bleeding."

Meanwhile, I peeked back over the trailer's edge; Ahimoth was catching back up, rising higher in the sky. *He's trying to get an angle on the cab!*

The floor beneath us lifted before tilting downward. Flames lit up the night beneath the trailer, keeping it between him and the truck. *He doesn't want to shoot us through the trailer?* O'Meara thought, *then I'm happy to keep it between us.*

The living statue of a magus broke his impassive hovering stance. Thrusting his fists forward, he shot through the sky over us.

"Incoming!" I shouted, losing track of the magus due to him being eclipsed by the truck's air dam. He entered O'Meara's vision though, dead ahead about half a mile. Those great wings swirled like fabric as he turned around to face us. One of his hands lifted towards us and his aura darkened in my eyes.

"Keep going! We've got it!" Willow shouted. The cabin below me lit with interwoven purple and gold magics.

The shot fired and the windshield flared with purple and gold, the spike of black pierced it, bent around O'Meara's head, curved around the width of the cabin and back through the windshield where it missed Ahimoth's head by less than a foot. Willow and company had remained on the floor; the gold and purple spell between them spun like a generator, complete with arcs of power.

Another shot and the spell slung it back in Ahimoth's general direction. O'Meara poured on the speed, turning the entire truck into a flaming meteor. I had no idea what the wives and their familiars had built, but it had started shaking after that second shot. Whatever they were doing they couldn't do it for long.

Glancing up through O'Meara's eyes, Ahimoth was slowly growing in her view but far slower than the pace of the scenery. Not taking O'Meara's challenge of chicken but staying as distant as he could. Which meant... he was afraid of fighting us in close quarters.

"Everybody! Hit him with anything you can reach him with! Swarm him!" Another shot and Willow's spell flickered uncertainly. I grabbed the inquisitorial sword and unleashed its swarm of projectile spells. The kinetic bolts blew the windshield clear off the truck cab and cleared the way for the elemental and death spells to arc out through the swirl of fire that surrounded the truck. His next shot hit Willow's shield directly in front of me, bouncing back and striking one of his wings. It shattered, and he wobbled, throwing his arms out as if he suddenly found himself on a tightrope. He quickly found his balance and banished my swarm of spell missiles with a wave of his hand. A ball of tightly focused energy streaked out from the cab: Riona's. It struck him dead center. Black flashed over his white surface a moment too late and he reeled from attack, bouncing onto the road once before catching himself.

"Keep it up!" I shouted, or attempted to, as I had a mouth full of sword and released a second salvo of spells.

At that point, Ahimoth saw the writing on the wall and gave up maintaining his distance; black blades, both nearly as long as his body, appeared in each hand as he hurled himself towards us. My spells were outrun, Riona and Tack's second sonic bomb was parried by one of the long blades, and he blasted through a huge granite stone that Farah summoned into his path like the Kool-Aid man through a wall.

"Focus on that remaining wing and hang on," O'Meara commanded, and I hunkered down. The truck swerved to the side with such speed that it felt like a side impact.

He shot by us. The tip of one black sword slicing left a cut through the wall of the cab. I leapt back up through the hatch and found him immediately behind us, racing toward the truck, arms outstretched as if for a hug except each hand held a blade composed of black hole material. "Rudy! Hit him!" I urged the rodent, but he wasn't in the perch where I had left him. Where'd he go?

That left it up to me. I released the last salvo of magic from the inquisitor sword and dropped it from my mouth. As he swatted the deadly little spell balls out of the air, I grabbed a long black staff and pulled it from its magic dampening holster. It flared with black fire and tasted like ash on my tongue. Without my telekinetic thumbs, aiming was awkward, but the eyes on the side of my head made it much easier to target the wannabe angel. "The bitter end!" I spoke the command word, and the rod spewed a widening beam of blue-black fire. Sending cold instead of heat blasting against my forward side. Ahimoth's white body turned black as the beam struck him. A ward powered by his anchor of *No*. So the question now was how long he could keep that black field over himself.

O'Meara! Get Riona and Naomi to attack!

She was opening her mouth to spur the other magi when the back doors of the trailer opened.

"Hey Negative Nancy! I got your rainbow-sparkle knuckle sandwich right here!" Rudy shouted through a loudspeaker before Stompy launched out of the trailer, the giant robot blazing with wards. I cut off the beam of anti-heat at the last moment. I'm not sure if Ahimoth can't see well when he's using his *No* shield, or if the sudden appearance of a giant robot snapped a sprocket in his brain, because he made no attempt to dodge the rocket-assisted fist to his torso. I heard the crunch of metal on stone as both robot and magus fell onto the road. They immediately shrank into the distance.

"Rudy! Get back here!" I shouted, the staff falling out of my mouth.

"Keep going! I'll catch up!" His voice screeched with feedback but even with my ears I could barely catch the words as both combatants sprang up from the road.

An explosion of black, peppered with white sparks, filled my vision, Rudy had set off an anti-magic bomb. When it cleared, we'd crested a hill, obscuring both Stompy and Ahimoth.

He'll be fine, O'Meara's thoughts answered my worries.

Better be, I growled back. Stupid squirrel, he hadn't needed to do that. We had it handled. *How's he going to catch up? He doesn't know where we're going,* I worried at her.

He's Rudy, was her only comment before she briefed the others on what the crazy squirrel had done. I remained up on the roof of the cab, watching for any sign of continued pursuit while those below tended to Naomi's wound. They stopped the bleeding, but we needed an experienced healer to regrow the arm. We had always relied on House Morganna for that. Fortunately, the road behind us remained empty. At Crystal Springs, we rolled a die, and it pointed us toward Reno. We all argued whether or not that was a smart play, but it turned into a simple one. The Death Magi knew of our association with the Lions of Reno. If they wanted what we took from the casino that badly, they'd pay Shina a call regardless.

14

THE GRINNING FACE OF the Cat's Meow Casino loomed over central Reno. A cartoon cat's head composed of concrete and glass nearly ten stories tall seemed totally generic to most viewers, but something about the expression, the wideness of the mouth, the squint of the eyes, I could only see Jowls in it. The bold orange cat who'd done his damnedest to both kill me and then undo his misdeeds. Eight months ago, a group of idiotic magi activated a god egg in an attempt to convert the entire city into tass. We'd stopped them, but the God egg needed a mind to direct it and consume in the process. Jowls had stepped into that gap and been woven into the fabric of Reno's reality along with his wishes. The Grand Sierra casino had become the Cat's Meow casino, and far more changes were hidden beneath the ground.

In theory, nothing remained of Jowls' spirit or intellect, but I wondered, and the lions straight up worshiped him as a living god. The building's grin always seemed to widen as I got closer to it, and as the truck crossed the threshold into the parking lot, my ears heated as if they'd been filled with Jowls' assorted flirtations. I found myself staring up at the face until the angle got too steep. The entire casino was the tomb of my greatest frenemy; I kinda missed the jovial bugger. Then felt guilty for missing someone who'd coldly left several thousand people to die. Emotions are hard.

Brain full, I stared at the dashboard while O'Meara maneuvered the truck into a parking spot.

"Hey like, did somebody call ahead?" Farah asked, "Cuz like, I don't think Shina usually sits on the front stoop like that."

I jerked my head up from my memories to see the outlines of five lions perched on the roof of the valet structure. They sat in a row facing us and the center one's aura glowed with the force of an anchor I was intimately familiar with. "No, she's expecting us," I said, knowing this would be an epic "I told you so" moment. I pawed down the sun visor to get a look at how Weaver had rearranged my face. Six eyes stared back at me. Two on my temples, two from my cheeks, and my original pair. The last pair were right beneath my ears, too far back to glare forward. They were, thankfully, not the blank orbs of a natural spider but smaller copies of my own gold-yellow eyes. Still creepy. With a few moments of practice, I figured out how to close the new eyes and keep my original pair open. Closed, they were subtle slits in my fur.

Weaver tsked, *Why hide your pretty eyes kitty?*

Because I'd rather not have five hundred lions know that I am sharing my body with a vulnerable spider god.

Let us both hope that my body is near completion; my legs itch to stretch. With that, the bones in all my legs strained widthwise, forcing me to feel the spider legs crammed inside. It made every hair along my back puff. O'Meara inhaled deeply beside me and slid a calming hand down my spine.

When Weaver said nothing more, O'Meara reached across me and opened my door. "We'll sit tight until you give us the all-clear. Everyone else look around; if you see five lions, then there are more you don't." She gave me a tight hug before she allowed me to jump down to the ground.

I slipped sideways as I approached the valet, hiding my approach from unmagical eyes and unpracticed magical ones. Sidestepping can be seen as subtle purple ripples in the air if you're watching closely for it. With the entire casino in a shallowing of its own, it's extra-difficult. Curiosity made my tail lash as I climbed up the nearest column onto the roof of the valet. Shina sat in the center, projecting a stony grace, channeling lightly, transforming her golden hide to actual stone, although the occasional flick of her tail tip, and the heave of her breath, prevented any onlooker from perceiving her as a statue. Sitting a head taller than the four lionesses that flanked her, Shina remained a regal queen among her children. I stifled a groan when I saw that the lioness to her immediate right possessed fur pink as the dawn: Sunrise. Her ear flicked in irritation. Had she spotted me somehow? Oh well, better get through her now-traditional hello.

Treading a wide arc around towards Shina's backside, I watched the muscles in Sunrise's legs tense beneath her skin. She saw me! Somehow. Had Sunrise awakened or was she somehow hearing my footsteps from outside of physical reality? I checked the other lionesses: no response from them. Although Sunrise's neighbor had noticed her tension.

I strode up between Shina and Sunrise, curious what would happen. They stood two lion-widths apart. The young lioness whipped her head around towards me, teeth flaring with the glow of tass. Forewarned, I jerked back, slid back into reality, and bapped her nose with my own paw as she attempt to rip open the air. She flinched, springing up onto all fours and backpedaling into the other lioness. Catching sight of an amused twinkle in Shina's eye, I tsked once before Sunrise got her bearings and pounced, sending nearly four hundred pounds of claws and muscle hurtling towards me. I threw myself down onto my back, twisting my body out of harm's way. She sailed over me and I delivered a donkey kick to her soft underbelly, popping her rear high into the air so she nearly tumbled head-over-tail when she landed. As she fought to recover her footing, I took O'Meara's heat and infused it into the fur around my neck and down my spine. Signaling that play time was over.

Sunrise stared at my flaming mane for about five seconds before pressing her nose to the concrete. "Welcome back to the pride, Giver," she said to the floor in growl tongue, a language invented for feline vocal chords.

"I never left," I told her in the same language.

She lifted her head and gave me a dubious stare.

With a chuckle and a small eye roll, I turned my back on her, snuffed the flames and leaned up against the warm flank of Shina, rubbing my scent across her ribs in greeting. "Teaching your daughters new tricks; that's not very fair."

"As if you'd ever fight my daughters fair." A laugh started to roll from her but choked off. I realized my vision had become a bit wide. I swiftly closed the extra eyes. She gave me a wary stare, her magical sight prickling across my face.

"Later," I said very softly, then continued the conversation. "I'd rather not fight them at all. They might actually hurt me one of these days, and then you'd be sad." We usually kiss at this point but I totally understood how spider eyes and a spider inside makes one a bit less inviting for cuddles.

"If you let them hurt you, then you probably didn't want to see this old lady that badly anyway," Shina countered.

I declined to argue further; this augment went round and round. The tribal culture of Shina's lion children still held that males had to fight for membership in a pride. Her daughters, Sunset, Noon, and Sunrise, had decided that my constant coming and going was shameful to their mother, so I had to be challenged every time I rejoined the pride. AKA whenever I made a visit and I saw more of Reno than the inside of Shina's room. Such fights usually boil down to "I have magic and you don't, so back off." Sometimes they're fun; other times they're annoying. Sunset in particular takes each loss personally. Shina definitely enjoys making me fight for her, probably because they're reminders for everyone that their great goddess's mate is a bit more than an overgrown housecat. Still, without O'Meara's flames, I'd likely be crushed even with my sidestep trick.

"Glad you saw sense and came home," she said, casting her eyes toward the truck.

"They hit us harder than we thought they would, and weren't satisfied with chasing us out of town. I think they want something we have in that truck. I don't know how long until they'll arrive here." Guilt for endangering her and her family ate at my stomach. Either that or Weaver was having a snack. I waited for her rebuke.

Instead, she groomed the back of my neck. "Then let Reno be either the graveyard for the house of the dead or ours. Tell your O'Meara to go around to the loading docks and park in front of bay U."

Got it, My magus confirmed. and distantly I heard the truck rumble back to life.

"Thanks," I breathed, and realized my body trembled, muscles still amped up for a fight that hadn't happened. Shina always claimed I was part of her pride but I couldn't quite believe it. Not yet at least. I waited for the lioness to name her price or at least imply that taking us in balanced our accounts.

"Come with us. We've had to move your friend below." She nipped my ear and moved her bulk away. I followed her across the roof towards a square door in the building's side. With Shina on one side and Sunrise on the other, I couldn't see much other than that door.

The gray metal opened into a softly lit room; lion-sized body pillows were scattered across its floor. I ignored the pillows and took a long drink from the fountain that babbled against the wall. The water was crisp and clean, and the sound of quenching my thirst forestalled any more conversation for after the floor dipped beneath my feet. Once I finished, I looked up into the face of a mosaic orange cat, "Thanks, Jowls, I needed that."

The mosaic didn't respond; none of them ever did, but I could feel them watching me from almost every surface of the casino.

"We give thanks to the maker," the lionesses beside me mumbled, as if my words had been a call. With a high-pitched *ding!* the door slid open with a soft hiss. I immediately caught the heady musk of excited felinity on the warm air that flowed into the elevator. Instinctively, I flehmed, lips pulling into what a human would read as a snarl, and my tongue forcing the incoming air against the roof of my mouth where the fuzzy taste of the air clarified. My brain buzzed as it attempted to identify the individual scents. Shina's other daughters, along with every lion I had a name for, plus dozens I did not. "A dinner party?" I asked Shina. "You shouldn't have."

"They're not here for dinner; they're here for you." She gestured with her nose, and I had little choice but to follow her out. Right beyond the elevator sat a semi-circle of yellow clay brick buildings. One of which was actually two stories tall. That biggest one had a sign, in a script made out of slash marks and then in English, God Hall. In it, my magical sight registered three active anchors being channeled through bodies that were clearly quadrupedal.

I sat there and stared at them for a moment. Two of them had extended yellow glowing tendrils of force to wrap around objects. The last, the green of a summoned substance. *Blood and ashes*, O'Meara whispered into my mind. *They're awakening.*

15

SUNRISE GRINNED PROUDLY AT me. Coating her teeth with tass hadn't been a trick at all. She'd done it the same way I did, and she'd seen the ripples I'd caused when I moved beneath reality. Not quite enough experience to determine precisely where I was, but she'd seen them all the same.

"How many?" I heard myself ask as I stared with all of my eyes.

"One in fifty thus far." Shina whispered. "All anchored in an elemental plane of some sort, but I think it will be more when it's said and done."

In the aftermath of the collapse of House Hermes and Shangra-La, the world they had created, the number of Hermes lions that survived had been around four hundred. That meant Shina had at least eight awakened lions down here. Not simply familiars but channelers, who didn't have the human handicap of not being able to perceive magic. They could pair up with a familiar with a different primary magical sense and learn advanced magics faster than any human – animal pairing.

Shina continued, "Started right after House Morganna concluded that our shallowing produced no harvestable tass and left. Thank the maker."

"Why didn't you tell me?" I asked.

"I dare not speak of it outside these walls and you were busy creating your link." Shina said.

"Which you need." There, it clicked into place now. Shina had no desire to subject her children to the perils of a permanent bonding. If House Khatt could manufacture them, then she'd do well to protect us. If more lions awakened, the Lions of Reno could be a dominant force in the post-council world. Battle magi without com-

I cut off the thought as I noticed Shina had loomed over me, shaking her head. "Stop it, Thomas," she said, her deep voice light with rebuke. "More to see." Then she was moving again, leaving me bewildered in her wake. I followed her out of the circle of buildings towards what I called the Rock 2.0. A pile of boulders that served as a speaking platform. It was gone entirely, and in its place a huge circular amphitheater with wide stone risers stretched before us. At its center a circular platform rested on the heads of two massive stone cats, a lioness, sculpted as a feline Adonis that could only be Shina, and a much rounder jovial form, Jowls.

Clusters of lions lounged about, watching us through the corners of their eyes. One male with a black mane broke away from his group, shouting "God Mother! God Mother!" Nearly as large as Shina, he made the ground bounce beneath my feet as he bounded toward us, skidding to a stop to touch his nose to the ground.

"Thomas. Meet Joystone, the sculptor." Shina reached out and patted his head.

His head snapped up with startling speed. "Ss rn howrrrr." He said in tortured English, the first time I'd heard a Hermes Lion even attempt human language. House Morganna had fitted a few lions like Kia with talking spells. Joystone hadn't been one of them.

"This looks amazing," I said.

Joystone preened, closing his eyes and almost wiggling under the praise. His attitude would lead me to peg him as an excitable cub but scars criss-crossed his shoulders, one of his fangs had been broken in half, and despite the energy in his eyes they were weepy in the corners. At least middle age. Abruptly his eyes snapped back open and his huge head prodded into my personal space. His head cocked one way, then the other. "Snap me claws, that muzzle of yours is very short and nobody told me about the eyes. I'll have to make adjustments!" He ducked his head. "Many apologizes, Giver, of the three, you're the only one I don't have a good likeness for. I had to use flat pictures and none of them have so many eyes."

"The eyes are temporary." I gulped, my likeness? My stomach fled for my bowels as a wave of anxiety washed up over me.

"He can't see it from this angle, Joystone, no matter how many eyes he possesses," Shina said gently. "You'll have to show it to him."

"Intended!" He declared firmly before meekly adding, "You are the least present of the old Gods. While both Mother and Maker are present in everyday life. Those who come in from the Savannah are reminded that without the Giver the wonders of the Maker would not exist and our Mother would be dead."

"Old Gods?" I asked in horror as Shina gave a soft chuff of amusement.

He winced, "Sorry, it's words, growl tongue only has so many. I and Sunrise are new gods so-"

"Joystone," Shina cut in, "Just show him it."

"Yes God Mother." He turned and jumped up on to the middle rung of the five risers.

I followed, whispering to Shina, "Maybe teach them the difference between gods and magi?"

"I don't teach them anything anymore, Thomas; they teach themselves. Besides, they're all perfectly aware that Gods are as fallible as everyone else. More so, even." she responded, and I had no more words as we walked around the statue. The platform balanced on three feline heads, not two, and the third was mine. My steps faltered and Shina swatted at my rear to keep me moving. Until I stood in front of my stone self, except three stories tall and bit more leonine in build but it was definitely me, in one of my dog harnesses, stylized flames surrounding each eye. A life-size depiction of O'Meara stood between my paws.

Joystone's gaze bounced between me and the statue, tail whipping back and forth behind him with enough speed to bruise flesh. Still with a nod from Shina, he puffed up his chest and kneaded the ground once. "The gathering is the center of our life in these new lands. And so, each time the prides gather, they will be reminded of the Trinity that brought our lives to be. The Mother, The Maker, and The Giver." He bowed to me, "I hope you find honor in my work, imprecise as it is."

"Why am I the Giver?" I finally gave in and asked, straining to keep my ears politely forward. Shina had created them; Jowls had used his life to create this place. I'd what? Let half of them chill on the roof of the MGM for a week while I ran around trying to save a council that in the end refused to be saved.

"Do you not like it?" Joystone asked in the manner of anxious artists everywhere.

"No. I mean I do. But- I uh. I uh, don't deserve to be there with those other two." I stumbled as if his hurt expression was kicking me in the ribs.

"HAHAHA!" Shina exploded with laughter so loud I jumped like a startled housecat and turned to her. "What is this? Too late for modesty now, Little Lion. What's one more title? Magus Khatt of House Khatt. Slayer of Hunger Demons, wrecker of the TAU." She sauntered toward me until we were nose to nose.

"That's... different," I growled. "I'm not a god. I was only there because you tricked me."

"Trick, huh?" She rumbled softly. "Was it a trick that you fought tooth and nail to save my children? That you opened a portal back to your territory and waited for the very last of them to escape before you and O'Meara jumped through? You laid with me while I dwelled in a pit of despair. Then, when it isn't even your fight anymore, you came here to correct my mistake and prevent the misuse of the god egg. Without you, without your influence, then Jowls would never have become the Maker. You are the link between the Mother and the Maker, and without you none of us would have survived. You gave what they and I needed: your strength, a place to shelter, and finally a home." She curled around me, wrapping one paw around my ribs and squeezing me to her chest.

"Shina, I don't-" I started, but she grabbed the scruff of my neck and pulled the loose skin taut against my throat.

"Let me put this in terms that might get through that thick skull casing," she growled, "Allow yourself to be honored or I will break you, Little Lion, and not in the way you like." Claws larger than pocket knives pricked my ribs so I got the hint.

I chirped in surrender. The teeth and claws withdrew but she squeezed me even tighter, holding me still as she rubbed her cheeks up and down both sides of my neck. Her body rumbled with affection. "You're a mountain lion, solitary by nature, so I forgive you for not grasping what pride means," Shina whispered, "but don't make me remind you again."

"I got it, I got it. Just stop crushing me," I insisted, rubbing the top of my head against the underside of her chin. She let me up and I approached Joystone. He smiled with his ears, completely unfazed by the public talking to/wrestling I had just survived. "Your work honors me," I said after taking a moment to consider my words. "Thank you."

He did that happy wiggle again, a motion more akin to a ferret than a lion. "May the wind always blow in your favor. It will be even better tomorrow," he said with a grin. "I will go find a fresh stone." He called out to the lions he had been lying with originally and the group of them trotted towards the entrance.

If Shina's done showing you off like a new teddy bear, O'Meara pushed into my thoughts with a bit of a huff, *we're about to unload here.*

On my way, I sent back and turned to Shina. "You want to show me the way to the truck?"

She chuckled. "Oh, does your magus suddenly need attention?"

"Unless you know some other magus-and-familiar pair who can lift a forty-ton vault without setting off its defenses, then yes."

16

THE PATHWAY TO THE truck proved to be a bit of a hike. The savannah cavern was so vast that it was difficult to see the ceiling in the glare of the bright sun-lights that blazed in the middle of each set of four pillars. Each of these pillars, thick as a SUV, were positioned every thousand feet or so. The foundation of the casino above extended all the way to the bottom of the cavern as a pillar of rock. They called it the Maker's Mountain. Except for a couple elevators like the one I rode down in, and the freight elevator that the truck took, Shina explained, it appeared to be solid rock. Since the lions tried to keep out of the casino as much as possible, Shina, I, and an escort of four other lionesses, walked around it to find the truck.

A small swell of ground had us looking down on a second lion village, this one much more haphazardly constructed. Huts were a mix of casino castoffs and repurposed construction materials, pop tents provided shade from the withering heat of the cavern's overhead "sun" while cubicle walls provided privacy. Ethernet cables snaked between the huts and solar panels mounted on tall tripods sprouted like trees. These were the homes of the lions prone to exploring the human world instead of the familiar but strange Savannah. Shina had framed them as a small pride of honored outcasts who had developed friendships with the casino's kitchens rather than hunt.

The huts clustered around a large concrete pad about five hundred feet long on each side. In the center of it was the red truck. I spotted the stacks of pallets we had portaled here immediately, lit up by the magical glow of the artifacts, tass, and our statuesque prisoners.

House Khatt's familiars, Smiley, Morie, Reynard, and Tack sat talking to two lionesses, one with a dark gray pelt and the other so bright it was almost gold: Sunset and Noon. The humans hung back, leaning against the truck, except for Naomi who I assumed was resting within. A whiff of Noise's scent blew on the breeze, although I didn't see her. Instead, I found myself looking for a bushy tail and my stomach clenching when I didn't find it.

He'll show. O'Meara's green eyes found me. *It's a long walk through the desert when your legs are only two inches long. Check his strand.*

I nodded back at her. I could do that. Then I would know, one way or another. My stomach burbled with acid as I started to shift my perceptions, but Weaver interrupted.

No need to worry about that one dearies. So long as a seal remains intact, no brute will end him. And if the seal is ever undone... She trailed off to laughter.

Merlin's seal, you mean? I asked her. *Why? What's inside Rudy?*

That's a secret that's ancient. Would you like to bargain for it? she countered.

No! O'Meara cut in. *We appreciate you telling us he's okay, but we are not entering into any more pacts with you. Ever.* That last word she seared on the inside of my skull.

Weaver retorted with something about the nutrient value of fleshling words, but we'd run out of time for internal debates. Sunset had noticed Shina and me, calling out, "Mother! Here so soon!" The taciturn lioness had taken to the concept of sarcasm as a fish to water. Still, she and her mother greeted each other with a touch of their foreheads.

Curiously, Sunrise and Sunset did not touch, acknowledging each other with a cold, "Sister." I actually got a nuzzle from her. I had little time to ponder what was going on with the two of them, because Noon's enthusiastic forehead bump had me seeing stars and wishing for a kinetic ward.

As I shook the sparks from my vision, I heard Noon whisper excitedly, "Do they have the keys with them?"

"Later," she hissed back before raising her voice to address everyone. "I would have delayed Thomas' reappearance a bit longer, but he tells me he's needed for some... heavy lifting."

All the lions looked at me, examined my tininess compared to them, and laughed. I sniffed haughtily in response. If we survived this, we'd have to rebuild the MGM, if only so I had a place to live where I didn't feel like a housecat.

"Well, you can all help, then!" O'Meara declared, walking down the length of the trailer. "They're only the artifacts that are too unstable to shove through a portal. I'm sure none of you would mind putting your mouths on them."

The lions shuffled somewhat uneasily as O'Meara punched a code into the keypad and the trailer's doors opened with an ominous whirr. I trotted over, propped my front paws on the bumper, and peered in. Stompy, who had taken a full quarter of the trailer, was gone, of course. Leaving a puzzle wall of tightly packed crates. Center to it was the long lock box that contained the spear of Remus, the real one. Just seeing it triggered dark thoughts, like where I was gonna shove it if Rudy didn't show up.

"What are we going to do with all these?" I called back to Shina. "They're too dangerous to leave lying around here." Particularly if some lions have awakened. Half these things were dangerous to the user. The majority of them had Death magics we didn't understand. There were also a few space-bending weapons that were quite powerful so long as you had time to practice with them, which we had not.

Shina came up and stared at the collection, wincing as she studied the objects' auras. She was the one who had IDed most of Death's collection. "I have a vault. It's not warded though, but it will put a few feet of stone between these and anyone who wants them."

"Farah and Smiley will ward it then," I said, unable to prevent the annoyance from creeping into my voice, "And there's a bunch of stuff sitting out in the yard that needs to go in, too." Shina had been a familiar for over eighty years. She should have at least moved all the stuff we portaled over! She'd just left over ten thousand groat of tass sitting out unguarded, not to mention several pallets of weapons. Was it even a good idea to put all this stuff in the same vault?

"Vault's this way," she huffed, and turned with a toss of her head. We followed her out of the yard before she spoke again. "I was getting to it. You try managing nine apprentices while sorting out petty conflicts between 12 different prides and see how long you take to sort your mail."

O'Meara laughed. "And I thought you knew: Thomas, the more stressed he gets, the twitchier he gets about organizing stuff. He's practically got a spreadsheet in his head and is wondering how quickly we could build a half dozen vaults deeper into the Savannah."

"I do not!" I sputtered. I'd been imagining a series of descending buckets. Categorizing the stuff I remembered into various threat levels.

Shina's tail swatted my flank. "While I don't have a mind link, I'm sure that was a lie."

I growled at them both and switched the subject. We were about two hundred feet away from the yard. "How's Noise doing? Why's she down here?"

Shina gestured to an event tent the size of ten huts put together at the far corner of the yard. "She's... large, mostly."

Oh dear. The massive lioness hit the scale in the neighborhood of five hundred pounds; for her to call Noise large meant we were talking about elephantine proportions.

Poor girl, O'Meara thought as silence rose among us until Shina came to a halt in front of a sheer rock wall and placed her paw against the stone. Her claws extended into slits in the rock and a large section of the wall slid down into the ground, revealing a large room. Jagged clusters of quartz in the upper corner glowed, illuminating the concrete-like floor and dingy white walls. A super-sized version of a suburban garage, it even had red bicycle hooks studding the ceiling.

"This work?" Shina asked.

It did for now. House Khatt spent about an hour schlepping things back and forth. Then we came to the last half of the trailer, where a rectangular cinderblock structure stood. It was about eight feet wide and twenty feet deep with a square black metal door on its front. Dead center was a large combination wheel. Frozen lightning arched across its surface, skipping between the floating graffitied runes we had used to put it in stasis. In my magical sight, it shone searingly bright. Its aura a tight weaving of protective wards, death magic and something else flittering between the strands, an entity of some type. That combination had defeated every single attempt we had made to crack the vault. It seemed to swallow tass bombs. Farah and Smiley had poured a solid month into it, resulting in little more than frustration. I knew of only one item held within it. A book penned by an Erebus Archmagus named Ghenna, who was known for her cruelty. Michael the 2nd, the current leader of House Erebus, wanted something in this vault. Either the book or something else. Question was, did Michael the 2nd have the combination to this vault or did he simply fear I did?

We locked it behind the stone wall and left Farah and Smiley designing wards to magically protect our possessions. Shina had peeled off, lying with her daughters, discussing something. Fearing we wouldn't get another chance, O'Meara and I stole across the yard to peek into the large tent. "Noise?" I asked, before poking my head through a flap.

"Noooot dooooone yet," Noise answered, her voice so deep it rumbled through the very ground. I swallowed as I looked upon her, perhaps not quite as terrifying as she had been when a hunger plane had possessed her, but the distortion of bovine features into those of a predator's made for an unsettling combination. Despite the udder that hung between her legs, the dappled Holstein black-and-white pattern of shaggy fur, and long fly-swatting tail, her body retained a wolf's proportions. Muscular legs ended in skull smashing hooves; while her head had the bovine broadness, her heavy muzzle extended further, with heavy horns that came out of the sides of her head and curved forward. From one of her horns my telekinetic bracelet hung. With a shoulder height that nearly reached O'Meara's head, if I was a housecat next to Shina, standing next to Noise would make me a kitten. I had to fight an instinctual urge to arch my back and look bigger as I approached her.

"Just seeing how you're doing," I said. She stood in front of a set of eight folding tables pushed together to make a working surface. On it lay a partially assembled wooden depiction of Weaver about half the size she'd appeared to be on the back of the NOW. Six of the spindly legs were reattached to its body, but the face had been shattered as if by a hammer, and the remaining legs lay in splintered pieces. A bottle of wood glue stood next to a curved mandible, held together with several clamps.

"Hmmmm," she grumbled, shaking her head so her ears flopped this way before baring her mouth of fangs at her work. "Noooot goood. I have the woooood but, the fangs were shattered to dust and one of the ooopals eyes is goooone."

"Where'd you get them the first time?" I asked.

"Don't remember. They came to me."

Because I helped the first time. Weaver chuckled to herself.

Noise slowly curved her thick neck around toward me and her nostrils flared as she took in my appearance. Ears flicked as her gaze lowered to stare into my chest, her huge horns encircling my head as she did so. "Leave him alooone."

Perhaps you have another body in mind? Weaver hiss-laughed as my eyes drifted to the fluffy contents of a basket set beneath the table. Wickett, Sprocket and Gear lay on top of one another. *An even tighter squeeze for sure, but far more malleable.*

"No!" A feral hiss came from my throat as I jerked my gaze from the pups. Yet, out of my... it wasn't really the corner of my vision but definitely my side eye, I saw Wickett pop his little head up.

Not talking to you, kitty. Simply proposing an alternative.

Noise stared back at me, us. Her huge eyes simultaneously grew wet and wide with horror. The soft patter of small but outsized paws filled the space as Wickett pranced his way over to his mother, displaying zero fear. Slowly, with extreme caution, Noise sank down to the ground, penning the pup in with her forelegs. With a tiny yip of excitement, Widget rushed the side of her face, forcing Noise to close her eyes to avoid getting a tongue in one. Her ear flicked and the pup immediately pounced on it.

Were you not steeling yourself to give him up, Child? Weaver asked. *If we had not come for the bargain and upended your life, how strongly would you have resisted? Would you have left on your own?*

Widget had the tip of Noise's floppy ear in a death grip and shook it hard, emitting the fiercest of puppy growls. *Grrrrr.*

Her head moved; Widget yipped in protest as his mother gently squeezed him between her muzzle and leg. "No. Not this one."

Weaver shifted, and my attention went back to the basket. Gear and Sprocket were yawning, watching us with half-closed eyes. *Another, then? The spitting image of her father, then? Giving his favorite to me would be a delicious revenge, wouldn't it? And it's not like you would lose her entirely. This is still not my home and I cannot stay with her all the time. Although she will know me as her mother and will be my first priestess in a millennium. Trust me though, you'll no longer see her father in her face.*

Noise continued holding Widget.

Unable to hold my peace any longer. "There's no need for that, Noise. O'Meara can create the obsidian you need and we can go find the opals. Simple fetch quest, right?"

She let out a miserable moo. "Stay out of this. It is my task. My fault. The lions tooooold." Her jaw open and closed with a solid click of teeth as if she attempted bite the moo that slurred her speech. "They told me that if you came here, Death would follow. They are your pack. Not mine. You have to focus on that. I will finish this, ooooone way or anoo," she paused, swallowed thickly and continued, "another." With a snort she stood, nosing Wicket back toward the basket, but he instead ran around her ankles and barked at his siblings, tail wagging to play. The glue lifted from the table, enveloped with the yellow glow of kinetic energy.

Three days. I can remain with Thomas until your full moon. Weaver's voice grew soft, almost tender. *Without a meal, hunger will drive me back home. He will have to live with my marks on his body. Meanwhile, the meadow will spread to your children and will not vary with the moon. They will never be human, ever. The sensations that you struggle under now will never leave them.*

Noise stopped breathing for a moment. "Raise a family of cow-woooolves or let one become a spider moooonster. Leave me to work, Thomas. Take care of your pack."

"Good luck." I told her. Hoping to hell she could do this, for everyone's sake. O'Meara glared at us as I slunk back to her;

anger smoldered through the link but a note of relief flittered among it.

Weaver plucked at this note. *Yes. Rejoice. The Great Weaver has a time limit to her stay in your kitty but he'll be a very odd one when I'm done.* Her legs flexed within my bones and sent pain like four simultaneous Charlie horses rocketing up into me, forcing a strangled chirp from my throat.

Don't you dare! O'Meara's fist burst into flame.

The pain faded as quickly as it came, leaving me gasping for air.

Weaver laughed. *Oops, that still needs a bit more work. I best get back to it. I suggest you focus on squishing that fly who's tangling your threads. Otherwise, it's not likely any of you will see this full moon.*

With that, she settled back down into me. I felt the lightest of tingles in my paws.

O'Meara and I stared at each other for a moment, but both of us had the same thought. Before anything else, Archibald had to go.

17

SHINA AND HER DAUGHTERS' heads turned in our direction when we stepped out of the tent, but Riona was directing the rest of House Khatt in sorting through the mountains of stuff into things that might be useful when Erebus came a-calling. There'd be no running the second time.

O'Meara signaled Shina to wait a moment as I scanned the interior of my mental landscape. The link to Midnight's mind was easy to forget, stealthy as he was. He kept it tightly closed unless there was a need. If he'd been watching me since we left Vegas, he'd been subtle about it. I mentally scratched at the link and it opened a crack.

Survived the chase. Good, the cat commented. *You want a report, yes?"*

Yeah, how'd things shake out after we left?

He chuckled. *House Picitrix views the smoking crater you left of the MGM with high-nosed disapproval and grumbles that with all the tass we received we should have held them off far longer. As if we're a pack of suicidal dogs. Rumors are the hellhounds disappeared in the blast. The lower-rank magi are confused as to why they haven't been ordered to attack House Erebus yet. The appearance of Ahimoth seems to have spooked the higher-ups. Overheard Alice and Grace arguing with Ceres about Ahimoth's offer before they all stomped off to the upper chambers of the Luxor as I was on my way out.*

Out? Where are you now?

In the Excalibur, but I'm not finding many magi here, just a junior cabal who are not very talkative. I will go to Erebus tower next.

Be careful. I told him and he huffed haughtily. *You see any more of that strange color of magic that-"*

Time? No, but Scrags is still hunting your friend. He found me an hour ago to tell you that he's appeared several times around both Houses Picitrix and Erebus towers, but never long enough for him to catch him. Per usual. I think he has cold paws or puddles, or pseudo paws? Whatever.

Thanks for the report.

Midnight closed the link with a mental nod.

I found myself watching Riona, her usual bright colors dulled by time and the dust that blew on the wind. All the other magi and familiars were busy, and even Tack had left her for a moment. She sagged against a pallet, hugging herself as if cold. Her face dipped, and I couldn't tell if she had closed her eyes or merely stared at her boots. Archibald was out there, trying to engineer the circumstances so that O'Meara and I would be X-ed out of the picture without the destruction extending to her. Or maybe he wasn't being so careful anymore. If I hadn't followed him into time and been forced to deal with Weaver, I would have put my faith in Farah's wards. Ahimoth's first attack probably would have killed me. If Scrags had seen him several times in the last six hours then... what? Was he trying to tweak events so Erebus would roll up here in force to wipe out the Savannah entirely, or attempting to stop a cascade of events that would lead to Riona's death as well?

O'Meara patted my head. *We can't know that, but I think I know a way we could find out at least what is enabling him to do what he's doing.*

Riona finally sensed our gaze and forcibly perked herself up, smiling her brilliant stage smile. We went over to her. "Maybe a few hours' sleep is in order?" O'Meara suggested.

"Heh, I got a few winks between here and Crystal Falls," she lied.

"I watched you in the rear view," O'Meara said. "You stared out the window once Naomi was stabilized.

She narrowed her eyes. "And here I thought Thomas was the one with eyes in the back of his head. Hots, I'll be fine. I wouldn't say no to a cup of coffee, though." Her eyes drifted upwards to longingly stare at the summit of Maker's Mountain.

O'Meara crossed her arms and frowned with disapproval. "I want you to get some rest. We're going to need to do some heavy scrying this afternoon."

"Pffpt." She blew a stray pink strand of hair out of her face and answered in a whisper, "All I'm going to do is stare at the ceiling thinking about how insane it is that my father is trying to improve my life by killing the only two people in this world who have stuck their necks out for me. I don't go to sleep, I collapse. And it's not like I'll be much help. I can't ward, Tack and I are maybe a tenth as good as you two in a fight, and I've barely scryed. I could play a song on everyone's heartstrings, make everyone feel good but that is mindfuckery and not kosher, ya know." Tears welled up in her eyes, a black blur shot across the yard: Tack. He collided with her legs, making her grunt.

She wiped her eyes, patted him affectionately, and sighed. "Tack, I'm okay. No need to come to my rescue." The growl, combined with the glare he gave her, indicated he didn't buy that for a moment. I chuckled, then slipped forward to whisper in his ear. "Hey Tack, did you know that you can force your magus to sleep?"

His ear perked up. "Ooh?"

"Yeah, you just take all your tiredness and dump it into her head. She'll be out like a light." I winked, although several eyes joined in.

"I-I can do that?" His head cocked.

"Tack don't you da-uh!" Riona wobbled; O'Meara stepped forward and caught her.

"I can do that!" Tack's tail wagged. "I didn't have to give her any of mine, just opened a closet."

"Uuuuh." Riona groaned in protest as O'Meara picked the much smaller woman up.

"If you're going to do that, wait until she's at least sitting down," O'Meara huffed, and started carrying the punky magus toward the nearest hut. "Also, mind that your magus can do it right back."

Suddenly, weights pulled at all eight of my eyelids. I tried to shake them away and force them back open.

"Did I hear that someone needs a nap?" Shina loomed up next to me, and I leaned into her gratefully. Her chest rumbled with laughter. "Late morning naps are the best."

"No. Not yet. We need to talk about defenses and... Something." My train of thought ran into a mountain of pillows that O'Meara had tossed into my head. *Not fair,* I huffed at her.

Gotcha, let me put her loudness to bed and I'll join you. O'Meara's thoughts shone with "taste of your own medicine" smugness. I allowed Shina to herd me into a different hut. She's not the softest of pillows, but plenty comfortable when she lies on her side and holds my head between her forelegs. Sleep claimed me within the first deep breath.

A familiar pressure on my belly stirred me from slumber. O'Meara settling down on the thin mat that covered the hut's floor and resting her head on my lower body. One of her hands reached up to rub my chest. It struck me as odd to feel her weight on me while I, in turn, rested against Shina. My magus and my... mate. That's what everyone else termed Shina at least, except for Rudy. To him Shina remained my girlfriend in finger quotes that implied cooties. I had thought that once Jowls had made the Savannah that it spelled a slow end to whatever Shina and I were. We'd barely talked the last month, me busy figuring out how to create the link, and her trying to train almost ten newly awakened lions. I expected conflict, bargaining and hurt feelings. Instead, this. Whatever this was. It felt deeper than before. O'Meara had always made herself scarce in Shina's presence, for her to come into the tent was new.

I'm not letting some over-muscled lioness deny me my favorite pillow at a time like this. She smirked at the canvas overhead and pressed her knuckles to my sternum, giving me a deep scratch. *Now go to sleep.*

Can't you let a guy sort through his emotions in peace? I grumped at her and laid my head back down.

No. Because it's simple. You both wanted to use each other for different things but got your hearts all tangled up. You think about her every day. Trust me on that one. Her eyes were closed, but I could feel them roll.

You can shut the link, you know.

And miss my favorite soap? Felines of Our Lives? Never.

I slammed the link closed, although the "door" seemed to be little more than a gauzy curtain at times. Shutting my eyes, I slid back into sleep between my magus and my mate with a smile on my lips and a happy twitch in the tip of my tail.

I could have slept far into the evening. A natural cougar gets much more sleep than a human and compared to them, I ran a sleep deficit that would take a year-long nap to repay at this point. Instead, a voice in my head woke me long before I was ready to rise.

Thomas. I have news.

Midnight. The urgency in his thoughts stirred me awake with the speed of a flipped switch, my eyes snapped open. *What?*

An image came, a massive room of black stone bricks lit with sconces made from human skulls. Standing at attention with a man's pace between them were black lions, hundreds of them, their skulls bare, eye sockets filled with a sickly red light. Their auras swirled with green and black. They stood at attention, like soldiers but not statues; tails flicked impatiently; their weight shifted from side to side. Some looked to be solid, others wavered as if composed of gas. *What is this, Midnight?* I asked.

I am unsure. Took me a few hours to figure out how to get in. This is on the second level. Midnight's view was from high up on this assembly room.

Unless there was a magus with an anchor plane populated with undead lions, I had a creeping suspicion I knew where they were getting these lions. Hundreds, maybe a thousand of Shina's children had perished in Shangra-la. Those in the farthest reaches of the plains were dissolved into the void as Shina drew power from the world to defend the world-birthing egg. When the battle turned south, O'Meara and I had evacuated all the lions present to Vegas. Sunset had stayed behind, gathered those who did not reach the Rock in time for the battle and led them over the mountains toward the central city. I had never spoken to Sunset about that journey, but it had to have been harrowing; those snow-covered mountains were not meant to be climbed. I don't know how many she started with, but those who made it were mostly younger adults. Not the wide mix of ages that camped on the roof of the MGM. House Erebus had somehow reached out into the void and pulled those dead to earth.

For which there could only be one purpose. The only question would be: When?

Find out more.

I would rather hunt this Michael the 2nd. His death would solve all our problems.

Midnight, there is zero guarantee that his death would stick. Find out how they're animating these things and how we can undo it! I stood. O'Meara snorted as her head fell to the mat.

"What?" Shina asked with a husky sigh.

"Undead lions. They have undead lions."

18

"They've made shades out of my children." Shina growled long and low after I'd explained what I'd seen.

"Do you know how to kill them?" I asked.

She shook her head. "I've only had a few spats with Erebus magi when Freddy and I were younger. They never tossed undead at us."

O'Meara stared into space with a sour expression as she rifled through unpleasant memories. "I've fought with them in the war. We had a cabal of Erebus who would create them." She concluded with a grimace. "They were little more than animated husks, at least until they got close to someone they knew in life. Then they remembered themselves and became terrifyingly hungry. Their former friends would freeze in the middle of a melee when they caught sight of them. Twenty of the things won us a decisive victory early on." Curious, I tried to peer at the memory she held but she pressed me firmly back to my own skull. "If they had survived longer, that cabal might have won the war for us but all four of them were struck by lightning a week later. Their replacements didn't know how to raise any undead, or so they claimed."

"They're like the grief vampires, then. Weaponizing the silver threads of connection." My own memories made me shiver, poor Jet.

"Could be how it works but I don't know." O'Meara said. "It's clearly a weapon targeted directly at the lions."

Shina's eyes narrowed as she thought, "The prides traded members all the time. If they pull out only a tenth of the lions that were left behind, they could still affect every lion in the Savannah. Everyone but the youngest cubs knows someone who was lost." She closed her eyes and sighed. "If that's what they are, we can't even fight that. Not without wards against it. I'll have to send everyone out into the Savannah." Tail lashing, she started to pace. "At least they can't open portals directly here. The Morganna magi that were visiting tried a few times, but the shallowing actively resisted. Portals are only allowed in the parking lot, but there are entrances to the Savannah all over Reno. My plan was to let the magi enter the Savannah, cut them off from the surface. Avoid the senior magi with good battle wards and batter down the rank and file, but that's not going to work."

Stopping her pacing, she growled at herself. "I'm sorry, you have to delay your hunt. There's something you need to do first. You need to see the Maker."

I coughed. "Jowls is dead; he's not an active entity anymore. He can't help. Right?"

She laughed dryly. "The Maker provides, as they say. At the furthest edge of the Savannah, word's come back that they've found a door."

O'Meara unzipped an inner pocket of her jacket and pulled out two cartoonishly large skeleton keys made of bleached white bone. "Let me guess, it's got a keyhole that would fit these."

"I don't know, but I bet there is. I haven't seen it myself; it's days by paw, but if that truck of yours can handle some off-roading, we might be back before sundown."

Both O'Meara and I shared a dark chuckle causing Shina to glance between us.

"If it takes that long it will be due to what's behind the door, not the journey. Let's go get the truck."

Jowls had never struck me as a cat who had an expansive imagination beyond his own vanity. Therefore, I was awed as we rumbled across the Underground Savannah by how sweepingly beautiful it was. The colors were all wrong: the tall grass too green and the dusty dirt a bit too brown. We flew over and around a vast herd of what Shina termed "antelopes" that were strangely stretched rabbits. Rats the size of raccoons fought over a carcass as a small group of elephant-sized deer watched glumly from a safe distance. The landscape gently rolled and swelled beneath us, while the columns formed almost a tunnel in the extreme distance. A wilderness capped with a tiling of cathedral ceilings.

After a half hour of driving, I had to ask the question, "How much farther?" We'd been traversing the land at over sixty miles an hour, rocket boosting whenever the ground became less than flat. We had to be well beyond the limits of Reno and yet I saw no cavern wall ahead of us. Had Jowls and the God Egg hollowed out the entirety of Nevada? Surely it couldn't reach all the way back to Vegas? Could it?

"It's just beyond the river; keep going," Shina said as she loomed over my back side. O'Meara and I occupied the two bucket seats in the cab's front, with my mate perched behind me, head thrust out, hovering over mine.

"A river?" I'd just seen small muddy water holes so far. I looked ahead imagining a dry water bed. Another ten minutes, a flock of pink and purple bats glided in the truck's wake. They reminded me of flying fruit and made my stomach rumble. When they departed, I found the landscape had shifted, become lush with plants, the greens vibrant; O'Meara had to lift the truck higher as the shrubs grew into trees. The stone columns morphed into woody trunks here. Then the ground sloped away into a valley choked with flowering plants, like a suburban garden that had burst the fences that contained it and gone feral. A rainbow of roses choked the banks of a snaking river.

O'Meara brought the truck to a hovering stop and rotated it slowly so we could take in the beauty of it. Awe flowed through our link. "And House Morganna left? After this?" O'Meara asked. "Not all of them are garden nuts, but this view alone would get a few of them to fight tooth and nail for property here."

"It wasn't here when they left about three months ago," Shina said. The cavern stretched only 15 miles from Maker's Mountain. The Savannah was all that was here. As soon as they all left, the walls started moving outward. Now we don't know if there are walls anymore."

"Jowls is still making this place?" I stared out onto the endless landscape. "Damn..." We'd viewed the God Egg as a bomb but maybe it was more akin to a loom. And if it had the intelligence to wait for the Magi trying to study it to leave, then Jowls, at least some aspect of him, was less dead than I had thought. It had been one thing to appreciate all this as Jowls' legacy; dealing with him as an active entity was far more concerning. "Where's the door?" I asked.

"Little farther; the lions that reported it told me it's difficult to miss."

She wasn't kidding; in Jowls' typical subtle-as-a-jackhammer style, the door appeared standing in a field of orange and red flowers, gleaming in the sunbeam like light cast from the ceiling. Metal framed glass with one of those broad plate handles that you could never be sure if you were supposed to push or pull to open it.

"Is that?" I started.

"Yeah, that's the door to Jules's shop." O'Meara swallowed and descended. Jules had been Jowls' magus. The one who had twisted the apparatus that had once imprisoned a dragon into a tool to grind up the entirety of Grantsville, including the residents, into tass. Despite having a familiar, passion for technomagic had led him to strike out without being associated with the houses, and open shops that traded tass, foci, and information. That door represented a time I wasn't eager to revisit. The truck landed, and I followed O'Meara out, curling around her legs and sniffing the air. She had her hand spread out, ready to dish out fiery doom to any threat that presented itself.

Nothing stirred in the clearing and we opened our link wide, readying spells.

"Is it dangerous?" Shina asked as she followed behind us.

"We're just being cautious," O'Meara called back. Slowly we approached the door. The door frame rested on packed earth, a black rubber welcome mat in front of it. The dark glass reflected our anxious selves and gave no hint what lay beyond it. Shina crept up behind us as O'Meara alternately pulled and pushed on the door to no avail. She fished a bone key out of her pocket. It slid into the lock without effort and turned on its own. The door opened with the sound of an electronic chime and a heavy scent of one chubby tom cat.

"Jowls?" I called, stepping up to the doorway. It moved, surging forward and slamming closed behind me. As if a building had swallowed me.

Thomas! O'Meara threw herself at the door, trying to pull it back open but the door remained shut.

I'm fine. I told her. *It's okay. Maybe Jowls wants a private conversation. Joke's on him; I've got Weaver in here.* A clang of metal echoed from its darkness and lights snapped to life. I stood on a great iron catwalk over blackness; a strange console set in what appeared to be a pipe organ waited at the end of it.

Tell him he's about to find out the limits of fireproofing if he has any thoughts about settling old scores, O'Meara mind shouted at me.

"They always come crawling back in the end." A distorted chortle echoed all around me. "Fab-u-lous."

"That's creepy, Jowls," I called out as I walked over the metal grates that prevented me from falling into the abyss. "I don't really have time for games at the moment. The entirety of House Erebus is going to attack the Savannah. We could use some help... From the Maker, as it happens. Did you come up with that? Or did the lions?"

No response to my babble.

I had been wrong about the organ; it had no pipes but the long things that jutted upwards were bronzed bones, wrapped in fine chains of silver and gold. Energies danced among them. The console comprised a wide screen glowing blue. Large paw-sized buttons decorated a control panel below it. All dark except for the green one at the edge, labeled START.

Not seeing any point to delaying, I pressed it. With a whine, the brass bones turned and the chains rattled as they coiled around their lengths. From above, the earth groaned in protest as the chains became taut and strained against whatever they connected to in the darkness.

It just went dark out here. O'Meara reported, *All the suns in the Savannah went out like a light switch.*

"Jowls? What are you doing?" I asked the air, and to my shock, it responded.

"Booting." Jowls' voice answered with an electric buzz as a progress bar appeared on the screen. Lightning raced down out of the darkness along the chains and into the machine. With each bolt the progress bar filled until the bones traded arcs of energy among themselves. An orange dot appeared and whirled around to reveal Jowls' face, rendered as if someone had thrust him into a Pixar movie.

"M-M-Meow!" the face glitch-stuttered. "Oh, Thomas! You're so gosh d-d-darn adorable when you're stressed." The eyes narrowed and his whiskers sparked, "Not that you'd be here unless you were! As if you'd visit poor old Jowls unless you needed s-s-something."

"You're a complicated cat, Jowls. I like you best as a villain who redeemed himself through a noble sacrifice. Seeing you alive and elevated to godhood cheapens that a wee bit," I said.

"Don't w-w-worry your pretty head." He laughed, spinning on the screen. "Beyond this machine, I am but a dream. With each inch that I build, the more my thoughts slow, stretched out over everything. This m-m-machine pulls me back together for short time. I am the glittering chains that direct the gears, but I cannot resist the engine of creation for la-la-long. Behold the heart of a f-f-fabulous world!"

The great darkness beyond the catwalk lit with the molten red hue of a furnace. Shadows of twisted machinery formed a tunnel to a pulsing, spinning egg, twisting itself in dozens of chains. The grey glow of tass dripped into the top of it from a series of interweaving parts. I stared out into the mechanism, then sidestepped as far as I could, pressing myself against a neighboring plane. The tunnel shifted; its walls bore massive drill bits driven by chains strung across the interior. A massive four-dimensional machine, a spell. We'd believed that without tass, the god egg would simply fizzle, like a bomb without fuel, but it had become something else entirely, whether because it had access to Jules' knowledge of space-bending through Jowls, or simply its nature, I can't say. The shallowing of the Savannah produced no tass because it funneled every single mote back into expanding itself, consuming our reality in the process.

"My j-j-jelly Jules would be so proud of me." Jowls' purr intermingled with static. "I built a wonder of a heart."

Awestruck and blinking I turned back to the console. The other controls had lit up; in the center of it sat a large keyhole. Around it, several positions were marked: On, Off and Harvest. Below Jowls' floating head sat a display labeled Harvest Yield (Groat): 74,088.

"The hell is this, Jowls? Harvest what?" My ears folded back to my head as my hackles rose.

Jowls laughed, "Why it's the keyhole to my lovely heart of course, you silly puss! It's pretty self-explanatory. I'm On now. I can't stop myself; eventually, if you leave my kitchen running, this world will tear away from earth, becoming its own."

"And destroying the original." I gulped, the original fear of the god egg had merely been postponed.

"Fabulous, right?" Jowls grinned and his background turned red. "If you set me to harvest, then it's your own personal G-G-Grantsville, Thomas. Take the tass and run. You always went on about how I should put have put my paw down and stopped that total fiasco. You were right, but a little, uncharitable part of my lovely self has always wondered: what if you stood on my paw pads?"

"I'm never doing that, Jowls," I growled at him. "I'll just turn you off now. This is plenty of space for the lions and more."

The light turned back to blue. "C-c-course! The noble Thomas. Selfless, to a point. Trouble is, you turn me off, the heart dies and the lights go out, like they are now. Then the whole thing collapses within a few months." He tossed his head and chortled.

My own laugh was bitter. "So, you're telling me I have to choose between the destruction of the Savannah or Earth itself?" Where would the lions go?

"No, no, no. That would be a terrible thing! W-w-what sort of friend would I be to force you to do that? A totally unfabulous one, that's for sure."

"Then give me a middle road, Jowls. Because I'm not seeing one now." I cast my eyes over the rest of the panel but none of the other buttons were labeled. What else could I do here? Or were the extra buttons on the console all for show?

"I'm expanding too fast now for you to safely s-s-switch me off. In the future, before we reach the breakaway point, there might be a point of equilibrium with a bit of elbow grease on your part." The cat head danced from side to side, cheek fluff bouncing with his own cleverness.

"You're not going to tell me when that is, are you?"

"Nope, I don't know. I am growing into a new world. When you stop me, or if you stop me, is up to you and that gorgeous tail of yours. You can cut and run now. Get the lions out, shove them back into the world of mundanes and magi. Or wait, try to find the key to that middle road. The stakes go up once I reach Vegas. All those magical creatures bottled up in there will find my virgin soil below them."

"So will the magi. Hell, that's the entire reason I'm here. House Erebus in its entirety could invade within hours. We need the assistance of the Maker to fight them off."

"T-t-the entire house? Er-r-rebus?" Jowls glitched hard and a flood of water hit him from off screen. Dripping shiny blue droplets clung to his rendered whiskers as he stared wide-eyed at me. "Why? There's nothing here for them! No tass that they can g-g-get at!"

"They want something I have, not sure what it is yet. Since you clearly want me to live here for some strange reason, now would be a good time to tell me how well the Cat's Meow is defended. Shina and the rest of the lions have faith that the Maker provides," I said.

His ears sagged unhappily. "I am the land. The Casino is part of that land. It has constructs, pretty things, hidden in the walls but fragile. My perceptions outside of this box are slow as the seasons. In time I will build you fantastic mountains to fortify, jungles to hide in and caves to hide your tracks within."

"That doesn't help me now, Jowls."

With a shake, Jowls' rendered image became dry and fluffy. "I have faith in you, Giver. You'll figure it out. It will be fab. My time here is up." Over his head, the bones and chains shook with effort. "Goodbye for now."

"Jowls! You're the one causing the lions to awaken. There has to be more you can do!" I shouted.

"You're the one with the paws T-t-thomas." Jowls glitched in half and blinked out. The screen going black with a single fading point of light at its center. The catwalk beneath me lurched along with everything else. A thunderous clank echoed as the chains unspooled from around the bones, drawn back up into the massive machine. The tunnel to the World egg irised closed as the many limbs of the world maker returned to their tasks.

Having the land on your side can help in a war, but it can't be counted on to win you a single battle, O'Meara opined from outside as I made my way back down the catwalk.

"It wasn't an entire waste of time," Shina concluded once we were all back in the truck and I filled her in. "The golden cats in the casino will at least be able to fight the initial wave of shades."

"You don't seem very upset that this entire Savannah is a ticking time bomb for the rest of the world," I grumped.

She rested her head on top of mine. "I'm not worried about that. I have experience with world stability. A decade of research and I'm sure we will have it all figured out."

O'Meara chuckled, "I didn't really care for living in Vegas anyway. One step at a time though. I don't want to slip in mineral oil while I'm fighting House Erebus."

19

THIRTY MINUTES LATER WE stood around a casting circle with Riona and Tack. Riona was chugging a large cup of coffee while Tack and I looked on with envy. About the only recreational drug that has crossover between humans and dogs is weed. Cats can't even handle that, at least not in normal human doses.

Riona crushed the cup and tossed it into a bin before looking at O'Meara skeptically. "Okay, run this by me again. You want to directly bind Tack to scry into my past? While I bind Thomas? Why can't I just bring Tack with me instead?"

We had a fey chain in front of us and the totally untested link we had manufactured a day ago.

O'Meara fiddled with a small crystal in her hand. "When the inquisition was investigating a magus, we'd always scry the locations where the crime supposedly happened. Not the history of the magus. All magi in a House have a ward placed on their own timelines to guard their secrecy during initiation. Only the owner of the timeline and their familiars can traverse it to visit their past. That means Archibald's past is sealed, but Nick Fessbender's is not. You should be able to follow your timeline back to his. And with this," O'Meara held out the crystal, long and slender, with a wickedly barbed hook at the end. "You can latch on to his timeline. Then follow it forward."

"But why can't I just bring Tack?" Riona asked. "Why do I need Thomas?"

"Because," I started, "there's a chance he might sense what we're doing, and I'm far better equipped to deal with him. And..." I took a deep breath, "I'm not sure you'd be able to bring yourself to kill Archibald." Better to get that out in the open or the mental link between us would go sour fast.

Riona frowned, her eyes sought Tack's, and they broke eye contact a moment later. "Fine on one condition. Thomas and I use the untested link. If its flawed, I don't want him getting messed up."

Tack barked in protest. "No! You're the one in danger. You need the stable bond."

"If something's wrong with the bond, I can reestablish it myself," I said.

"But only if you have to," O'Meara said firmly, squeezing her end of our link.

With some trepidation and a bit more debate, we bonded as a square. The link we had forged was far less gentle than a fey chain, feeling a bit like a drill to the skull as the connection was made. It snapped open, drawing us further into Riona's head than our previous connections had. I glimpsed a stage where a rock band of four Rionas performed. The spotlight focused on the glittering singer with a brilliant smile. Directly behind her, looming with one foot in the cone of light, the guitarist strummed a bloody double-headed axe. The bassist plucked at her instrument with morose disinterest, while the drummer, younger than all the others, didn't play at all. Instead, she hugged the German shepherd puppy in her lap.

Why hello there, dearie, no need to stare. Weaver's voice echoed through me and then she laughed.

Both unsettled, I pulled back to my own mind as she did the same.

Sorry, we both whispered to the other before turning our attention back to the casting circle.

Together, with O'Meara leading us, we wove a spell that to my mind's eye appeared to be a magnifying glass with spider legs. The lens focused on Riona and the world around us blurred out. I heard a snatch of that malevolent buzzing that had chased me in the future threads, then the world refocused and a doorway of glimmering gold confronted us. The color of time shone through the keyhole. Riona stood right in front of it, a key gripped in her hand.

I didn't see O'Meara or Tack; I felt them distantly through my main link. The doorway was the only thing my sight perceived in the darkness, but the black beneath me had a familiar fleshy warmth to it. We were back inside the Now.

Riona put her key in the lock and the door flew open. Although I perceived zero movement, it drew us through it, depositing us on a thick strand about five feet wide. It glowed feebly, its surface cold and sticky. It stretched out into a black void, devoid of light. Yet at the edge of my expanded vision, a glow beckoned.

Don't turn around, dears. Weaver whispered, *You're too far to see your futures, but not far enough back that its keepers can't see you. I'd rather not meet them today.*

"Thanks for the tip." I closed my side eyes tightly.

Better. Weaver's voice flowed through me like a breeze and I felt Riona shiver.

"Right," Riona announced, taking a step forward. "We have to find a spot where me and my fa- I mean Archibald interacted. That can't be too far." Another step and she bent, peering down into strand. "Okay this is me taking my unscheduled and totally unnecessary nap. Maybe an hour ago?" She continued walking, almost toe to toe, arms out to her sides for balance.

I followed closely after, trying to imagine the thread as a spider's silk thread and not a string of Now poop. Memories or visions from the thread flowed from Riona. I watched our flight from Vegas in reverse, then scenes of Riona and Tack working with Rudy to wire up the various contraptions, mostly unused, they'd installed to defend the casino remotely.

Then the talk with Scrags right after I'd come back from the future.

Another step and a scream jolted me from the display of her memories, Riona's arms were pinwheeling as she tipped forward, her mind desperately clawing for the power of her anchor. I rushed forward, clapping four paws around her waist, and hauled her back. A wave of unfamiliarity hitting me as far too many legs moved to accommodate my desire for backward motion.

"What the hell happened to the thread?" Riona asked, but I was too busy staring at the second set of limbs that gripped her. They had fur the right color, but were segmented, bowing far out to my sides and ending in digits that were hooked claws. I risked opening my side eyes to look and saw that two sets of furry spider legs had burst from my sides, ripping two holes through my harness just below my shoulder blades, and the other pair extended above my hips.

"Weaver!" I nearly shrieked, letting Riona go and scuttling backwards. The limbs, both old and new, worked in a disturbing harmony, propelling me faster than I'd intended.

Thomas, what's wrong? Riona halfway turned before Weaver froze her with an icy hiss.

Stop! No looking back, remember. Thomas is fine. He's even better now. She chortled.

"Yeah! D-don't look at me, Riona! I'm perfectly fine." My voice cracked with panic. While I had been expecting this eventually, I hadn't felt the shift at all and that disturbed me more than the extra legs. My mind was already adjusting to the new body plan, my awareness flowing out into them as they took their share of my weight. My original limbs had changed too, longer and thinner, I'd gained at least half a foot of height from the ground. I'd watched Shina be taken aback at the eyes; with these she'd probably never want to touch me again. My entire body bristled with a sense of violation as the spirit radiated smugness.

Oh, mammalian love is so basic. My mate offered himself up as a snack after our first coupling. I always carry a piece of him. Now that it's a little less cramped in here, I'll think about function next. Spinnerets would be useful and homey, but the way you digest your food inside here is disgusting.

I shivered hard, every strand of fur prickling. *No no no no. Please no.*

She laughed that stolen laugh of hers, sending it echoing through me. *Perhaps we will discuss it later. I am tired now, and you have things to attend to. This magus is worried you have lost your mind.*

"Thomas!?" Riona kept her head fixed forward, toward the infinite thread through the black void. Still, she had a hand reaching back for me. "Maybe we should go back. I'm not sure I can jump this without some sort of magic, and I can't reach my anchor here."

Careful not to touch her with my new legs, I approached, pressing my muzzle into her palm. She squeezed my face briefly, which I found odd, then swept her hand over my ears to scratch them. That was much better. The panic eased, and I saw what had stopped Riona. The timeline in front of us had gone rotten. Its surface had gaping cracks in it, sagged in spots and in others fine threads bloomed from the surface, the exposed guts of a cable. The rot was only about five feet long.

"I think that's the entire time he was with me and more," she said.

Weaver peered through my eyes with interest, *The keepers have been here, dearie. Tracking the thread that shouldn't be here. You won't be able to access his thread from here.*

"Then we'll have to keep going," I said, intending to step around Riona, but the wider stance of the extra legs forced me to sidle farther, and I found myself standing on the thread at a forty-five degree angle. Experimentally, I stepped again; the claws on all my legs hooked into the thread and held me there to the side of the thread. Disturbingly, my rearmost legs extended backwards and my paws flipped around to provide grip.

Oh Gawd, what did she do to you? Riona's thought ripped through the link, along with an image of myself through her eyes. Beyond the legs, sections of my torso looked too smooth, as if there was chitin beneath the skin instead of muscle and bone. Weaver's red mark, the interlocked triangles, blazed red from my backside. Riona forcibly shut the link with a squirt of embarrassment and fear. She took a steadying breath before asking audibly, "What are you doing, Thomas?"

I ignored the shock and hoped to all the entities that Noise finished that body today. "Stay there." In for a penny, in for a pound, and I skittered beneath the thread. Beneath it were a myriad of smaller threads, that came up to Riona's for a time and then left, diving back down into the darkness below. They all shone with the faint glimmer of silver. Connections.

But the rotted section had none, as if they'd been ripped out or simply fallen out. I probed it for solid handholds, but it had the texture of brittle paper; it crunched and tore. What would happen to Riona if her timeline broke entirely? Not wanting to find out, I braced with my rear legs and stretched out with my front four. They easily hooked into the undamaged thread beyond it. Then letting go with my rear four it was simply a big step. Careful not to look back, I circled back up to the top of the thread.

The link opened a crack. *That's one of us across. I guess I'll have to jump it. I wish we had brought Naomi; wings would go well right now.*

Open the link wider so I can use your eyes in case I have to grab you. I can't look back either, I reminded her.

I don't think that's a good idea. I'm really sorry, but I'm not great with spiders, Thomas.

Yeah, well, so long as you don't rush into my head trying to torch Weaver, I can deal. We need a better connection to do any magic at all. You can't use your anchor, but we can still manipulate tass if we need to. That will be more than Archibald can do if we encounter him. So, ovary up, I guess. It won't kill me if you think I'm ugly, I thought at her.

Right, you're just a helpful cat spider. Nothing to be afraid of. Her link widened and with it came knee-trembling fear and nauseating worry for me. With it came a vision of me through her eyes. After some debate, we decided it would be easiest for me to lift her across. So I edged backwards, walking only on my front four limbs. After a little experimentation, the spider limbs proved to be stronger for carrying. She grabbed my rear paws without hesitation, but it took some coaxing to get her to put her knees on the lowest joint of the spider legs. Only after sharing the way my back had begun to scream did she place enough weight on me that I could pull her across.

We both needed a long moment to breathe after that. She forced herself to pet one of my legs as she chanted, *a spidercat isn't scary, Thomas isn't scary,* in her head.

Afterward we walked down the timeline. I lifted her over a dozen more rotted sections before they stopped appearing. Occasionally she would stop, kneel, and peer down into the thread, only to shake her head.

Finally, after walking what felt like miles and miles, she swore in disgust. "Ah fuck, here we are. My ninth birthday party. All those times he said he was watching me he wasn't. It's like that shadow monster said." She sniffed hard. "I hate this day sooo much."

She placed a casting circle down on the thread and together we made a small knife of tass blended with a bit of the thread itself. Using it, we sliced open the thread and slipped through.

20

WE LANDED IN THE middle of a child's birthday party; the colors were washed out and faded. Bit like stepping into an old Polaroid photo. A crowd of ten children or so gathered in a living room festooned with photos of a little girl in a princess dress enthusiastically ripping open presents. Her hair was dark and fixed into two pigtails, her frame a bit pudgy, but by the way her voice carried through the room, there would be no mistaking her for anyone other than Riona. Nick Fessbender hovered over the back of her seat, whispering reminders for her to smile and thank the gift giver. And she did. When she frowned at a box of crayons, a jerk of a magic string plastered that smile right back on her face.

Nick's head was awash with magics, purple at the core of his head, and then a blue meshwork of mind magic extended through his body.

Riona stood at the other end of the table as the festivities commenced, her eyes fixed on Nick's smile. I showed her the magic that infested him.

I know... She sent with seething anger and resentment as Nick stood.

"Who's ready for cake and ice cream?" He announced to a chorus of meee!

He used it on you, too. I prodded.

Let me watch it! The thought came with Tack's growl. Taking the hint, I settled back to observe as Archibald, playing as Nick, herded the children into the kitchen. He used magic on them twice to quiet them as they jockeyed for positions at plates with a Disney princess staring up from them. The light blue magic originated from a ring on his finger; from the looks of it, the magical equivalent of hypnotic suggestions.

A woman marched into the party, her movements almost robotic, deposited a large sheet cake at the center of the table, and then left the room. Blue magic ringed her head as well. The child Riona grinned at that cake, clutching a plastic knife and fork as nine candles were lit. The suggestion ring pulsed as Nick commanded everyone to sing Happy Birthday. It all played out perfectly, the wish was made, the candles were blown out, all the children clapped. Then the purple within the spell in Nick's head winked out.

Nick fell to his knees as if the spell had been holding him upright.

"Daddy?!" Riona's voice was pitched high with alarm.

Slowly, Nick pressed a palm to his forehead, face scrunching with pain. Cautiously, he got to his feet, running two hands across his closely shorn hair before opening his eyes. He scanned the room, pulling the leather jacket he wore tighter around him as if it could protect him. Zero recognition in his eyes.

"Daddy?!" Riona asked again with more of a pleading tone.

He turned to her, stared down at her face, before slowly shaking his head side to side. He answered her, "No." Turning he stopped, staring through the adult Riona at the front door. "Hell, no." He addressed the adult Riona as tears streamed down her face.

He lowered his shoulder as he walked towards the door, passing through his daughter as her younger self shrieked, "Daddy!!"

"No," was still his answer as he turned the knob, jiggled the door once before reaching up to undo the deadbolt.

Riona, use the hook, I reminded her, but she was already moving, the crystal in her hand. She struck his back with it as the door swung open to the wider world. The moment it contacted, he disappeared, a single thread in his place, within the small crook of the hook. Everything around us became threads, spent and dead. They slipped around us, we fell, no, we slid along that single thread. I grabbed for Riona, hugging limbs around her waist but there was no need; the hook's magic guided us together. It was like the door, the void seeming to move around us rather than us moving through it.

As our feet touched the solidity of another thread, the link between us shut tight. Riona put her face into her hands and sobbed. Getting a serious "do not touch me" vibe off her, I settled down to wait, spider limbs folding somewhat awkwardly beside my adjusted originals.

"Hate it," Riona said after I had groomed two paws and spent a good long while staring at the hooked pincer-like things that were spider feet, not quite having the courage to groom them as well. "I hate it all so much," Riona elaborated helpfully. "I think about my childhood and that comes back every time. And now I got to see it again from a brand-new shitty angle. So, thank you very much for that, Thomas."

"Sorry," I said, and I meant it but didn't see what I could do to make it better. I was slightly jealous that she remembered much from her childhood at all. My own memories only appeared to start when I had moved to Grantsville. A side effect of either the way Archibald had prepped me to awaken or getting taken apart and reassembled by a dragon. Perhaps a bit of column A and column B.

Slowly, our link irised back open; Riona climbed back onto her feet. The scene still spun through her head like a record stuck on its turntable. Voices within her whispered arguments about it. I tried not to listen. "So, we do this like O'Meara told us. Walk backwards until Nick becomes Archibald again."

"I don't have a better idea," Riona conceded, and thus began the longest backward hike I can remember. We peeked into Nick's life periodically. He'd been diagnosed with amnesia, granted a divorce, and never stopped moving for the next ten years. Living out of a van, busking, and playing piano when he found a gig. He stopped being a nomad around the same time Riona awakened, floored by stomach cancer. It looked grim; he didn't have the money for treatment. Then there was a gold band around the timeline. A ring representing the space of a week. We couldn't get into it. We guessed Archibald had somehow slipped out of his house arrest to do something there. On the other side Nick was back in the hospital, bills mysteriously paid, laughing with his nurse whom he later married. But the man wasn't okay. He hated mirrors; he'd glare into them, not at himself, but at something standing behind him that we didn't see. Yet he settled into a sort of normal life, always nervous, muttering to himself when he thought no one was listening. We stopped looking closely, hurrying to get close to the present.

My paw then sank through his timeline as if it were a rotting log. We couldn't turn around to look at how long this rotten section lasted. After some debate we decided to try walking through it from within the time line. We paced back a few paces, cut into it, and jumped through.

We found Nick perched on the edge of his bed. The room smelled of blood and gun smoke. He typed into a phone in his hand while a gun lay on the nightstand. The body of his wife laid next to him, blood leaking out from under the pillow over her head. The doorbell rang. He stood, his posture that of the father at the birthday party, not of the haunted musician we had been peeking at. Archibald had returned, but I didn't see any magical puppetry rig this time. He took the gun and checked the slide. "I did warn you not to get too close to people," he said.

Riona and I watched in mute horror as he murdered thirteen people over the next two hours. Just walked to up to them, asked to talk to them in private, and once they brought him aside, he'd shoot them through the head and calmly walk away. Riona closed herself off to me again as the events swept us along, invisible witnesses to the carnage. We both knew his purpose, severing all of Nick's silver threads. All the murders were local; several neighbors were first, and then spread throughout the city he lived in. As they progressed, cracks appeared in the world in which he moved, as he drove out of town in his last victim's car, apparently unpursued and undetected, the scene lost all semblance of color. For hours he drove through back roads, without referring once to his phone or to a map.

Riona finally broke the silence between us with a soft laugh, *And here I had thought I had run out of depressing song material for open mic nights. I'm glad Tack isn't seeing this. He would have been sick.*

Yeah, I don't know what happens if you vomit in someone's timeline, I joked back.

O'Meara said he might know that we're here? If he shows, what's the plan? she asked.

I was either gonna bite him or shoot him, I responded, although the spider legs exploding through my harness might have damaged the electronics; biting him would be more satisfying.

Sound. She took out a shiny silver pistol and cocked it. I had a paranoid vision of her pointing it at me, but she lowered it to her thigh and held it there in her lap. *I want to talk to him so badly, but it seems we're past that stage now.*

Archibald pulled to the side of a forested road; there was nothing to mark the spot. No trail head, no creek, no sign. An unremarkable bend. From the signage we had passed, we were about an hour outside Grantsville. Abandoning the car, he walked into the forest, threading through the trees until he came to a snow-white boulder. I couldn't tell you if it was actually white, or if that was the washout effect of the timeline's decay. An archway appeared in the stone, and from its depths I heard that insistent whining buzz. As we followed him down a narrow stairway that led into the earth, I noticed silver flecks drifting through an increasingly black and white world.

I saw it with my magical sight before we emerged into the small chamber at the bottom of the stairway. Solid matter blocks magical sight to a degree and this thing was bright enough that he'd had to bury it quite deeply. A blazing purple orb strained to contain a twisting thing of silvered time within it. In the room, the walls vibrated with the keening buzzing. In my confusion to make sense of it, I reached out to Weaver but she didn't respond, all eight eyes closed. Archibald did not slow his pace. Mundane sight only perceived the thing as a shimmering shadow, but it was enough for him. He donned a pair of gloves that had been laced with tass, grabbed the thing and shoved it into his chest.

The scene froze, his scream and the buzz combined into a single skull-piercing note that stretched out to infinity.

What? It can't stop here! That doesn't tell us anything! Riona stepped forward into the chamber. *Other than he has a magic time thingie! And we knew that already.* Something crunched beneath her foot and she stumbled as a piece of the floor fell away, revealing a different sort of black, that of the time void. *Shit!* She held herself still, arms spread out for balance.

Careful! I warned her. *This must be the end of the thread, and it's definitely damaged.* If we fell, our only hope would be to hook onto another thread and hope it led all the way back to the present. Slowly I made my way over to Archibald, testing the ground with my spider legs, and walking around small white cracks that were hanging in the air and slowly getting larger. Whatever we were going to do, we had to do it quickly.

I guess we go back. Try to figure out precisely what this thing is.

We don't have time for that, Thomas. We're not leaving until we find my father. She looked at the frozen eyes of

Archibald's puppet and shouted over the sound of his frozen scream. "You cut all of Nick's connections, but you couldn't help to make one of your own. Hang on to me, Thomas, this hook is probably not made for this." Putting her gun away she closed her eyes and clapped. From her mind I heard the beat of a snare drum each time her hands collided. Her hum harmonized with the frozen scream and warbled around it as the prelude to a song. Music flowed through our minds as each part of her joined into the song.

Daddy-O, Oh Daddy-O
Where have you gone?
Daddy-O, Oh Daddy- O
You left me there.
Cold in my chair.
Where did you go?
Oh Daddy-O!

As she sang, her thoughts spiraled around the two men that had combined to be her father by dark magics, and around her head, silver threads waved as if in a breeze. I slid over to her and wrapped my forelegs around her thin waist. One of the threads pulsed with her mental beat, glowing brighter than all the others. She reached out and snagged it with the hook O'Meara had given us, but we went nowhere. No zipping sensation. Her song warbled uncertainly.

Keep it up, I urged her. Coating the end of my spider legs with tass, I reached out and gripped the thread. I could feel it between the pincerlike digits. I pulled.

We moved. Still no zip, but we hung above Nick Fessbender's thread, all crumpled and broken below us. Remembering the motion Weaver had used to haul me in, I took it in two legs and soon we scurried along the line as a spider crawls up a single silk strand. The Now loomed ahead of us, its great undulating wings propelling it through the black void. A great wind seized us and we rose as if we were a kite attached to a car careening down the highway. The web of possibility stretched out before the mouth of the Now. It had changed since I had seen it last. More than half of the strands were tied into a giant black knot that far fewer threads continued out from than went in.

21

WHAT IS THAT KNOT? Riona asked, and I dumped everything I knew and guessed about the strands into her mind. She revised her question. *What the hell is that knot? Can the Now choke?*

I'm going to guess it's not good, I responded, pausing my scurrying to try to follow the silver thread. It led to the spiraling threads almost directly in front of the Now's mouth. Around which silver somethings swarmed like a cloud of angry bees. A few of them separated from the swarm's churn to spiral around our tether. *Oh, that's very definitely not good.* Were those the Keepers Archibald had been terrified of?

Charge past them, Riona thought. *It's the only way. Get down there, grab my father, and ride the threads back into the present. This strand ends at my head. They can't follow it to us.*

There were so many assumptions about how this all worked in her logic, but I didn't have a better idea. I rubbed my rear spider limbs together and coated them with tass as well, using the dimensional dust I carried with me to act as climbing chalk, grabbed the silver thread, and pulled with all the strength the weird muscles within them could deliver. We launched down the thread: left side grab, launch, right side grab, launch, and repeat. Not running but more skating along the strand, each stroke building more speed. The silver things resolved from gnats to terrifying combinations of spiders, mosquitos, and wasps, their carapaces cast from mirror-polished chrome. The terrible whining buzz grew as three of them charged along the strand, each tethered to it by a single appendage, be it leg or antenna.

Keep going! Riona writhed in my grasp until she pointed her gun ahead of us. She waited until I could see the face of the lead monster. It had no eyes that I could see, but its mouth opened, a flower full of needles. The gun barked to life, but the bullet shot out only six feet in front of us before stopping and falling back past us. The second shot bounced off my nose.

Its many limbs reached out to catch me. I did the only thing I could do to avoid the game ending grab: I jumped, snapping out my left limbs. Letting go of the thread. Riona and I tumbled as we shot past. The creatures, still tethered to the trailing strand that looped back to Riona's head, crashed into each other as they tried to reverse course. Two of them went spinning off, but the leader hung on, the silver thread stretching out behind us like an elastic band.

What are you doing?! Weaver woke with a brain-slicing shriek.

Being dumb! I shouted back at her as I reached out and managed to hook a claw around the silver thread. The weight of the creature had pulled it taut, bringing it close enough for me to grab hold. Our momentum had not faded; we shot along its length as if it were a zero-G zip line.

Too fast! The spider spirit tried to grab control of my limbs, but ceased when I pointed her attention to the creature behind us. It had completed the turn and was pursuing us with gaining speed. *You idiotic larva! You cannot oppose the Keepers!*

We're not opposing them! We're running away from them! Riona pointed out as I bent my own efforts into resuming my rhythm. Left. Right. The strands were looming closer, but so were all those other Keepers, as Weaver called them.

Sever this strand! Weaver ordered. *With it latched on like that, it will follow us even into the Now!*

Sure! We'll spin up a casting circle and work complex magic while falling at terminal velocity! Riona shouted back inside my head.

I had found the rhythm though, and the creature, while pursuing, wasn't gaining on us anymore. Remembering the time-spider's anger, I only hoped that it might find the Archmagus's ghost a more tempting target if we got close enough.

With an inarticulate hiss, Weaver reached up toward my back. *Then I will do it!* Here, she didn't need a host.

I had to laugh as the spider panicked. *Please keep all your limbs and fangs inside the cat until I come to a complete stop.* Twisting the eldritch parts of my body, I shoved her back down. The spider jolted with shock. *There's no other body to deliver you here, so you stay put.* Ahead, a second group of Keepers circled the line curiously, forming a ring around it.

Insolent- Ahhh, what are you doing?! she shouted as I leapt from the line, which was only solid to me because of the crystal hook and the tass coating. For the Keepers it had mass, too. While O'Meara and I together might have been able to construct a wall of tass and toss it behind us, Riona and I would need a circle. So, without that as an option, the only way I could knock this Keeper off our string would be by using other Keepers.

Their buzzing whine sounded like a jet engine convention as we fell past them. The closest one, a great chrome wasp with dragonfly wings, rotated towards us curiously, only to be crashed into from behind by the silver meteor that was our pursuer. Both shattered into a cloud of silver shards. I let loose a whoop of victory and latched back onto the silver thread right before we plunged into the whirling web of time.

The world fractured into an insect's viewpoint as millions of possibilities assaulted my mind: a storm of people, decisions, and random chance. Yet the thread before us remained singular; Riona and I clung to it, focusing only on it through the sensory overload. It drew us to one specific thread, one possibility looming larger than all the others, expanded and drew us inside. The sense of breakneck speed vanished and my paws stepped down onto concrete hot with the intensity of the sun.

The hazy skyline of Vegas welcomed me, among a sparse forest of metal ventilation ducts and mammoth air conditioning units. We were on a roof in the northern part of the strip. A set of pigeons hung in the air overhead, wings frozen mid-flap. Everything still, except for one Archibald-possessed Nick Fessbender, who stared at the gun Riona pointed at him. He held in his hand a fist-sized wad of white clay with a kitchen timer set into the top. Enough C4 to blow the roof off the building.

"Hi, Dad. It's time for your swan song to end," Riona said.

"Princess. No y-you can't be here. You'll throw everything off!" Terror lit his bloodshot eyes, sweat shone on his dark flushed face. Feverish. Was that because I bit him? Cat bites can be prone to infection. He laughed, "This is all for you!" He shook the bomb at us. "We're ten minutes from the Now. Let the threads carry us there. I'll place this bomb, you get off the roof before the shipment arrives, and your chances of survival go up five percent. As long as Thomas dies first. Seventy-five percent chance of that, at least it was before you came here." He grinned uneasily.

"Put the bomb down, Dad," Riona said, but her insides were roiling with conflicting emotions, and she hadn't flicked the safety off either. There was still a good thirty feet between us. I chanced it, dashing forward. The motion of the birds resumed their flutter upwards as Archibald pitched the bomb towards my head and I swatted it out of my way. It cost me a tiny stumble and bought him the time to get his arm between himself and my jaws. Still, my paws hit his shoulders, bowling him over as I bit down on the offered forearm. It was like chomping the arm of a statue. My longer legs allowed him the space to drive a booted foot right up below my ribs. Driven back, I took a section of his sleeve with me, revealing an arm coated in the same chitinous chrome as the Keepers.

Thomas, I had him! Riona hurried closer, firing a shot over both our heads.

"I surrender!" Archibald called out, thrusting his hands into the air.

Kill him! Weaver demanded, and I agreed with her.

Stay out of this. Both of you, Riona mentally hissed at us. "Whatever you are trying to do, it stops now. Or I will shoot you where you stand."

"Does that mean I can stand up?" he asked, still sitting on the ground.

"No! Take that thing out first!" Riona demanded.

"Before I do that, you have to see something." As he finished speaking, the area right in front of Riona flared with the purple light. She fired, but the bullet hit the side of a crate, a stack had manifested there. The purple light pulled back into a small familiar figure perched on top of them, a white barn owl with a bow tie. The crates glowed with tass. Oric!

In that moment of distraction, Archibald threw out a line from his silvered arm, into the owl, hooking on a flickering decision point within him and disappeared in a glow of time.

Both Riona's and my minds sparked with curses as she ran around the crates. *If you had just fucking shot him!* I thought at her. At least Oric gave no sign of seeing us as black-robed Erebus magi came out onto the roof from a doorway.

I can't shoot my dad in cold blood!

What else are we going to do!? Drag him back to the present for trial?

I need to know why, Thomas! Why is this so damn important?

What if it's not important at all? We watched him murder thirteen people as if it was another day at the office. There's no reason to expect his reason to be sane.

She grimaced, *I... just don't want to do it, Thomas.*

You killed Neelius and would have killed Veronica too if you'd gotten a chance not too long ago. Can't you be a little harder hearted for this? He's the entire cause for why we had to flee Vegas, I thought even as I watched Oric deliver a load of tass to the House Erebus magi.

That was different! Personal. Veronica and Neelius tanked my entire career on the off chance it'd force me to awaken!

Archibald's fingers were behind that. Scrags can tell you. He made sure that Veronica found you. He'd been staring into the future for a long time. Your future. He was old and washed up. You're supposed to carry his torch to... whatever cause he's fixated on. Probably destroy the Veil.

What if I want to destroy the Veil? It's what keeps me from actually having a music career. I can't have fans outside Vegas, and those I have, I don't know if they like my music or want to get in with a magus.

I can't say it's a bad idea in the abstract, but the fallout would be cataclysmic according to Rudy. It was Rudy who betrayed him to the council. Rudy stopped an explosion that would have blown up a massive 4th-dimensional creature. Think about that.

She laughed. *That must have been a very tough decision for him.*

I'm all for lifting the Veil, Riona, but I'm not here for destroying the world, civilization, or even a single country to do it. Although there are certain individuals I'd gladly sacrifice to the cause. I gestured at Oric with a long leg.

Riona slid the clip out of her gun and examined it. *I've only got three bullets left. You don't have any nine-millimeter in your harness, do you?*

No, it's point forty. Rudy designed it so it's always one step bigger than practical. I talked him down from a forty-four round.

Riona closed her eyes and took a deep breath. *I can do this. At the very least, I won't get in your way next time.*

A whining buzz cut through the air. We were out of time here.

22

STILL HOLDING HER GUN, Riona nodded, took out the crystal hook and began to sing. I circled to her back, wrapped my forelegs around her chest and re-coated my spider limbs with tass. Soon as a thread manifested, she hooked it, making it solid enough to grab onto. With a yank, I launched us back into the chaos of possibilities. We surfaced back into the void among the now-familiar whine of the Keepers' wings, but they were sluggish to notice us. Below us the spiraling strands of possibilities broadened from a crowded wedge into large, fibrous bundles. The silver thread I pulled us along ran outwards into the future, past the huge black knot where so many threads ended, to where the futures resembled more of a web than threads being spun together. Massive spiderlike beings plucked their way among the strands, moving with a purpose unknown to me.

Weaver stirred. *Do not think we have escaped the Keepers. We all trail strands they can follow. They will find us. When they do catch you and force you to pay your passage, I am not here. If they discover me, both of us will wish I had never answered your call.*

Noted. I gave her an internal nod and kept my eyes forward, those that pointed that way, at least. The strand led us to a section of the webbing dense with threads, a web tessellating within a web. As it loomed closer, I saw the strands were massive, thicker than the entire swath of probabilities we had left, composed of many threads that writhed together and through each other. We splashed down into it, and again my senses were assaulted by a sea of futures, but while those closer to now had seemed impossibly sharp despite their multitude, these were fuzzy. Then they cleared; I landed on a floor of smooth, cold metal. A golden balcony, centered on an ornate podium inlaid with the circular symbol of the Council of Merlins. A woman dressed in a white feathery robe stood at it, holding up a hand encased in a shining gauntlet of magic to quiet the applause roaring up from below. Embroidered on the robe's back was the symbol I had submitted with the paperwork creating House Khatt. A thick circle broken at the top with an equalized scale in the center, a paw on one side, a human hand on the other. I hadn't really liked it, but it had been the best we'd been able to come up with at the time. To see it emblazoned on this finery was jarring in the extreme.

From this angle I couldn't see the woman's face, but the German shepherd sitting by her side gave both of us a pretty good idea who she was. As I squinted, I saw dozens, if not hundreds, of sliver threads entwined around those fingers.

I spotted the glow of Archibald's time parasite moving inside the building. Riona, my Riona, went to pull open the glass door as this Future Riona spoke in a booming voice. "It has been ten years since the sundering! And we have done far more than survive!"

Cheers erupted again. Riona glanced back at herself, at the adulation, and recalled herself screaming into a microphone amid cheers and flashing lights. She shook off the memory and opened the door for me. Beyond stood an office of sorts, desks set up among pillars of white stone. It had a familiar scent of age and the mingling of magical beings. The council building, we were inside the council building.

Archibald lurked behind a pillar at the end of the room, Riona leveled the gun at his position. "You see how high you can climb?" He called out. "I've already given you the key. You're already using it to find me."

We split up. Riona took the main pathway while I crept around the outside wall. Most of the desks were empty and the bodyguards posted at the entrance made no notice of us. She called out, "Why would I ever want to be that woman out there? She looks like a politician, not a singer!"

"She is the most powerful magus in the world. She reestablishes the Council after Great Houses annihilate each other and gather the scattered mundanes after the Shattering comes!" His voice echoed off the marble walls. Then I spotted him, ducking behind a pillar near the far entrance to the room. "She is the pinnacle of your potential, Riona! Undisputed power!"

The door next to him exploded as if the world were answering Archibald's claim. A huge boulder sailed past him, crashing through all the desks with the misfortune of being in its path.

"Mostly undisputed!" Archibald amended as a familiar and short figure charged into the room in the boulder's wake.

"Your time's, like, totally up Riona!" The figure declared, throwing back her hood to reveal Farah's wrinkled face. A boa constrictor coiled around her neck as she drew in power. In her a branch point formed, a choice between three spells. Archibald leapt for it, his magic surging. Riona fired a single shot before he disappeared. Then we were after him. Riona hummed a few bars of his song and grabbed onto the silver thread with the hook. We passed through a blaze of time and landed on a crumbling sidewalk.

Up ahead, Archibald stumble-ran through a debris field of rubble from the shattered buildings on either side of the street. Time for this game to end. I charged at him, my many legs carrying me up and over the obstacles.

"No! No! Get away! You were supposed to die!" He screamed at me, grabbing bricks and tossing them behind him with startling accuracy, forcing me to duck or dodge lest he nail my noggin. With a hiss I threw myself sideways and into the insectile world of possibilities, but there was only one possibility here; there were no people to make decisions. He'd jumped into a thread without immediate branches. In the sideways space I tore past him and cut him off, reappearing a few feet in front of him. With a shriek, he stumbled into me.

This time I bit him with teeth coated with tass, crunching through the carapace covering his midsection. An inhuman screech of pain accompanied a wave of physical force, tossing me end over end.

Twisting hard, I caught the wall of a building with my limbs instead of splattering against it.

Two distant pops sounded as Riona emitted a mental scream of sheer horror. Archibald clutched at his side, fighting in vain to stop the length of a silver ribbon with an impossible number of legs from squirming out of his chest cavity. The thing fended off his hands with ease as it continued to crawl out from the magus and his stolen body. It snaked upward before bending into sharp angles, legs grabbing hold of each other to form flat angular surfaces.

The building I clung to vibrated; the high buzz of the Keepers flowed up my spider legs. I felt Weaver's presence shrink into a tiny speck and it was as if a boulder had disappeared from my stomach.

"Don't go!" Archibald pleaded with the thing still worming its way out of him. "We're not finished!"

Riona stood, empty gun trained on the thing, mentally clawing for her anchor for any bit of power she could reach. I too wracked my brain for options. I tugged at my link to O'Meara, trying to recall Mr. Bitey, but it felt as if he were pinched in a drawer; time was simply not the domain of a dragon. But we needed to know more about the scene unfolding and only one head contained that information.

Disconnect. I thought the command. The link between Riona and me irised closed, accompanying a painless squirming in my skull as the roots of the link pulled themselves from my consciousness. It manifested midway between us, falling to the ground with a gentle clink.

I scrambled for it, snatching up the delicate-looking cylinder and charging for Archibald. The thing had started to take shape, a weirdly polygonal octopus with tentacles ending in either scorpion claws or lancelike stingers. Archibald's hands had been ripped to shreds, but he still futilely tried to prevent the thing from leaving. As I held the link out toward him my rear eyes caught a silver shimmer in the blue sky as two Keepers pulled themselves into this time strand. The roots of the link reached out and touched the side of Archibald's head, grabbing hold of him, then me. The links require consent and something in Nick's head pleaded for help. A mental passage yawned open between us. I leapt through, unsheathing mental claws.

A storm of physical agony hit me like a hurricane, trying to sweep me away into it. I armored myself with my own memories of overcoming pain. This too could be overcome and I swam in the wind. The storm had no calm in the center, but surged with frantic desperation and black dread. Archibald and Nick Fessbender both screamed with their shared pain. The ghost of Archibald had been welded to the back of Nick's consciousness. Their spines fused near their hips and Archibald's fingers ended not in strings but tendons. They were all routed not through Nick's head, but through wounds in his neck, turning him into the most grotesque of puppets. I extended my claws into a set of sabers.

With them too distracted by the pain to even react to my presence, I cleaved them apart with a single wipe.

Immediately, Nick Fessbender erupted into a geyser of dark memory. In it, the cold, clinical murders replayed with the same rapidity as the pull of the trigger. Nick's voice, pleading over the steady beat of the silenced gun shots.

Oh, god. Please stop. Phht!
Please no. Phht!

No. Phht!

By the twelfth he had fallen mute to the horror of the death of everyone he'd cared about.

I shook off the memories and stood knee deep in a lake of despair and hopelessness. The storm of pain had parted. Perhaps the parasite had finished leaving the body, or Nick had simply moved beyond the ability to perceive physical pain.

Floating over it, Archibald cast about. The tendons at the ends of his fingers dipped down into the muck as if seeking to reattach to something. He stopped when he saw me. "You! You titanic fool. You are a metastasizing mistake. So long as you are alive, my daughter will never seize her legacy."

"I'm not here to debate you." I growled, stalking forward.

He came at me, those stringy tendons rearing up like snakes. They struck, not at me but zipping back towards the entrance to my own mind.

I scooped up the slime of Nick's hopelessness and threw it in his face. He staggered back, sputtering. Before he recovered, I had grabbed him with my paw and slammed him down. "This mind is not yours. It doesn't defend you; it won't attack me."

"What?" He protested as I tore him open and peered down at the contents. Inside, I found a tiny Nick, floating in a sea of foreign memories. His head was pierced with a pulsating crystal. I touched it and the little Nick screamed, "My daughter will sunder the Veil! Build Atlantis anew!"

This didn't help us now. I dipped my paw into the memories, looking for something about the parasite. Before I grabbed hold of anything, made any sense of it, something tapped me on my shoulder.

I turned to find a hollowed-eyed Nick staring down at me. "No more," he whispered. "Leave."

"I can help. Let me find the answers I need," I asked him as the mindscape shuddered, and the construct of memories I held dissolved. "Let me figure out what he did to you."

"No. No deals. No. Out. Out." He stopped looking at me, his eyes dissolving into bleak emptiness. "Out," he repeated as the mindscape flickered and a frigid wind blew through. Nick was dying, his mind calling out for it. I dove back to my own as Nick surrendered himself to his trauma.

I stood over Nick, his blood soaking into my paws. Our connection broken with his death, the link splashed into the red puddle. Over me the parasite, timecyte, towered. Its claws snapped warningly, and I backpedaled away from it. It had grown massive, an undulating ball of weaponized limbs that moved through each other, unbothered by solidity. The two Keepers that had followed us: the wasp thing and the mosquito spider, buzzed back at it with menace.

"Thomas!" Riona waved from the doorway of a ruined building. I snatched up the link and ran to her. More Keepers shimmered into existence as I reached him.

"So, you killed him?" she whispered as we shrank into the building, taking the link from my mouth.

"I freed him, Nick I mean, but he was..." That bleakness flashed through my mind, "Done." I focused on our surroundings; calling it a building was a stretch. Buildings have roofs; it had four walls, depending on how generous you were towards piles of rubble being walls.

"After what he went through. Maybe this is better." Riona said, offering me the link.

I gave myself a deep breath to push the horror show of Nick's mindscape away from the front of my mind, then we rebonded without ceremony.

Sharing her vision, she peeked back outside. Two more Keepers had appeared; now with six against one, they flew at the timecyte. The multilimbed creature snatched one of them out of the air and neatly severed its head with a snap of a claw.

A second Keeper caught a sting in its abdomen. It did not pull up with its fellows, but crashed into a wall, wings buzzing out of sync. Above, the entire blue sky seemed to shimmer with the sheer number of Keepers coming into the thread.

I started climbing up a pile of rubble. *Come on, we gotta go.*

But where? she asked as she hurried to follow.

Anywhere there's people. We have to find a branch point and... I paused, Neither Archibald nor Nick had opened the way back into the time void; that had been the work of the timecyte. Even if we found a branch point, we might not be able to crack it open. *We'll figure something out.*

I picked my way over the lowest wall of rubble. Riona kept close; we got over the wall and onto a back alley as the sounds of the battle escalated behind us. Something about the street pinged as familiar, although all the buildings were unrecognizable. We hurried on, looking for any sign of current human habitation. Then I spotted a bent and rusted street sign: Koval lane. This was right behind the MGM! Or where the casino had been. The piles of debris blocked my view of the strip entirely, but at least I knew where we were.

Come on. If this a future where you're a warlord, then maybe there's some civilization on the second strip. I said to Riona.

Would I put the council tower back in Vegas?" she asked as we jogged along the road. *Is it still a shallowing?*

"Best idea I got," I said, suddenly realizing that Vegas' usual purple haze wasn't present here. Had it been there when I'd first fought with Archibald near my own memorial statue? The wreckage of the MGM came into view. Well, more the wreckage of what they had been building in place of it. The shattered husk of a partially constructed dome. Rusting girders arched high overhead, some bending away from their fellows, others snapped off. Below it all sat a massive beetlelike Keeper. A dozen arching spider legs carried its armored bulk while a blossom of needles, ringed by segmented antennae, served as its head. Every single one of all those needles pointed toward us.

A Queen. Run, came Weaver's voice, trembling with fear.

I agreed wholeheartedly. Riona and I turned as fast as we were able. The extra legs were great for sprinting, not so great for turning. Riona ran out in front of me.

Suddenly an image of Tack burst into our brains, running, teeth bared, before a black bolt struck him. He tumbled forward, eyes widening in shock and pain before black briefly engulfed him and then dissipated, leaving a withered corpse behind.

"No!" Riona screamed, pivoting around. "Not him!"

I hooked her with a spider leg and drove my head into her hip to keep her moving. *Not real!* Reaching through our link I batted the horrible image away. *We have to keep going.*

Riona lurched back into a sprint as she choked back a sob. We had rounded a corner when something pierced through my head and yanked like a fish hook embedded in my mind.

She has your threads. Don't look, Weaver urged but for all the eyes I have no eyelids inside my skull. O'Meara and Shina rose in my mind, their skin textured as dark stone, their veins pulsing with magma. Lions of darkness swarmed them, tearing at their stony flesh even as their bones caught fire. The pair lashed out with sweeps of elemental magics, but I could see my loves tire. Their heat fading. A dark spell caught them, consuming the heat and leaving them still and stone.

My own scream of protest wasn't as articulate as a word. A feral call of agony ripped from me, too, tried to face the Keeper Queen but Riona grabbed hold of my harness. She jerked hard, kicking two legs out from beneath me. "If I'm running, so are you!"

Run. If she catches us, then all of our futures will only hold disaster, Run. Weaver urged and I found my feet.

We both pounded down the street, but she had hooks in us both now. With every step, the tension grew and the devastation of that initial vision spread. A creeping rot spread out from the entombed O'Meara and Shina, flowing over grasslands, draining the life from every lion and animal one by one.

I can make it worse, far worse, the giant bug seemed to say.

Weaver vibrated within me, jiggling my organs with fear or excitement. *Run.*

Where? I cried back at her. Our bodies moved but the tension piled in strained as if our very consciousness were about to tear. Ahead of us stretched only more barren streets. *There's no branch points here! Archibald's thread was the only one we could follow with the hook. All the rest are diffuse; they're spread through time.*

Behind us the domed shape of the Keeper Queen's carapace rose over the rubble of a ruined building like a chrome-plated sun. In two of her many limbs, she clasped a pair of silvered threads that led straight to Riona and me.

Weaver made a series of popping clicks that reverberated along my ribs, a gruesome sort of cricket call. Time's color flashed from every visible surface around us and collated into the burned-out skeleton of a hotel to the side of the road. It flickered, a split, a sudden possibility that the building's remains could collapse.

We didn't pause to ask why or how; Riona and I charged. Leaping towards the building's crumbling brickwork. Weaver extended herself into my four forward limbs and twisted them, like going sideways but on an entirely a new axis of motion. Pincers and claws hooked on something slick and filmy. The color of time flooded through us, and I felt the cool of the time void kiss my nose before my vision cleared and beheld the mirrored eyes of another titanic spider crab staring down at me.

Now hook that thread, Weaver instructed, and I wrenched my eyes from the creature to take in our surroundings. Riona had grabbed hold of my harness and we floated just above the surface of that massive thread of possible futures that we had pursued Archibald into. How were we supposed to hook all of that?

But that wasn't what Weaver had meant: a pair of tiny silver fibers plunged into the side of the thread, shimmering with strain. I grabbed the surface of the possibilities below me and hurled us toward them. Riona deftly snared one with the crystal hook as we drew close, solidifying it so I could latch on.

Go. Do not stop until we reach the Now. Weaver reached a limb out of my mouth and cut both lines with a deft scissoring motion. The strain in our heads disappeared instantly.

I obeyed her instruction, wrapping my feline legs around Riona I skated down the thread with as much speed as I could muster. The dizzying kaleidoscopic journey that we had taken played out in reverse, the massive network of distant possibilities slowly funneling down into a funnel of probable.

Where's this thread taking us? Riona asked.

To the future it's connected to. From there, we'll be close enough to jump back to the Now, Weaver answered after a moment; she felt even smaller now within me. *Do not get snared there.*

23

THE PATH OF THE thread we traveled on dipped into and through many possible futures. My vision fragmented into cells of possible futures, all playing in a rapid rewind. At the start they were all nonsensical, random people and places. All too crowded and tiny for any one image to make even the faintest impression in my mind. Yet as we continued, those cells start to merge and patterns began to emerge, one set happening on a darkened landscape and the other alternating between rich browns and greens. Seasons. Life flourished in those futures, animals, lions, and magi wandered in and out of those frames. While the dark half merged faster, the stillness only broken by the traversing of black-robed figures or creatures of rotting flesh and exposed bone.

The rot spread across the entire swath of my vision, the grasses shrinking back down into cracked and blighted soil. Each side depicted the same patch of ground, as the possibilities dwindled down to two. In both, the removal of O'Meara and Shina's stone-frozen bodies played out in reverse, but the teams who did it were very different. In one, a jovial apelike man led a pair of hooded figures to load them up on a cart. In the other, a pride of lionesses bore them away on white stretchers.

"No!" I cried out at the uncaring surroundings and let go of the thread, shutting my eyes to visions. They crept in through my eyelids. The pack of lionesses arrived on the scene only after wrestling a thin and wounded cougar with extra limbs away from the bodies. Then I watched them both die in reverse. On the periphery I saw other possibilities, the moment remixed, with me in place of Shina or O'Meara, a few tiny cells contained only one of us.

I saw no future where either my blood or that of my loves did not christen this patch of earth.

The light of day faded out to night and brightened again.

A flash of time's color and all eight of my feet landed, snapping stiff grass beneath them. I stood there, my mind reeling, processing the sensory overload. We weren't far from the cargo elevator, maybe a thousand feet or so.

Thomas! You're back! O'Meara's thoughts found me before I was prepared. I recoiled, trying to corral the visions away from our link. *What happened? she asked. Where are you?*

We're fine. Everything is-

"I won't let it happen!" Riona declared from some distance away from me, hands tightened into fists. "We. Won't. Let it. Happen. Right, Thomas?" She looked down at me with eyes that vibrated with determination. The mental link between us had shut with a door of iron that glowed hot with shame and anger. "I won't let Tack die because I got tricked."

She must have gotten a different angle on the future. We came back via the Keeper Queen's threads of prophecy. Did that lock us into it? Would the Keeper Queen funnel us back into those situations? We couldn't give her the chance. We had to make sure that tomorrow's battle never happened. At the very least it couldn't happen here.

"We'll find another way, Riona. There has to be a different option." I gave her a nod and stood, but even as I did so, O'Meara snatched the memories that still loomed on the surface of my mind.

And what are you two being so bloody dramatic about? she asked. I latched onto the memories of her and Shina's death. *Show me!* She insisted.

We engaged in a brief mental tug of war, and she pried the memory from me like I was a dog who wouldn't drop a ball. *Can't! It's time stuff, O'Meara! We're not supposed to share it,* I protested as she skimmed through the entire adventure like a book and shoved them back at me.

You got the bloody bastard. Good. Come on back to the hut you left. We have a lot of work to do before tomorrow. Her thoughts rang with steely determination but the note waned to a sad one.

O'Meara! I growled at her. *We are not going to let any of that happen. I won't be losing you or Shina.*

She answered with a laugh. *Is that what you see in that? You know what I see? A possibility that we can win. We're going up against an entire house, Thomas, there's going to be a cost. If we're not willing to pay it, then we will lose it all.*

I don't use my loved ones as currency, O'Meara. I stood up and snarled at the empty air. Riona didn't flinch, engaged in a similar argument with Tack, although louder. A frustrated howl came from somewhere in the lion's village. I nudged her. "Come on, let's get some supplies and the spear." Time to do what I should have done right after Ahimoth threatened us the first time. I'm an ambush predator, not a turtle. We had the spear of Remus, and it was time we used it.

Thomas, we'll need the spear for defense; we have very few right now and we need to move stuff away from Maker's mount. We can't waste time on an ill-timed assault now, O'Meara argued as we walked back to the storage yard. O'Meara and Tack met us at the village edge, her arms crossed and his ears back.

I tried to do the whole "push up against her legs" thing, but the spider limbs tripped me up. Also, I swiftly found myself in a headlock, her cheek pressed against the top of my muzzle. "O'Meara, you can stay here and use Tack. We have to try to head off this fight," I murmured against her.

"We do it this way; if we let them come to us, we now know there is a chance of victory, that this place survives, that you or Shina, maybe both, survive. If you go it alone, then you might be throwing that chance away, Thomas," she whispered.

Riona's mind touched mine. Tack was on the same page as O'Meara, unsurprisingly, given that we were all bonded in a circle. Our desires to protect one another clashing. "We don't see it like that," she said.

I picked up the thought. "That vision didn't give us any probabilities along with it. There's no telling what will happen. Any defenses we make in a day won't be wonderful. There's too much risk to allow the fight to happen here. If there's a way to head it off, I'm going to take it."

O'Meara loosened her grip to stare me down with her green eyes. I returned it without blinking, mostly; the rear pair might have closed due to a speck of dust, but she didn't see that.

"Blood and ashes, you stubborn cat." She scruffled my ears. "And if you're going to ignore proper tactics, you're not going anywhere without me." The scratchings turned to grips and she forced us forehead to forehead. "Got it?"

"Got it," I agreed.

She let me go and frowned at one of my longer limbs. "Now, where's that spider?"

"Dormant at the moment," I said, "Little too much excitement, I guess."

I have news on a certain rodent if all those emotional storms have receded, Midnight's voice glided through my head. O'Meara and I froze.

Tell us. Our thought simultaneous.

Without any more prompting, a scene opened before us. Ahimoth stood, his alabaster body cracked and chipped, at the entrance to a lab of some kind. It had a large slab table in the center, with magical apparatus crowding the walls. He held a struggling Rudy by the scruff of his neck, for a thin, ungroomed owl to inspect.

"What you looking at, Birdie?!" Rudy snapped at his captors, his tail waving threateningly behind him. "Stick that beak a little closer and I'll crack it open like a nut! Then I'll rip your brain through the hole in your head."

The owl leaned back away from Rudy and lifted a set of talons from its perch. "I don't need a hole to pierce your heart, rodent." He snarled.

"He's baiting you, Vivi," the last occupant of the room warned. A white-haired woman wearing a leather apron studded with tools. "Keep scrying."

Rudy kicked, wriggled, and called everyone in the room lower than peanut butter stuck to a bottom of a shoe, but Ahimoth's grip held firm.

"Merlin's Mark," the woman declared. "And here I thought Oric was the only one left."

"Now you see why I couldn't kill it?" Ahimoth said in his heavy monotone.

The woman sighed and scanned the room before grabbing a heavy glass jar. Wards flared to life across its surface as she pulled off the lid. "It will be interesting to see what's beneath that seal. Pop him in here for now."

Ahimoth dropped Rudy into the jar. He immediately tried to rebound out but the dead magus' anchor flared, and Rudy slammed his head into a field of "No" right above the jar. The squirrel fell back, stunned just long enough for the Erebus magus to clap the lid back onto the jar. She put it to the side as Rudy scrabbled his claws against the glass. The woman then turned a critical eye to the damaged statue and tapped him on his chest. "This took me a year to construct, and you've nearly destroyed it in a single night. Charging after an entire cabal by yourself armed with Death's weapons and military hardware? The 2nd is not happy with you."

"He is not capable of being happy, but he is correct about this House Khatt. They are craven lunatics. That bomb that destroyed the Hell Hounds would have wiped out half of

Vegas if their containment had failed. Such reckless magic must be brought to heel." A chip of stone rolled down his blank faceplate.

The woman tsked and caught the chip with a snakelike movement. "I did not make this body for trading punches with war golems. The one House Khatt uses looks ridiculous, but it's fast. You are to keep your distance in future conflicts, and call for others when you are outnumbered in the open. I will make you pretty before you meet with the 2nd, but these deeper cracks will take longer. Your arrogance was your downfall the first time; I suggest you keep that in mind. Now get on the table."

The scene faded. *This occurred an hour ago,* Midnight thought.

Where's Rudy now? I asked, my chest tightening.

Still there. She's still working on that walking piece of masonry. Jar's reinforced. I tried knocking it off the shelf but it didn't break. I suspect if I keep close to Ahimoth, he'll lead me to Michael the 2nd, but I'll have to leave the rodent.

Here it was, this had to be the branch point. Have Midnight stick close to Rudy and attempt to spring him when the Erebus were distracted attacking the Savannah. Or we go get him. This complicated things. We had to get him out before destroying the Tower. *Midnight, stay close to Ahimoth and figure out how to reach the 2nd, but don't get trapped in the building. We're coming to rescue Rudy.*

"Bloody Ashes," O'Meara grumbled. "Rudy just has to make it complicated. Come on, we're going to need some of the squirrel's favorite things." She led us into the storage at a march and stomped up to a pallet I hadn't gotten to. She opened a small chest perched on top and grabbed a fistful of tass-infused M-180 firecrackers.

"So much for doing this stealthy," Riona commented; her own eyes had fallen on a collection of swords. I didn't see Tack anywhere.

"Stealth works up 'til you bungle something," O'Meara said, looking at me. "Then our only chance is to hit them hard enough to jar the marbles bouncing around in their empty skulls." With a flick of her wrist, purple flashed from a bracelet, and two swords appeared on her back along with the golden blaze that was the spell ripper.

A bellowing roar pulled my attention from both women to see Shina and Tack approaching. Shina made the German shepherd look like a toy poodle, although a particularly smug one. "And none of you are going anywhere without me," she declared, shining with numerous battle wards emanating from her collar. Stalking directly up to me, she raised a paw and swatted my muzzle with it. Not hard enough to knock my head off my shoulders, but it probably would have removed a portion of my face had she extended her claws.

"I wasn't going to leave without telling you," I said, speaking in the direction she had knocked my head. "Wouldn't be possible, anyway. I need a few things we locked in the vault." Contritely, I nosed her chin with a light chuckle, and her rigid anger relaxed a fraction.

O'Meara laughed and scruffled the top of my head. "Don't worry. I'm going to make sure he comes back to-Ack!" The fire magus fell down to her knees, putting her surprised eyes level with Shina's. The lioness had struck O'Meara in the back of her knees with "blink and you'd miss it" speed.

"I'll say it nice and slow. Neither of you are leaving without me." Shina's glare had room for both me and O'Meara. "And I know precisely how you'll object to that. That without a magus, I'm limited. So, fix it and bond me."

O'Meara's and my jaws dropped simultaneously. Shina was only eight months removed from being violently separated from Freddy, her magus of over six decades. "Uh," I started, "My head's a little crowded at the moment, Shina. I've got O'Meara, Midnight, and the Weaver crawling around in here."

"I'm not requesting a bond with you, Thomas." Shina licked my ear before returning her gaze to O'Meara. "I'd prefer a buffer between me and my mate."

Fear sparkled in O'Meara's eyes. "You think I want to be in the middle of a pair of mated cats?"

"Tack had told me of the prophecy Thomas and Riona came back with. O'Meara, your willingness to die is unacceptable, particularly paired with Thomas' desperation to live." Shina reached out and stroked one of my spider limbs. I shivered from both the sensation and the call out. "I will accept a temporary bond for now, but if Thomas is the one that doesn't make it, then we will make it permanent. Together we will continue what he started."

"Shina, please. Ask Riona. Or Farah; she and Smiley are still using a fey chain. I've sworn to myself that Thomas is my last familiar. His mind is grand central station lately but mine's a graveyard. He's my seventh. If he goes, I won't survive the grief."

The lioness nuzzled her and then with a growling purr hugged her, forcing O'Meara to hug back by the sheer dint of her weight. "I thought the same thing when Freddy died and we lost Shangra-la, but I'm still here." O'Meara gasped with pain and surprise when Shina gave her face a solid lap with a cheese-grater-rough tongue.

I had to laugh at that, and Shina snagged me into the hug, her strength rolling me onto my back, leaving my limbs to claw helplessly at the air as she squeezed O'Meara and me together. "I have more to live for than I did a year ago, and no matter what happens, I want this pride to continue. So bond me. If you will not take another familiar, then you can be mine. You can wear the collar and I'll try pants."

The image of that hit me so hard that all my breath exploded out of me. Had I been drinking anything I would have snorted it a mile away. Then I collapsed into a breathless giggle.

"It's not that funny!" O'Meara roared back at me, but I could feel her cracking at the edges, lips trembling as she fought off her own laughter. At the image of the muscular lioness straining her blue jeans and red shirts, while O'Meara lay on the couch with a dog harness over her back and shoulders. It wasn't funny, simply ridiculous, silly. Then she started laughing, a sad slow chuckle. *I am not going to withstand being bossed around by TWO cats!* she protested, but images had already bubbled in her imagination, seeded by the nap together in the hut. Stepping over the both of us, the massive amount of meat in the fridge, and the dread of having to block both of us out when Shina and I "played together." Sharing me but also having Shina. Slowly she hugged back, wiping tears in Shina's somewhat bristly fur and squeezing around my chest. "Okay," she breathed, "Okay, we'll try it."

"Do it now," Shina insisted gently.

O'Meara reached into her pocket for the fey chain and it eagerly encircled their necks. They both took in startled breaths, and I felt them slip together, exploring each other's minds. I shut the link to give them a moment's privacy, and escaped from Shina's loosening grip. Riona and Tack were having a heart to heart of their own, with Tack being hugged so hard I feared he might pop.

The link opened; that had been fast. Had it not gone well?

O'Meara assured me with the mental equivalent of a pet. *Ground rules first. If this is going to work, I want you to talk to each other the old-fashioned way. Unless we're doing magic, or it's involved with safety, no using me as comm channel. Two, never ask me to mediate between you.*

Knowing you? You'll do that before we ever ask, I quipped and then endured a noogie.

Third, you are my primary familiar. Shina is secondary. You get priority on my anchor power. Let Shina handle herself with her knack. The more she uses my anchor the more likely her connection to Freddy's anchor will decay. She suspects it won't last more than a year regardless, but would like to hold on to it as long as possible. Fourth, you remain, not allowed to die. I love you. Got it?

My magus is not allowed to die, either, I agreed, touching her hand.

"Right, then." She said out loud, then stood up out of Shina's grip. "Let's go rescue a bloody nut-brained rodent and break all of House Erebus's windows."

24

With O'Meara, Shina, Riona, and Tack all carrying enough magical armaments to violate several arms treaties, I felt rather naked with just a few tass bombs carried in my sideways stomach. Well, that and the spear of Remus. Thanks to Weaver's "gift," none of Rudy's Wizard Phooey harnesses fit. Speaking of the spider spirit, she hadn't responded to any of my prodding thoughts since I'd met the Keeper Queen. I wondered if the bug of time had told her to keep her mandibles shut for some reason. Still, in the quiet moments I felt her scuttling in my neck, so she hadn't left.

We feared the parking lot around the Grand Meow would be watched, so we took a passage deep in the Savannah up to the surface, a full five miles outside the scorching Reno city limits.

The entire Second Strip was locked down with anti-portal wards and all the houses would sound the alarm if they spotted what we were packing. Midnight provided the layout of the Tower. It was nearly an entire realm unto itself. It appeared the majority of the entire house resided in that tower and when they needed more space, they made another room that was bigger on the inside than it was on the outside. Midnight was getting around inside by essentially squeezing between those layers of folded space. So, he didn't have a great mental map of the building, but more of a vague sense of what connected to what. The more they bent the space to fit the room, the easier it had been for Midnight to get in.

Hence, he first arrived in the huge staging area where they were building the lion army. The higher in the tower, the less space bending. They appeared to know that the space bending was a security risk. Sensitive areas, such as the lab Rudy was held in had less. Michael the 2nd and a cabal of the most senior Erebus magi lived in the top. Midnight had tried to followed Ahimoth up the stairway, but found things prowling the shadows up that way and backed off.

Our plan was vague. I'd scout ahead, try to use the same entry points that Midnight had found. Get as far as I could and then blow out the side of the building, hopefully damaging the wards enough for O'Meara and Shina to join me via rocket propulsion. Outside, Riona and Tack would be unleashing nearly literal hell on the building's defenses while we sprang Rudy. Once we got the squirrel, then it was crater later time. O'Meara would heat the ground beneath us to the point we'd rocket down into the earth. Once we were deep enough, I'd take out the Spear of Remus, fire it upwards and blast the entire building from existence. Taking out Michael the 2nd, the army of lions, and a large portion of the House Erebus.

There was absolutely no way this would go wrong.

A two-story-high wall of iron and bone had sprung up around Erebus tower since the last time I had visited. The bleached white skulls perched like pigeons along the serrated metal spikes that dared one to climb it. The interior of the skulls had a sickly greenish gleam, which meant something had been summoned into them: spirits of some sort. I stared at them from the opposite street, concealed from most eyes by being slightly out of phase with the rest of reality. The spirits resided there, too, as did the ward that extended up over the fence and below the ground.

Midnight had slipped in by hiding beneath the cloak of a magus who had entered the gate. Not exactly an option when you're a two-hundred-pound cat-spider. I'd have to ring the doorbell.

O'Meara, tell Riona I'm in need of a door knocker, I thought.

So much for subtle, she quipped back before relaying the request.

Fortunately, Death's stash had included what amounted to a high-quality door knocking kit. A small catapult that was magically accurate for over a mile, along with some very interesting ammo. A soft whistle through the air and a glass globe struck the pavement with a sharp *Tiiiing.* It bounced high into the air; the skulls tilted upwards to follow it. It glowed frosty blue to mortal sight and a brilliant green to the magical.

With a light *pfft,* it burst and released its prisoner. A torrent of shining ice erupted up from the road, screaming with rage as it manifested in the middle of a scorching summer day. Spells exploded out of the ward like bursting blisters, raining caustic magics down on the elemental. The ice wrym's nearly transparent body turned white with hairline fractures as its skin steamed; it reared back, opened its four-mandibled jaws, and slammed its huge body against the ward. The ward rippled out from the impact unevenly, as if certain parts of the ward were stiffer, and it tore right above the wall.

I raced across the street; the massive spirit extended well into my sideways space and I scurried up its length. Above, at the top of the tower, a black shine darkened the sky. I leapt for that rip in the ward as a beam of negative energy lanced down from the top of the tower. I passed through, landing hard on the other side of the fence. The elemental let loose an offended hiss. Its body sheathed in the black radiance from above. The beam faltered, the great wyrm shook itself and then immediately resumed maneuvering for another smash. I had to laugh, ice itself is the absence of heat; while ice spirits come in all sorts of conceptual varieties, true ice elementals were essentially hunger spirits. Negative energy blasts would only make it colder. Sadly, I had no time to see how they eventually dealt with the wyrm. The Tower had an immense door set into its base, charred black and framed with gray stone, but I wasn't going there. The building itself was ringed by a sculpture garden minus the plants. Mostly statues of hooded fellows posing with books and scythes; a few bucked that style, playing with how many skulls one can attach to clothing without getting bit.

Okay Midnight, I sent to the stealthy feline. *Where's this crack you mentioned?*

Around the back. Step lightly.

I slowed on his advice, and stopped when I saw the rows and rows of small tombs constructed of black and white marble. They were diverse in style, from miniature Greek pantheons to pyramidal to cornucopias constructed of tentacles. In front of each stood a shade of an animal, red eyes in a body of shadow. Dogs mostly, standing at attention, ears perked. A few birds perched in a stone tree. Bone white collars were secured around every neck, the spells within entwined with green and silver threading.

They were dead familiars, chained here. None of them looked at me, standing still as if on display. If I could cut those collars, what would they do? Would they attack me? Or simply go free?

They are just dogs, Midnight huffed. *It is the cats you have to worry about. They guard Michael the 2nd. Do you see the crack?*

I did, along the wall of the building was a meshwork of purple seams, protected by a tattered ward. In it, a small hole had been torn. Getting to it would take me within ten feet of the dog shades closest to the wall. Instinct told me to slide up along the wall but physical contact with it might set it off. Carefully, holding my spider limbs out in front and behind me, I crept towards the hole. As I passed by one of the largest doggy death-houses, its resident growled.

"Caaat." The shadow spoke with a rasp, its silhouette a thick snub-nosed dog, a heavyset boxer perhaps. "I smell you, Caaat." Yet it didn't move from its statuelike pose.

"Do ya now, laddies? Do you really want to smell a cat while you're trapped by the sunshine?" A Scottish accent rolled across the graveyard, Scrags. "A cat that slices stone?" Space rippled through the statue's neck and the dog's stone head toppled from its shoulders, the collar bisected.

A yip echoed as the spell unraveled. In the sideways space two bright eyes opened, opals in the dark, followed by an outsized grin; the fangs within were more akin to a tiger's than a housecat's. I couldn't see the rest of him; his face hung there without any of his gooey body.

"Thanks, Scrags." I risked a whisper. "We need to talk, but this isn't the place."

"I will make it, then. One moment, lad."

The chorus of growls rising from the statues fell silent. The magic in their collars winked out.

"Did you just...?" I let the question trail off.

"That depends," Scrags answered as he strode forward from the shadows of the sideways reality. A tiger with tiny eyes, his torso extended like a snake's into the dark, the stripes merging and splitting in unsettling patterns. He no longer fit entirely in reality, grown beyond it. "House Erebus holds that so long as the chain of memories remains unbroken then one don't die. That these shades, their minds so narrowed to service without question, represented immortality for those familiars honored to be placed here. Rubbish. They are, were, mere memorials. They couldn't dream, cannot grow. They'll all better off, lad, gentler too, for it to be me than that spear you carry."

I took a sharp intake of breath, He was right, my sudden concern was misplaced. Once we got Rudy out, everything in the building would be vaporized. Had to be if we were going to avert the battle and its consequences. "Course," I agreed, then looked over his strange form. "Looks like you, uh, found out that I got Archibald. His shade, at least."

He chuckled, "Laddie as soon as you did, I realized that damn spider inside you was right. I've got wings. They were always there. Now that I've spread them, I see so much more."

"That's good for you, Scrags. Happen to see a back door in this tower?" I asked, glancing back at the small hole in the wards.

"Why bother, Thomas?" the shifting tiger asked. "Our sire built you crippled without wings, but you have seen how tiny this place is. There's so much more out there; we're crammed in here. Come with me. In time I can spin you wings of your own."

I felt the trill of alarm from O'Meara but she stayed silent as I shook my head.

"No," I said. "This is... this is where my family and friends are, Scrags. I'm not leaving them, especially not now. Rudy's in this tower and there's a future we have to avert."

"Please, lad. I cannot stay here much longer, it's too tight a fit now that I've spread my wings. Its crushing. We're brothers; if you could see what you really are, then-"

"Then nothing." I cut him off. "I've seen my scales in the voids, I know there are pieces of me that push against the sides of reality. My own timeline, it probably begins with our sire as you call it, but I will not do anything that makes it difficult for me to stay here, Scrags."

He bared his teeth and the expression spread through his stripes; they were all a part of his mouth, stripes of fangs flowed as rivers over the dark hide, similar to the way the dragon's maw stretched down his length. "Be that way. Then I won't help you. I'll go without you. When you tire of the squeeze, I will be too far away to hear you. Bye, lad."

Before I could get another word in, all that mouth yawned open, reality around him shone purple as he disappeared, the

space unbending like a portal coming undone. "Scrags! Wait!"
I called out but there was no response. Although O'Meara
wrapped me in memories of our many embraces.

Weren't even tempted a little, she whispered.

*I'm on a mission here, and well, I know what I want out of
life now.* The memory of our shared nap loomed large. *I won't
find it out in the connective tissue of the universe.*

25

I DROVE TWO PINCERS into the purple seam beyond the rip in the tattered ward. It didn't tear open into a portal like the rips that Oric had left in space but fought me. It took six legs to pry it open and shove myself through into the purple void. Didn't get far, though. It was like being stuck between two tightly compressed mattresses. Had to use all my legs to press against the space on either side of me and slowly peel apart the space ahead of me.

Go up, Midnight urged. *Find a thin spot.*

Easier said than done. I did my best to angle myself upwards, but I couldn't tell if I was angling upwards or doing a loop. Every muscle started to burn. A soft whisper tickled my ear, a voice. Couldn't make it out but I re-angled down towards it. The words clarified.

-deliver us from evil.

A whispered prayer. I crawled towards it. Someone was reciting the Lord's prayer in a fervent manner in the Tower of Erebus. Unease rolled through me. Then I found it, an edge, a thin membrane I could peer through. Putting an eye to it, I looked down on a casting circle set into a large granite slab. The prayer came from the sweaty man strapped to it. He had his eyes closed. A hooded Erebus magus stood at one end holding a skull in his hands that pulsed with tass and the blue of the conceptual plane. Opposite to him, a black snake curled on a perch. Judging from the bloodstains on the slab this wouldn't end well for this guy.

I don't recognize that, Midnight commented. *I can't guide you from there.*

The Erebus magus raised the skull, and a sent a pulse of magic through the circle.

Crap. I couldn't see any details of the room or whether or not the pair had any backup there, but I coated a claw with tass. The smell of fresh meat hit me as I ran my claw along the slit in reality.

The man's eyes popped open and he stopped praying as I eased myself through the hole. A roughly circular room, doors in all cardinal directions. Each door had a guard clad in black plate armor, with each holding an iron-tipped cudgel. All of whose heads lifted up at me to reveal fleshless skulls in their helmets.

So much for subtle. I threw myself down from the ceiling; the man on the slab screamed. My feet touched the slab only for the briefest moment as I pounced on the magus. He threw the skull behind him and tried to toss himself from my path. Too slow.

Knocking him flat on his back, I sank fangs deep into his shoulder and felt his collar bone crack. Something squeezed from behind my jaws and the magus squealed below me; his arms, which had been reaching for my face, flew out and his back arched. Another squeeze.

Behind me, the snake launched himself from his perch, traveling over the helpless man, fangs swinging forward. I drew on O'Meara's anchor, focused the heat down into a rear pincer, and neatly cleaved his head from his body.

The guards moved then, taking heavy steps toward me, clubs raised. I tried to release my prey, but my jaws stayed locked on his shoulder. Weaver. I felt her, eight legs grasping the back of my throat. There was no time to address her. I filled my longest limbs with fire. With upward slashes I cut arms from torsos, but the armored skeletons barreled on, throwing themselves down at me. Slipping sideways, they collided with one another. Only part of my prey came with me, and he prevented me from doing more than pivoting around. I slapped the two fallen with sun-hot paw pads, popping their skulls. White-hot spider limbs stabbed through the eye sockets of the remaining pair of guards.

The magus in my jaws lasted a few more seconds after the guard fell before he stopped breathing. I had to get out of here. Someone had to have heard that scream.

O'Meara tried to look through my eyes but I held her off and assured her I was okay before turning my attention to the spider puppeting my jaw.

Weaver, let him go, I growled.

Patience, she hissed back. *If you let go, then all his tasty tangles will evaporate. Usually I wrap my meals so I can enjoy them longer, but since we're in a hurry... Did you know he's been down here for months making golems? He's become quite numb to the screaming.*

How do you know that?

You think I go to school? The best way to learn is by eating the learned. Sadly, no one teaches me much new about the universe anymore, not since Atlantis fell. It boils down to gossip, which can be juicy on its own. As she talked, the magus's body shriveled, and I closed my eyes to the rest of it. Then I noticed the slurping.

Oh, don't be squeamish, kitty. You came here prepared to kill everyone in this tower. I can say that everyone in the holding cells will be thankful for the instant oblivion of ceasing to be instead of having the cores of their beings entombed in the hearts of golems. Weaver chuckled as she grew larger within me, swelling from a tarantula to the point where she strained against the sides of my neck.

My jaws sprang open with a gasp with the spider retreating down into my chest. I opened my eyes to find that the magus' corpse had shriveled away to a mere husk of skin resting on bone. Green fluid still dripping from the empty eyes and gaping mouth. "Oh gods!" I recoiled, tasting bile, and backed away from it until my tail hit a wall.

O'Meara charged into my mind, eyes glowing with fire. *Weaver! This is hard enough without you interfering.*

This time Weaver skittered back, deep into my torso. *I am only helping, Ash Bringer. We both needed the food. All of you are poisoned with adrenaline. You're both running on two hours' sleep and have barely had a snack since you left Vegas.*

Leave Thomas' body. This isn't your bloody fight; we don't need your sort of help. O'Meara sunk into a fighting stance, and it felt like a furnace switched on in the center of my skull. I started to pant.

I tried. You think I voluntarily cast off most of my power to be reduced to the point where you could threaten me? Thomas prevented me; he's trapped me here. She laughed musically.

Thomas! Her anger turned on me as the memories of the time void flowed through her fingers like sand.

We couldn't leave Noise like that, let the meadow spread to her cubs. I shook my head, trying to ignore the pain of O'Meara's searing anger, and scanned the room. No one had burst in from the scream. Then again, as Weaver noted, screams were probably not uncommon in this room. I rose up on my eight legs; my stomach protested, full to bursting. *And I'd be stuck like this.*

My magus was searching through all my memories involving Weaver, and then I felt her heft a blazing fist. *Hospitality? You offered this monster hospitality in our home?!*

Deep shame flooded me. *It was that or die.*

That was not something you had the right to grant without me, and you should have called her on it. O'Meara pivoted back to the spider. *Renounce that part of the deal or I will cast you out right now.*

No. Weaver reared up defensively, tickling my kidneys. *Without that, I have no incentive to help you and yours. My designs require both a body and a safe harbor. Banish me and*

Thomas will remain in my debt. While I am weakened, I will recover.

They glowered at each other for a long while and Shina's voice broke in, striking a polite note. *Grandmother Weaver will need to negotiate the precise terms of the hospitality with each of us, but NOT while Thomas is so exposed.*

The spider god lowered herself cautiously. *I agree with the lion. This is not the time.*

Bloody ashes, O'Meara swore and snuffed out her fists. *Alright. Get moving, Thomas. None of this matters so long as Erebus threatens the Savannah.* With that she stepped back into her own mind, still burning with an anger fueled by a cold fear.

Sorry, I sent to her and Shina before pushing my attention back outward. Had to find Rudy. Focus on that. A whimper and grunt made my ears flick.

The guy on the slab! He was still alive. When I turned to look at him, he struggled anew.

"Relax, I'm a good guy." I said, unsure if that was really true now. He certainly didn't believe it as he pulled at his bonds. If I let him go, how far would he get?

Leave him for now, O'Meara suggested. *We don't have time.*

I loomed over the man and smiled. He froze, shutting his eyes. "Listen, now," I told him. "Your prayer led me here."

The eyes opened with horror. "No! You can't be an angel."

"They were all busy today. I'm only here for the "deliver me from evil" part but really between us, I'm much better at the "slaying the evil" part. What's your name?"

"Winston," the man squeaked.

"Okay, Winston. I'm going to cut you loose and you're going to hide until you get a sign to run. Probably a very large boom. Can you do that?"

He nodded, although it might have been a tremor. I cut his ropes.

An image fluttered through my mind, a map of spun spi-derweb. *You're Welcome*, Weaver sent. One of the four doors was a closet. Winston sat up, rubbing his wrists and I pointed towards it.

"Hide there," I told him.

He hurried to obey, opening the door, and the air grew heavy with fresh meat. Winston made a noise but hurried into the darkness and closed the door behind him. When we blew the tower, we'd have to do it from this level up.

I opened the door that led into a hallway, and peered out into a dungeon of rough-cut black stone. Slipping sideways, I followed the path on Weaver's map through an absolute maze lined with cells. The doors varied. Some with iron bars dis-played their occupants, which ranged from captured tourists, shivering in their shorts, to enormous beasts of bone that roared and rattled against the iron. Other doors were stout wood and warded so strongly they created a glare.

Several times I heard heavy boots, and ducked around cor-ners until they passed. As I drew near the center, where the map indicated a stairway or elevator, the traffic increased; there were no living humans, but vast varieties of moving corpses, human and inhuman. Enough to flood the streets above. O'Meara watched through my eyes with growing un-ease. *I know what they've been up to while we were perfecting the link*, I sent.

When they attacked the MGM they stuck mostly to the rules, not involving the residents and tourists of Vegas. These are all for the war on Picitrix. If any of these are infectious, then Vegas is going to be a city of the dead.

Why? Why would they do that? Did these creatures have a purpose? Or were they art to the Erebus?

I shook away the distractions as I came to a central cham-ber, built around a magical elevator comprising rectangular floating platforms that floated up and down the shaft. The stone platforms traveled down on the left and up on the right.

It hardly fit with the tomblike theme of the building, but I had to be grateful that even undead magi didn't fancy climbing up fifty stories of stairs.

Midnight rose in my mind. *I recognize that. It goes all the way up to the labs.*

A pair of Erebus magi guarded the magical elevator, along with a squad of those skeleton goons and three giant chicken skeletons with teeth: velociraptors.

These guys would definitely have access to an alarm of sorts. Clearly, they were there to guard against the undead getting out of control, not intruders. Still, I took the cautious route. I climbed the wall up to the ceiling and passed over the heads of the guards. Then I simply stepped onto a platform as it moved past.

Going up.

26

I ROSE THROUGH THE tower. It bustled with activity as several clusters of magi and familiars rode down opposite me. Almost all were armed with weapons and armor that shone with dark magics. My stomach tightened with each one that passed. Were they usually so armed? Or were they assembling for an attack at this very moment?

At the top of the elevator sat a domed room. The platform I rode smoothly swung over to the downward side of the pillar without stopping. I jumped the eight-foot gap to the floor.

As soon as my feet touched solid stone, I heard Midnight's voice. "The ice wyrm has them on high alert. You shouldn't have used it to get in." It took me another moment to spot him. It shouldn't have been that hard; his gray, black stripped coat contrasted plenty with the smooth black stone he stood against. Yet, my eyes wanted to slip over his still form. Only the agitated lash of his tail gave my eyes something to focus on.

Worked so far, I huffed at him. *Let's get Rudy.* The room had three exits: two closed doors on opposite sides, and a much larger entryway set between them. It opened directly to a stairway, the black stone steps edged with gold. Illuminated by purple flames flicking out of cat skulls, the shadows crawled with eye-drawing movement. The wards that guarded it promised a thousand flavors of pain if one were to brave the stairs uninvited.

"Stand next to me and be quiet. We wait for someone to open this door," Midnight said, taking a single step toward the closest closed door and tilting his head to listen. I moved to stand over him and strained my ears for whatever sound Midnight might be waiting for. *Oh, don't move a whisker.*

As soon as he said it, my left ear itched, but it also caught a noise coming from that well-fortified stairway. A sharp tap followed by a double soft shuffling that repeated over and over. A blaze of magic stepped down in my field of vision, Michael the 2nd himself. He leaned heavily on a, not a staff, but a scythe that roiled with black and golden energies. His skeletal body used it to carefully navigate the steps, his body held at an odd slump as if it were supported by strings instead of muscle. Interlocked wards encased him as a suit of armor instead of the normal bubble shielding. A bleached-bone cat skeleton slinked past him. It had been either an enormous housecat or one of the smaller wildcat breeds. Very little tail to speak of, so perhaps a bobcat. Its empty eye sockets held the same pinpricks of light that graced Michael's withered face. Within its ribcage beat a bright white flame of magic that extended green and silver threads through the skeleton, moving it like tendons.

Unlike Michael, this animated skeleton moved with vigor and grace as it passed through the wards that guarded the stairway. It glanced incuriously around the room before scratching at its nonexistent ear.

My itchy ear flicked involuntarily. The bone cat yawned and cast its gaze in Midnight's and my direction. I'd never seen Michael's familiar before at the council meetings. Had it always been there at his feet, or was having an undead familiar gauche somehow? Didn't matter, what mattered now is that I remained unseen. It didn't appear to extend itself into the sideways space I occupied and it had several wards around it, including a shining heat ward. So as long as I stayed a nonmobile bump under the rug of reality, it shouldn't see me through those wards.

To distract myself I scryed at the wards protecting Michael, who took his sweet time walking towards the door I stood by. They were complex buggers, constructed not as barriers but as siphons, shunting energy away from the body and dumping it somewhere, probably in negative energy planes. Depending on the siphon, you could overload them with enough energy and, failing that, I had the spear.

Thomas, you are not taking on an Archmagus without me. O'Meara batted the idea away from me. *You hear me?*

Yeah, yeah, I agreed, but the original plan of disappearing the entire building wouldn't work if they had captured tourists in the basement. Maybe we grab Rudy and vaporize the top of the building instead. Still, he'd see the spear long before I could point the damn thing at him. We were too close to use it. So I stayed still. As Michael walked past, cold brushed my fur and I shivered. Instinctively, I shuffled away from it. Wincing as purple shimmered around my limbs. The bone cat, intent on the door, didn't appear to notice, but Michael himself paused, peering down at me with those pin-light eyes. I mentally reached for the spear, held in my extra-dimensional stomach. Michael cast a shadow into the sideways space. At a distance it had been impossible to see, but this close it was a huge, apelike thing that moved the desiccated body as a puppet. Its neck bent down and thrust through the back of the body's skull.

The door slid open to admit the bone cat, and Michael the 2nd's gaze lifted from me. The bone cat's long neck curled back, upside-down head cocked curiously at its magus.

"Shadows," Michael told the cat. "Many shadows." He resumed his feeble trudge using the scythe, that could probably slice an aircraft carrier in half, as a crutch. When he reached the threshold, a shadow moved. Midnight darted from where he had pressed himself against the floor to position himself right behind Michael's dragging feet. Mimicking him, I crouched down low and cursed the width of my spider legs as I did so. We both belly crawled behind the Archmagus. Once my tail swung clear of the descending door I stopped, allowing Midnight to continue on. The bone cat led his magus down the hallway. While still composed of black stone, this one had little resemblance to the dungeons below. These were even bricks, polished to a glossy shine; cables snaked along the ceiling, powering long fluorescent lights that illuminated arched doorways that broke the perfect tessellation of the brickwork. The doors were bone-white and entirely feature-less. It felt like a gothic spaceship that had outsourced its lighting to a Home Depot contractor for budgetary reasons.

You do shimmer some when you move, but not as much as you fear. He's about to pass where Rudy is hel- Midnight bit off the thought as Michael gestured towards a door and it slid open. He stared into the room. *Not good,* he commented and sent me his vision. The lab was far bigger than the one that he'd shown me previously. A large ritual chamber with a golden casting circle set into polished black marble. Rudy floated in its center beneath a spell bristling with twisting blades that had already cut into a light emanating from his chest. That same white-haired magus who'd put Rudy in the jar stood at the circle along with the frizzy-feathered owl. Raised seating boxes on either side of the circle hosted other magi and their familiars who now turned toward them with various expressions, from annoyance to outright fear.

Weaver crawled forward from my bowels to peer at the vision. *The fool has already damaged the seal. This will be interesting.*

What do you mean by that? I hissed at her but she didn't answer. Meanwhile Michael the 2nd began to berate the other magi.

"Hecate! Did you not hear the announcement or have your ears rotted from your head? We have been assaulted. You all should be at your stations." Michael's disconnected voice rolled with anger.

The woman did not look up. "That's what happens when you start a war. I'm sure you have handled it admirably. I am involved with something I cannot interrupt. Unless you'd like whatever forsaken god Merlin sealed in this rodent running free through the tower."

Midnight slipped past the archmagus. *The woman has no wards up. Give me the heat when I call for it.*

Channeling O'Meara's power to him would light us both up like a pair of Vegas Christmas Trees. He'd need a distraction. I counted eight Magi including Michael; he was the only one who had more than a basic ward over their bodies and his familiar was not nearly as well protected.

Thomas, O'Meara warned me and I heard Shina's growl echo. *Set the charge first.*

I had to laugh internally as I set myself for a pounce, dredging up a set of tass grenades from my stomach. *Get ready for a Rudy-style entrance and exit. One distraction coming up, Midnight.* Launching myself into the air, I reached Michael within two bounds. The bone cat's neck twisted around to hiss with alarm as I slipped back into reality just long enough to spit a lit tass bomb at its head. The cat jumped straight up as a panic ward encased its body.

"Assassin!" Michael the 2nd cried out as the bomb exploded in a flash of white light. His wards flared as the blast flung him back down the hallway.

Inside the lab, as all gazes whipped toward the door, Midnight reached and received O'Meara's burning power. A second flare illuminated the now enlarged doorway as the housecat coated himself with hot plasma and leapt through Hecate's back. Her familiar shrieked. Midnight kept running, dodging around Rudy as he fell, until he slipped beneath the risers and extinguished himself.

Outside, Michael's magics caught him as I reached a T intersection of the hallway. I kicked off the wall, gathered a massive amount of heat into my body and channeled it into my teeth to the point that the red orange light of them shone through my skull. I opened my jaws, and the air met the surface of my superheated mouth and expanded violently. Pumas can't roar, so I call this move the world's loudest meow. It sent a concussive shockwave back the way I came. The lights, the brickwork, everything shattered in its wake, except Michael the 2nd. He floated in the middle of the hallway, supported by a dark miasma. It swept out from him and captured the bone cat, encased in a hamster-ball-like panic ward.

I dodged down the next hallway, coughing up the shaped charge cobbled together from Rudy's box of explosives, lit it with a flick of my tongue and batted it down another hallway. Behind me, twin snakes of miasma curled around the corner. Whether born of an artifact he carried or of his anchor, letting it touch me would be a bad idea. I slipped sideways.

"Bold. I'll give you that." His shout echoed after me.

I let the blast of the shaped charge answer for me. Dazzling light flooded as reality itself reeled from the explosion. Briefly the black of the void shone before space twisted to fill the hole. The walls bent, the stone shattering, spewing shards everywhere.

O'Meara shared her own visions of the moment. An eye-scorching white beam of power had blasted out from the black surface of the building. She and Shina shot towards it on a comet of kinetic energy. As they approached, they dropped three more marbles containing Kaiju-level elementals on Erebus' front stoop.

The hallway I stood in became a balcony; the remaining walls flared with magic, struggling to keep the building from collapsing. The brilliant afternoon sunshine made the broken masonry sparkle all around us. Michael slid around the corner to face me; the bone cat, freed of its panic ward, floated within the black miasma pouring out from the archmagus. "You had your chance. Now show yourself."

Simultaneous with his demand, two shining comets landed in front of me. Shina and O'Meara wore their war wards, auras swirling with the power of the weapons they bristled with.

"Bolder still." Michael lashed out with twin streams of miasma. O'Meara countered with a slash of her sword, sending out an arc of white light that sliced through the dark flows. As they dissipated to nothing, her other hand sent forth another brilliant beam, not from an artifact, but from the weave of a spell between her and Shina. It struck Michael's wards and crystallized around him. A stasis spell that trapped him within his own ward.

"I'll give you one chance to surrender, Michael." O'Meara said with a thickened Irish accent. "Refuse and we'll rip you apart along with this building."

He didn't struggle; the pinpricks of light danced in his eyes. "To threaten me with death is like holding a feather duster to my throat. I welcome you all the same. You're all going to be here for a very long time. Forever, in fact."

Incoming! Midnight warned, broadcasting a nimbus of gathering blackness. Ahimoth!

27

O'MEARA AND SHINA THREW themselves backwards to dodge a black spike, but instead, a black beam struck Michael's crystallized ward. It shattered and the Archmagus shot back behind the corner. I bolted forward, scuttling up onto the wall.

Deploying mana arc! O'Meara tossed out a red stick which burst into a brilliant light. Completely whiting out my magical vision and hopefully Ahimoth's bird's as well. If he fired, I couldn't see it. I swung around the corner, pushing another tass bomb into my mouth. Ahimoth floated in the center of the hallway, black wings obscuring the rest of it. He had his hands outstretched, angled towards where Shina and O'Meara were, the glare of the mana arc too bright for me to see any of his magic but the fist sized holes in the wall. He was firing blindly. I charged; lighting the tass bomb, I spat it into my pincer. Flickering back to reality, I lobbed it forward, a spinning tube of red cardboard and silver duct tape. His fists clamped closed, and he swung what appeared to be a mere shadow to my mundane sight. The firecracker exploded mid-bisection with an echoing crack. The impact drove him back barely a foot, but as he opened his hand to thrust his palm out towards me, the fingers crumbled away. Wary of his black spike, I dodged into the sideways space and flung myself toward the opposite wall. Instead, as his featureless head snapped up to focus behind, a wall of shadow appeared in front of him in time for a brilliant beam of heat to slam into it. O'Meara and Shina had rounded the corner.

Stay sideways, my little lion! Shina roared in my head as a jagged bolt of lightning sizzled through the hallway and struck the shadow shield.

The whiteout of the mana arc had begun to fade, so I could see how the shield rippled with each strike. It gave no sign of weakening, and worse, it filled the entire hallway. I retreated back behind my mate and my magus. Soon as I stepped behind their wards, the beam O'Meara blasted Ahimoth with doubled in width. The cracked edges of the bricks glowed with heat.

This is taking too long. We're going to get flanked! She thought at me even as she shouted, "I can do this all day, Ahimoth!"

"As can I," the Stone Magus called back. "Your mayhem ends here." Then the wall of black came rushing towards us.

O'Meara dropped her beam and slapped a bangle on her wrist. Force magic grabbed us and slid the three of us down the hallway. Ahimoth smashed into the wall of the intersection but recovered swiftly, shifting his shield to cover his entire body before Shina's bolt struck him.

I stepped close to O'Meara and together we wove together tass, rock and heat, recreating a volcano's eruption and pointed it right at the undead magus. A torrent of force and magma blasted out from O'Meara's hands. Blasting away another section of the building with it and Ahimoth tumbled out through the sky. Some element of the attack must have gotten through.

Way is clear! I thought at Midnight. *Bring us Rudy.*

Affirmative. I shall try, He answered, flashing me a vision of Rudy still suspended in the air, the seal on his chest glowing brighter than before.

"Hit him again!" O'Meara shouted as Ahimoth halted his fall and spread his wings. *Attack from every angle you can.* With that, she unsheathed the inquisitor's sword and sent a dozen spells streaking up through the air.

Let's bring down this elephant, Shina thought as the tip of one of her wands lit with green magic that belched out an entire swarm of silver daggers that streaked towards Ahimoth with the buzzing of angry hornets. Ahimoth covered himself with blackness and came at us, his remaining fist stretched out towards us as if he were superman.

Damnit, there has to be something that can get through that! O'Meara and I wove together another volcano eruption, choking it down into a solid stream of lava. It blew him backwards like a bee hit with a garden hose. But again he caught himself and climbed back up into the sky, rising faster than the swarm of daggers could follow. The black flowed into his hands.

Down! O'Meara commanded and dived on to the floor. Shina hopped to the side, lashing out with a narrow beam of force. They hit each other simultaneously. The yellow beam lancing across his legs and the black spike piercing her hip.

Got him! Shina beamed us a mental smile before the storm of agony ripped through her mind and through O'Meara.

O'Meara roared out in pain, shielding me from the brunt of it.

"Shina!" I screamed as I leapt over to her side. The black hole in her hip was expanding rapidly, already the size of a quarter. Gritting her teeth, O'Meara flung herself at us, grabbing my paws to form a circle between us. Together, we fumbled through the pain for O'Meara's healing plane and slammed it into the hole of negation. *Hang on, Shina. We got you!* The hole had reached the size of a small fist but stopped growing.

Let me go! It's fine. You're both exposed. I'm not sure if I killed the bastard, she thought with a pained pant. *Even if I did, they could swarm out of that elevator at any moment.*

You don't have to worry about that, Midnight commented. *They've all run away, Michael the 2nd as well. Something about a seal being uncontained.* The sneaky tabby illustrated the problem, while Midnight had the squirrel by the scruff, he now hung from Rudy. The light from his chest had grown to fill Rudy's entire body. He floated in the air, dragging Midnight up with him. *I can't let go, either.*

Our concentration wavered, and the hole surged larger. "Bloody fucking ashes." O'Meara and I cursed in unison.

Riona pushed through a thread of healing power from her and Tack. *Here! We're about out of gatecrashing party favors too. We've backed off some.*

O'Meara and I gratefully threaded the additional power into the literally sucking wound.

You can't amputate half my body, Thomas. Go help the squirrel and cat, Shina growled at us. *He's who we're here for.*

Rudy will hold on. I focused on the hole. It wasn't simply a projection of Ahimoth's anchor plane, but a whirling mechanism. It had to close. It had a sound of its own, a slow grinding hiss of nooooooo. Noooooo.

Streaming in the torrent of life energy had stalled it from ripping into Shina's flesh, but it still fed the weave of the spell. Sustained it. We had to unmake the weave of the spell itself.

A piece of it glimmered. *There,* Weaver whispered.

Without hesitation or question, O'Meara and I drove a thin spike of tass through the indicated strand. Instantly, the spell's negative energies turned on itself and it imploded with a soft pop. It left us with a gory tunnel through the lioness, into her thigh and out her backside. Shina moaned as her flesh began to reclaim the space.

Tack and I can sustain the healing spell. Get to Rudy, Riona thought at us.

O'Meara and I tied off the healing weave and pulled our perceptions back to our surroundings. Rudy glowed with the light of a bonfire further down the hallway. Midnight hung from him, rear legs kicking.

"Fight it, Rudy!" I shouted as I charged and then swung around to his far side. Scrying through the glare, I spotted Merlin's symbol in the center of it. A slit had been cut into it and cracks were spidering out from its edges and through them, loops of white threads poked through; they had entangled Midnight's head *What the hell do I do with this?* I asked O'Meara.

Rudy answered the thought, *run.*

A surge of fear pulsed through the links. Down the hallway Ahimoth rose into the frame of the ruined brickwork, one hand outstretched. A wall of rock and muscle slammed into me and O'Meara both, driving us into the lab; Shina on lay on top of us both. Where we had stood, a black line streaked, nearly hitting Rudy and Midnight.

"Would you just bloody die already!" O'Meara blasted a beam of plasma out from her foot as Shina struggled to get off us. It cut through several walls to splash against Ahimoth's black shield.

"I have no fear of any death you can mete out, Ashbringer. My soul key is safe from your meddling. I will gladly die again and again against you, who seek to hold us hostage," Ahimoth called back as he advanced.

Shina, Thomas, O'Meara thought at us. *Try to get Rudy and Midnight moving, I'll-*

Rudy went boom, cutting off the thought. A nova of magic drove all three of us into the opposite wall of the lab. Their wards activated, and I hit more flesh than stone.

Where Rudy and Midnight had stood, a squirrel filled the entire explosion-widened entryway to the lab. As big as starving grizzly bear, tail twice that in length. Every surface of his skin wrapped with those threads, spider silk. On the back of his neck, Midnight struggled, hopelessly entangled. He cast a large featureless red eye towards us.

"Rudy?!" I called out to him.

It twitched its head to the side, evading a black spike.

"Ratatoskr." He hissed back and leapt down the hall. Through the hole O'Meara's beam had cut, we watched him impact the death magus. With a chitter that shook rubble from the ceiling, Ahimoth came careening down the hallway. Wings opening and his remaining foot digging a furrow into the floor in front of us. The Squirrel tackled him, long teeth biting through the stone of Ahimoth's shoulder. His body flashed black; it blew the squirrel's paws off him but did nothing to dislodge the jaw's grip. Instead of reestablishing his grip, Ratatoskr kicked out his rear legs and twisted his long body like a corkscrew. The pro-wrestling move spun Ahimoth into the air and slammed him headfirst into the ground with a bone sharp crack of stone on stone. The arm popped off as if Ahimoth were a cheap action figure.

Gripping the wrist of the captured limb with both paws, Ratatoskr pulled it from his mouth. Ahimoth pushed up to one knee and Ratatoskr clubbed him with his own arm. The black shield appeared, and the arm passed right through it. The Squirrel chittered darkly as the blow knocked Ahimoth onto his side. "Nut Crrrrracker!" Lifting the limb over his head, he brought it down in an arc. Stone cracked against stone.

"No." Ahimoth lashed out with a black blade, but Ratatoskr avoided the slash and casually pinned the remaining arm to the floor with a hind foot. The raven swooped down toward Ratatoskr's head, only to be snatched from the air and crunched between sword-like incisors. The raven shattered like a piece of glass.

The stone magus screamed then, a wordless vibration of shock and pain that ended with another brutal overhead blow from Ratatoskr. It broke Ahimoth's head from his shoulders and sent it tumbling towards the elevator shaft.

"Hee Hee Hee." The massive squirrel laughed with glee, his tail waving proudly as the three of us stared, stunned by both his power and the malice emanating from him. Still the broken seal shone on his chest.

Midnight yowled, *Get me off this thing!*

Working on it, I thought as the three of us got to wobbling feet. Shina sneezed and sniffed as the aftershocks of the healing spell wracked her. O'Meara watched Ratatoskr with the wariness of a gunman at high noon. I approached him with cautious steps, "Ratatoskr. Hi. Do you remember me? Do you remember being Rudy? My friend?"

He flowed, turning toward me and bared his yellowed teeth at my eye level. "Thomas... Where is the tree, Thomas? Where is my tree?"

I blinked. "Uh... You moved it. Before we evacuated the MGM. You and your buddies."

The head cocked. "Nooo. Not Coraline. THE TREE! Tell me!" He took an aggressive step forward, and I backpedaled to avoid feeling those yellow teeth against my nose.

It's too soon, Ratatoskr, Weaver whispered from within me. *You need to go back to sleep.*

Flinching back with a bark, he raised his paw of hooked talons, his gaze flicking down to my chest. "Spider! Not Again! No Wrapping again." He shook himself, and Midnight let out a plaintive mew. Ratatoskr blinked rapidly and scratched at his muzzle. "Remember. Must remember."

We didn't have time for this. "Rudy, Ratatoskr," I snapped. "Let's figure this out later. We came to rescue you. Let us put a heat ward on you and we're going to show these bastards one huge boom before we get out of here."

"Booms..." He smiled. At least that part of his personality hadn't changed. On his chest, the broken seal still sparked with magic.

"Big one. Gunna, take out this entire tower," I said. "Come on, let's go."

His lips closed over his teeth, giant tail flicked back and forth as he thought. "Tree gone but seed buried. Too deep. But... boom," his voice murmured.

"Later!" I circled around him, trying to herd him back towards Shina and O'Meara, who were really not sure what to make of this. *Give him the heat ward,* I urged O'Meara, and she produced a tiny amulet which had been made for a normal sized squirrel.

Tentatively, he hooked it with a claw, held the tiny thing up to his nose and sniffed it.

"Now that's a squirrel-size ward, so if you could shrink back down you won't get burned," I told him, silently begging the universe to listen for once. O'Meara's eyes met mine. *When he shrinks, hit him with a stasis.*

She nodded.

"Better idea." Ratatoskr announced. His form whirled with impossible speed. One arm clamped around my neck and his other hand plunged down my throat. Shocked, all I could do was gag on a limb as I felt his fingers dance around the interior of my extra-dimensional stomach. "I take boom."

"Let him go!" O'Meara lashed out toward us with a scythe of fire. Ratatoskr jerked himself out of range. Inside me, his fingers curled around the shaft that sizzled away at the edge of my consciousness. *No!* I bit down, driving fangs through his web-covered skin, and muscles pumped poison in as I drew on O'Meara's heat.

With a roar of pain, he leapt away, heedless of the scorched flesh my teeth claimed. Wrenching the spear of Remus from me in the process, my magical vision filling with a scorching yin and yang of white and black. Shina and O'Meara struck out with a beam of white stasis, but Ratatoskr bent his body out of the way, and with a motion more liquid than flesh he rebounded from a wall. By the time O'Meara fired again, even his tail had pulled out of view as he raced down toward the elevator.

I stood there, sputtering, spitting out ash. Internally a whirl of chaotic thoughts and shock. *What the hell?*

Weaver answered me. *Once the messenger of conflict and war, Ratatoskr became the guardian of the world tree seed when it fell. As squirrels do, however, he forgot where he buried it. Seized with madness he digs and digs with whatever he has at hand. The remaining gods of the world sealed him away. A companion of Merlin's undid that seal and he called on me to help remake it.*

So... he'll use the spear to make a really deep hole? O'Meara stood and brushed off her jacket.

Spirit, you could have told us earlier, Shina rumbled. *Depending on how deep that spear can penetrate it could hit a vein of lava and turn Vegas into Pompeii.*

It wouldn't be the first time, dearies, Weaver said. *The seal is on his madness and power. We must repair it; I will show Thomas how.*

There were no disagreements on that. The spider was being suspiciously cooperative. No doubt as leverage she'd use later, but we had no time to deal with that. Exhaustion had made the divisions between us blurry. Blearily, we tuned into Midnight, who watched helplessly as Ratatoskr propelled himself down the central shaft; we couldn't see precisely what the squirrel did, but we got the gist. Defenders had thrown up hasty wards, but the squirrel gnawed through them in seconds. He danced around beams and spells before smashing the magi with the butt of the spear and continuing on.

Together, Weaver and Midnight included, we made a plan to recapture the squirrel god.

28

WE MADE OUR OWN elevator shaft. O'Meara knelt between Shina and me, thrusting the spinning spell ripper downward as she projected stone and boiling heat downwards. Ceiling after ceiling we slammed through, the spell ripper making quick work of the few wards we encountered. We felt a pang of guilt as the contents of the rooms combusted around us. Bedrooms, labs, libraries, a dining hall, all flashed into flames.

Through Midnight, I tracked Ratatoskr, who slowed as he approached the base of the building. He encountered resistance and screamed as several spells winged him, and then got distracted by his rage.

Near to the ground floor, we burst down into a vast room lit by green flames of human skull torches. The room where Midnight had seen the army of lion shades. Nearly empty except for a cluster of Magi and shadow lions hurrying through a purple portal at the very far end of the room. Michael the 2nd had fled our fight with Ahimoth to launch the attack on Reno. That's why we hadn't seen anyone in those rooms we'd cut through, not a single magus or familiar. He'd abandoned the entire building, the heart of the House. Only leaving Ahimoth to slow us down. And if it hadn't been for Ratatoskr, we'd still be dueling him.

Why? Why hadn't he simply fought us with Ahimoth? The pair of them could have beaten us. Ahimoth nearly had alone.

My soul key is safe, We thought together. Ahimoth's last words clicked into place. That he wouldn't allow us to hold his brethren hostage. That's what Death's vault had held that was so important. Death collected collateral for the gambling debts of his fellows; he could have included the key to their own resurrections. Had Death somehow stored Micheal's soul key in his vault? It had to be. Why else would he be clinging to that body? None of the other Erebus were that obviously dead.

If he had just told us what we had... I thought.

Shina laughed at me. *He couldn't let you know that. If you'd known, that would've given you leverage over the entire house. Nor could he allow the other houses to realize it either.*

Bloody Ashes, O'Meara hurled a huge ball of flame at the magi hurrying through the portal. *We need that spear back, then. Destroying this building is useless. We used the wrong threat. Michael has been baiting us into using the spear against his house. It's the only thing we have that can destroy that vault. Come on!* Tossing another fireball, she broke for the direction of an archway. I ran alongside her, but Shina hesitated.

Wait! We can't let that close! Shina thought. Feeble blasts of magic pinged off her wards. *If we don't use the spear, we'll have to run miles to get out of anti-portaling wards, and hope Willow and Reynard can grab us. The Savannah's defenses are not ready for an attack now!*

We paused. *That's what rocket-propelled O'Mearas are for! Come on! We can't do this without you!* I waved my paw at her and with a shake of her head, she loped towards us in a three-legged run. The last Erebus hurried through the portal and it snapped shut. We hurried out into the hallway and ran towards the shaft. The door had a ward on it, so we blew through the unwarded wall next to it.

Ratatoskr's deep barking chitter echoed down to us through the tube of stone. Ten feet up the shaft, he paused his chewing through a panic ward to glare at us. His bared teeth were stained with blood, as foam dripped from the corners of his mouth. The limb I'd bitten and burned had swollen, so it appeared as if several footballs had been stuffed beneath his skin. The blackened fingers still held on to the spear of Remus.

"Go away!" he screeched, "I'm making big boom! Biggest boom ever!"

The panic ward collapsed beneath him, out of juice. Ratatoskr made to dive down the shaft to the lowest level. The three of us channeled a wave of force too wide for the squirrel to evade and smacked him out of the air. He tumbled, but only got one foot between himself and the wall. The masonry cracked. Yet he bounced from the impact, landing on two feet. He swayed, tail waggling for balance.

We channeled heat and stone into the floor. The brick glowed red beneath us, and the portal to the dungeon closed like an eye.

"No!" Ratatoskr cried. "The seed is below us. I can reach it!"

"Rudy!" I shouted at him. "Change in plans, I need that spear back. It's important for everyone. It's the only thing that can blow the vault. You remember the vault, the one you couldn't get through no matter how hard you tried?"

He stared back, breathing hard, the poison, the burn, and the spells of the Erebus had all taken their toll but had not stopped the immortal squirrel. "Yes," he answered. "It is unimportant. The seed is all that matters."

"It's not down there. It's not on Earth, Rudy. It's in a different place, in a different time," I told him, creeping forward carefully. "We can try to find it together, but I need that spear first, for the sake of everyone else."

"Wrong." Those eyes shone with furor. "It could be here. It could be anywhere. Let us see." The spear twirled in his fingers.

Told you that wouldn't work, Midnight thought at me.

Had to try, I responded, channeling O'Meara through me and into the tabby cat. The back of Ratatoskr's neck burst into flame. The squirrel reared back in pain as he ripped the flaming feline from his neck and flung him. Midnight yowled as he cartwheeled through the air. *Here we go, Weaver.* I prodded the spider spirit, consciously yielding my tail to her as I charged the squirrel in full-out scuttle.

Burned and poisoned, the monster squirrel still moved faster than anything that big should, clubbing the butt of the spear on a spider limb with a wet smack. Pain howled at me as I rushed past him, leaping not at his body but at his tail. No longer under my control my tail thwapped against his calf and then the floor, stringing a white thread between them. Meanwhile I jumped into the fluff that composed his butt serpent, my jaws seeking the column of sinew and spine at the center. My teeth found only fur, so I channeled flame into it.

"Don't touch my tail!" Ratatoskr roared. From O'Meara's view, I watched him twist around towards me. I kicked out, swinging my body around the tail. His jaws met his own burning fur. Shina and O'Meara grabbed hold of the spear with force hands, and twisted it out of Ratatoskr's wounded paw. He didn't even notice as I leapt away.

He made to follow and face planted into the floor as the webbed snare snapped tight.

You're clear! Do the bloody thing now! O'Meara thought at me. *And good luck!*

I sent my love down the link and broke it. Mr. Bitey manifested beside me, a cobra of the finest silver chain. Whirling around, Ratatoskr beheld me with shock-widened eyes. "You're my friend!" He screeched at me.

"That's right," I said, "And I'm not leaving you like this." Mr. Bitey sprang forward, breaking up into thin chains that wrapped around his neck.

Nothing happened.

"Rudy!" I shouted, as Ratatoskr reeled back to bite at the silk that held his leg. "Let me in!"

No, you can't come in! Nobody's allowed in! It's too crowd-ed in here! Too much. You can't see! Rudy's panicked voice flowed out of the link.

"Rudy! I need to talk to Merlin!" I shouted as Ratatoskr snapped the bond and leapt at the spear as it floated across the room. It whirled away from his grip.

"Mine!" He bellowed.

You must subdue him, Weaver reminded me and I tasted the acrid flavor of her venom on my tongue. *One way or another.*

Working on it! I thought at her and shouted, "Rudy, if you don't consent to the bond, then you are going to spend the next week encased in silk and miss a battle. Again!"

Aaaaaaaah! Fine! Don't say I didn't warn ya, you peanut-brain cougar!

The link didn't simply open, it detonated.

29

SHARP SHARDS OF MEMORIES tore into my mind. I fell, no, leapt, feeling the air rustle through my fur and tug at my long tail. Landed on a shoulder but not one shoulder, a dozen different textures greeted my paws all at once, the experiences ramming together. The head that turned towards me held overlapping faces and spoke many names. Rudy, Rantallion, Raggabrash, Rube were among the ones I could make out.

I twisted out of the memory only to find myself shouting, "Fire in the hole!" and diving into a can labeled "peanuts". As an explosion rocked my shelter, I flung myself out of this memory too.

A zippo clacked, lighting a fuse of a battery of bottle rockets. As they caught, I called out, "Heeeya Moonbag!" The werewolf framed in the doorway downrange of the rockets turned towards me as the rockets launched, his bared teeth parting as his jaw fell open.

Tossing the memory away, more struck me, jarring scenes replayed as I reached for the link. I saw Rudy's life through the lens of a firehose: battles, trees, laughter, explosions, all mixing together in a torrent, which made it easier to not to get drawn into them. To section them off as Rudy, who I wasn't. I used a core of memories as a shield, where I was looking at him and his fuzzy tail. From our first encounter, his exclamation, "Holy Walnuts! You're huuuuuuge!" in my bathroom, to where I sat on the shoulder of Stompy as we stormed the casino in Reno.

So armored, I forced myself against the stream of memories and through the portal into the squirrel's mind. More and more memories, too many to count or process.

I arrived in a vast warehouse that looked like the aftermath of a hurricane, or rather several hurricanes, including one currently in progress. There were rows and rows of shelves that towered above me. All overflowing with nuts, acorns, cashews, walnuts, peanuts, most of them loose, with a few cans floating among them. On the ground, the nuts formed a wavy surface that resembled sand dunes. Up ahead, a great whirlwind spun, flinging countless nuts through the air. They rained down on me, each a memory trying to show me something, a relived moment. I shut them all out as Ratatoskr's voice boomed through the mindscape. "WHERE IS IT?" The roar made the shelves tremble, sending even more nuts cascading down from their shelves.

No sense digging around at the edges, I started running across the nut dunes. "Rudy!" I called out, but heard no answer, only Ratatoskr's frantic roar.

As I passed aisle after aisle, I noticed their labels; the first had borne my name, then Archibald, Death, and then names I didn't recognize, until I came right to the edge of the storm. The labels were crossed out and replaced with insults like, fuddy old fool, bitter acorn beard and Mr. Smarty robe. Too busy chuckling at the signs, I almost missed the man himself. Merlin's ghost, it could be no other, sat cross-legged on a pile of acorns. He wore an ash grey cloak, facial features obscured by the brim of his large conical hat with the point slumped to the side. A gaping hole had been blown in his chest, exposing the remains of a beating heart that had pieces missing as if it were a partially eaten pie. Merlin had died of a spell to the back while bonded to Rudy, to Ratatoskr. Rudy had lied about only being bound to him for a year.

"It's all gone to pot, has it?" He said by way of greeting. "Like everything else."

"Hello, Merlin. I need your help to put Ratatoskr back in his bottle. You have to tell me how you made the seal."

"I think it's better to let it end." He laughed darkly as he gestured at the relabeled aisles. "He's right; yoking a god of conflict and madness to keep my legacy alive was foolish. While stasis killed Camelot within the pace of a few lifetimes, the Council needed conflict, its ideas challenged. It worked for a while, but they still turned inward. The squirrel found and advised those who would challenge the Council, but he couldn't correct their focus on power over their fellows. Until he found you, and with the help of a dragon, shattered it entirely. Perhaps that's what needed to happen."

Growling I stepped up to the ghost. "I don't care about your designs and plots, old man. I want my friend back."

A mirthless grin emerged in his long white beard. "Your friend doesn't really exist. He is a mask over an insane beast. Now that mask is shattered. A new mask won't bring your friend back. Besides, maybe it's for the best. He was tired."

I lashed out at the pile of acorns he perched on, causing a minor avalanche that sent him sliding down to me. He cried out before I caught him by his throat with a segmented pincer. "Rudy still exists. He's here. Look at all these shelves of memories. That's all Rudy. And you're going to help me. So tell me how you made the seal."

Narrowed eyes shone from the beneath the brim of his hat. "You realize you're threatening a ghost, don'tcha? I wasn't bonded to Ratatoskr when I made the seal. I am only composed of the experiences during that time."

"You must have done things that were similar. Show me those memories," I snarled, my stomach twisting with anger at magi and their awful "legacies."

He laughed in my face, a bitter, hot scent. "Do you see a filing system in here? Go digging."

"No." I grabbed his sleeve with my teeth and pulled him from the pile of acorns towards the storm.

"What? Let go!" he protested as he stumbled after me and pounded at my back. The blows had no strength in them. The old man was just a memory, after all. We had no time to tease the answers out of him. Every second I spent in here left Weaver unsupervised in my body and Michael's attack on Reno further unchecked.

The acorns underfoot pricked at the pads of my paws as I first dragged Merlin's ghost out beyond the shelves of the last five hundred years or so. Fragments of the nuts whipped through the air, pinging off my head. I saw flashes of a grand tree, running along highways of bark, gathering acorns the size of watermelons, and a new world to explore at the end of every branch.

And I smelled that same bark burning.

The acorns grew mushy beneath me, becoming a paste, a blend of memories that had lost any distinction from each other. It was in this paste that Ratatoskr dug with mad abandon, his blood red fur plastered with the muck. Throwing up clouds of nut debris before coming up with a palmful of pristine acorn memories. He sniffed at them desperately, let out a despairing wail, "Not here!" Then he'd crush the nuts to fragments to toss them aside and dig again. Destroying his own memories to cross them off the list. His eyes whirled in utter madness, his fur crawled with parasites, black many-legged things composed of failure and fear.

"No, no, no," Merlin begged as we approached him.

"I thought you were tired. Ready for a long rest?" I taunted as I threw him down into the memory muck. As he landed with a wet splat, I finally spotted Rudy, a cheap plastic gray squirrel mask that stuck to the side of Ratatoskr's neck, its black eyes watching me with a shiny amusement.

"Told ya the place was a wreck," he called out to me. "You shoulda listened to that there old fool! We're all about setting things free, Thomas. Well, I'm free now. Look at me! The great Ratatoskr!"

The titanic squirrel dug blindly, compulsively, in the muck and the Rudy mask sputtered.

"Rudy!" I shouted back at him. "You're not a mask! You're still you! It's this thing that's a bad memory. Ratatoskr is no more real than this memory of Merlin. Help us shove him back into a bottle! You can fight him."

With a fierce chitter, mask Rudy melted into a gray sludge and swirled down Ratatoskr's arm. The paw wrenched up from the ground mid dig and the sludge engulfed it, swelling into a plush squirrel hand puppet with black button eyes. "If I'm not a mask, then it's worse! I'm not only a puppet, I'm this guy's puppet!"

He surged forward, stretching the still-oblivious-to-this Ratatoskr's arm out like a noodle. Merlin, who had just gotten up from where I had tossed him, suddenly had a squirrel puppet clamped around his throat. Rudy lifted him into the air. Merlin kicked feebly and made gurgling noises. "It was all part of your master plan, then! Huh, Acorn breath! Cycling through lost causes like some sort of addict! Free the spell dogs! Create a multi-house library! Destroy the Veil! Make familiars actual partners! And a dozen more causes that I can't remember!" He shook Merlin hard, and acorns fell from his robe.

I shouted up at Rudy, "What if it's not the plan at all, Rudy? What if he simply decided there was a plan to give this little fragment of himself a sense of control! Maybe even an excuse you told yourself when you felt guilty for wandering away from someone."

"Can't hear you! Too busy strangling this figment of my imagination!" Rudy shook Merlin harder and his very legs started to dissolve into black acorns that landed in the memory muck.

"All I'm saying, Rudy, is that you could be Ratatoskr! Merlin and Weaver just supplied him with anti-compulsion drugs and amnesia for therapy! Sure, they sealed away your powers, but that doesn't make you any less Ratatoskr than this asshole."

The shaking slowed, as did the digging.

"Hey, if you want to give up your shot at being a literal god who's bigger than any cat in the world, that's fine, too, but imagine how many bombs you could carry. Oh, not to mention you could actually carry one of those big tablet phones."

Merlin fell from the squirrel puppet's grip with a sharp *Oof!* Rudy slowly turned to face Ratatoskr. The giant squirrel snorted like a bull as he eyed him back. The now noodlelike arm stretching between them.

"Find. Seed." Ratatoskr groaned.

"Puma's got a point. So, I got just one thing to say to you, past me," Rudy said. The storm around us died away and a sun snapped on like a light bulb overhead: high noon. The puppet's stubby arm flicked, and a long ribbon of firecrackers unrolled from it.

"Seeeeeed!" Ratatoskr roared, making Rudy's plush tail whip in the wind of his breath.

Rudy shook his head, "Nope. That's not it at all. It's... GEEEERONIMO!" The ribbon of firecrackers whirled to wrap around Ratatoskr's head as the puppet charged his throat.

Ratatoskr squealed in surprise and pain as the firecrackers burst with a machine-gun staccato. He grabbed at Rudy and flung him away.

"I'll crack you open easy as a roasted pistachio!" Rudy screeched, swinging around to bite the back of Ratatoskr's skull. The pair whirled into a violent storm of claws, teeth, and suddenly manifested explosives. The smoke thickened to the point that it obscured all the details of the fight except for the whirling motion.

"You! Not real!" Ratatoskr roared, and an explosion blew apart the cloud of the fight, sending two long-tailed entities rocketing in opposite directions. The larger one hit the pasty surface and tumbled before catching himself. Ratatoskr stood, smaller, his red pelt pockmarked with burns and one eye swollen shut. The other bounced once before landing like a miniature super hero, one paw punching the ground: Rudy restored to flesh and fur, tail waggling with bravado.

"Got news for ya! You're nothing but unexploded ordinance that nobody likes!" He chittered at the squirrel god.

"I am eternal. You are nothing but a false face whose time is over!" Ratatoskr flexed his claws and bared his teeth.

"Eternity-smernity!" Rudy stomped on the paste of memories. "All you got to show for all that time is an endless plane of low-quality store-brand peanut butter! I do more living in fifty years than you did in a thousand!" He stretched his paws up over his head and the entire mindscape rumbled. Above him the entire contents of the warehouse section of his mind appeared, a battalion of massive shelving units, his memories swarming like clouds of bees. "I have friends!" A cloud of nuts swooped down with the speed of an eagle to pelt Ratatoskr, who threw his arms up to protect his face. "I have enemies!" Another swarm struck. "I've known pain!" A massive swarm blew Ratatoskr backwards. "I've even been in looove!" A tiny swarm about the size of a fist zipped in to deliver a nasty right hook as the squirrel staggered back to his feet.

Ratatoskr swayed but remained standing, wiping blood from his nose. "That is nothing! I-We are the messenger of the great tree." He gritted his teeth and reached for the ground. It shook. The paste behind him bubbled into a boil. "And this I remember! Our purpose is our power!" Greenery erupted into the mindscape, leaves the size of countries unfurled, branches longer than worlds, connected to a gnarled trunk that folded entire dimensions into its bark. It tickled my memory from when I had seen the entirely of the universe from very far away. When I had seen it all as a great organism. This tree had not been that, but a significant piece of it. An organ of the universe. As I beheld it, the leaves of the tree caught fire.

Rudy stared up at the tree and then shook himself. "Big whoop, it's gone. Like thousands of years gone. Time to move on. We just need a good coping mechanism. May I suggest... Giant Robots?" Rudy leapt up with a gleeful cackle, memories swirled, and Stompy assembled himself around the squirrel. Now building-sized, the mech brandished a huge gatling gun at Ratatoskr. It spun up with a mechanical whine before roaring to life. "I am old uncle Rudy! The Hercules to sentient rodents everywhere, with the terrible theme song! I am the squirrel who swallowed the sun and spat it out because it was too spicy! I'm the guy who fights for justice when all the magi are being stupid and dumb!"

I laughed," Don't forget the hider of bombs in the pockets of your friends."

"Oh yeah!" He called over the sound of the thundering firearm, "I'm the patron saint of unsafe explosive handling! You can't do any of that!"

Ratatoskr tried to protect himself from the onslaught, curling into a half-fetal position. The bullets were nuts, hammering him down into the pasty ground and piling up around him. "Noooo!" He cried out as the nuts reached his chest. "The seed! Must find it! Regrow the tree!"

"Oh, put a walnut in it!" Rudy shouted back. "I am you! I am Ratatoskr! I will find your silly holy nut when I get around to it! So, calm your little tail and stay down!"

Time to wrap this up. I darted forward and laid a sticky strand at the base of the nut pile.

"Hey!" Rudy cried at me. "Don't touch my mad alter ego with your gross spidey bits, Thomas!"

I sighed. "It's only a mental representation, Rudy. Let me help you contain him, otherwise he'll never stop fighting you."

"No making webs in my head, spider-cat!" he insisted.

"Fine." I reached into my own mental tool box and reimagined the spider silk into a silver donut and brandished it at Rudy. "Duct tape better?"

"That will do!"

Ratatoskr, now buried up to his neck in nuts, howled with impotent rage which I quickly cut off by wrapping a band of tape around his muzzle. With Rudy back in control and separate from Ratatoskr, wrapping up the personality proved simple. Once Ratatoskr was encased in a silver cocoon, Stompy picked up the still-struggling personality and hurled him towards the horizon of the mindscape, into the deep subconscious.

The big bot dusted off his hands as Rudy sighed. "There. No more mad squirrel god. Uh, Thanks for the help. Although I'm sure I would have gotten him on my own. Eventually."

"Sure Rudy," I chuckled, then meeped when the metal hand closed around my torso.

"Sorry, Thomas! No cats allowed in here. Top Secret stuff!" Rudy said as Stompy wound up like a baseball pitcher.

"Rudy, I can leave on my own!" I protested.

"Where's the fun in that! CAT-A-PULT!" He chitter-laughed and threw me. His mindscape shot by, and I hit the link between our minds as if it were a bullseye. I passed through the link so fast that it felt like I rolled around the interior of my head several times before my awareness spread out into my body.

I staggered dizzily before opening my eyes to find Rudy, back to being squirrel size, trapped in a cocoon of webbing the size of a football with only his head exposed. Magical knots were cinching closed across his chest, the strands held by Shina and O'Meara on either side of him.

"There! That will hold ya," O'Meara declared as the spell circle between them winked out. Rudy's eyes fluttered open and he immediately struggled.

"Hey, what's the big idea? Why am I small again?" he asked with a whine. "Thomas said you didn't know how to fix the seal!"

"We had no idea how to lock Ratatoskr's personality away. Weaver had plenty of ideas on how to seal up his power," Shina said, and the spider spirit laughed in my chest. "Now let's get back to Reno as fast as we can. I fear for my children. Thomas, get the spear, we'll untangle the rodent later." With casual ease, she picked up Rudy up with her mouth.

"Ewwww kitty drool!" Rudy squeaked. "Thomas, help!"

I focused on shoving the handheld worse-than-nuclear weapon down my throat before answering. The spear of Remus tasted even spicier than last time. It was definitely getting too much exposure to reality. Once it was safely in my interdimensional stomach, I grinned at Rudy. "I might ask O'Meara to carry you instead, if it weren't for recent cat-a-pult experience."

"Awww come on! It was a pun. I had to do it," Rudy proclaimed.

"Can't hear you. Too busy saving your tail," I responded, noticing Midnight limping towards me.

I would like a ride, he said, and I knelt to let him.

30

IT IS A FLESH wound, Midnight insisted as we ran down the hallway toward what we hoped would be the front entrance of the tower. The space was folded so it proved to be a long run, plenty of time to probe at Midnight's wounds.

Midnight, a torso puncture wound is not a flesh wound! I argued back.

We'll heal him as soon as we're clear, O'Meara thought back as she blasted out another wall. Daylight beckoned beyond. "Thomas, stick close. Shina's and my battle wards should hold against any remaining defenses. Apparently Riona's door knocking has attracted gate crashers. House Picitrix is assaulting the tower."

"Cavalry's a little late," Rudy grumbled as we peered beyond the hole and into a war zone that awaited us. Black auras surged over the ground and sky, clashing with a battery of magical beams and waves.

No house Erebus magi in sight but they had released all the creatures in the dungeons on their way out the door, apparently. "I don't suppose anyone's got a white flag?"

"We don't have time to explain what's happening to them. We have to get home right now." Shina snapped.

"We'll go under it, then." O'Meara grabbed hold of her anchor. "A tunnel!"

"Rudy doesn't have a heat ward!" I pointed out.

"No worries, I'll have to snuggle with your girlfriend here." Rudy had somehow escaped the webbing already and flattened himself on Shina's back. "These wards should hold unless you let magma drip on my head or something."

"I can try to dodge the bigger bits," Shina chuckled.

"One fiery exit plan coming up." O'Meara sent a spray of plasma down in front of us at a 45-degree angle. Shina and her wards deflected the backdraft of gas and stone as I hid behind them. A few insubstantial creatures came screaming down the tunnel after us, but nothing a few tass-enhanced claws couldn't disrupt. We came up a few blocks away, met up with Riona and Tack. We healed Midnight the best we could. Contacted Willow and Reynard to get ready to bring us back. They were waiting for us by an entrance to the shallowing and reported that the Veil was definitely getting stirred up. Gigantic shadows were reaching around the entire Cat's Meow casino but she couldn't tell us if House Erebus were inside the Shallowing yet or not.

We stepped through a glimmering purple from the heat of Vegas onto oil-stained concrete of an abandoned mechanic's garage, its cinderblock walls hiding the pulsing portal from mundane eyes, and therefore the Veil's. Still, I felt the cold prickling of its agitation along my spine as soon as I scented the sharp musk of Willow and Reynard. The pair were visibly straining to keep the portal open long enough for the last of us to come through, Shina panting openly from her three-legged run. It snapped shut, leaving a thin purple scar floating in the place it had been. Both Willow and Reynard sagged.

"You all made it back!" Willow pressed a hand to a heaving chest as a relieved grin graced her narrow face. "Farah set some wards in the casino to slow them down, but they didn't last long. Everyone's pulled back deeper in the Savannah."

"W-waiting for us," Tack barked, with his own doggy grin, although his tail did not move. "Can't d-d-disappoint fate."

"Don't talk like that, Tack." Riona said, grabbing his scruff and shaking it. "We did enough. This is different now. It's not a siege. There's lots of possibilities on how this can shake out."

She glanced up at me, eyes pleading. "We don't have to go down, we've done enough."

Tack's head whipped around, teeth flashed as he bit Riona's black-denim-clad thigh.

"Ow!" Riona jerked back, toppling down onto the floor to be confronted with Tack's fangs.

"I'm n-not a c-c-coward," Tack stared down his magus whose complexion had gone several shades paler. Distantly, through the link with Shina, I heard him mentally shouting at her.

Her face went from pale to red in record time and she threw her arms around Tack, "Sorry."

Finally, the tail wagged.

A gentle push on my shoulder, and I found Shina leaning against me. Her tongue ran across the back of my neck. O'Meara stepped down in front of us, her hands flowing over our muzzles, over the top of heads and down our necks. We both rumbled with the touch. None of us had any doubt what we were doing next. Didn't matter what the prediction was, no running now.

"What's with all the hugging?" Rudy asked loudly from the top of a rusty tool chest. "You gonna tell me what's going on, or do I gotta wait for the peanut gallery to write a Wikipedia article?"

I laughed, "Nothing much, we're all gathering our courage to go take on the entirety of house Erebus at once. They're invading the savannah looking for Death's vault, and probably plan to wipe us out afterwards."

Rudy's tail lifted to hook over his head and he chittered. "And you have some sort of plan to do this, right."

"The plan was to rescue you, then use the spear to vaporize the tower of Erebus with the house still in it. However, by the time we stopped Ratatoskr's rampage, most of the magi were already on their way to Reno. So, destroying the tower just would have been senseless property damage. So, we got about two thousand stairs down to come up with a new plan," I said. "Do you happen to know what happens to a House Erebus magus when you destroy their soul key?"

Willow opened a trap door in the floor. One of the many entrances to the Savannah below. We began to file down its steps. Rudy jumped onto my back as I passed his perch. "Soul Keys are in the vault? Oh, that tracks with Death. Talked about those all the time. Depends on how many times they've used it. The more they die the more entangled it gets with them. Worst case, their entire soul shreds apart best case, they get a massive headache."

The stairs were a broad spiral winding through the earth for perhaps three stories before the outer wall opened up into the Savannah cavern. The stairs now carved their way around one of the countless support pillars that supported the blue stone ceilings of the shallowing. Willow stopped and pointed, the Maker's Mountain clearly visible in the distance. It swarmed with black pinpricks of lights with occasional glints of gold. The black would be the shade lions and other undead troops. The gold would be those Erebus using traditional wards for protection. The largest concentration was at the foot of the mountain, near the village of the techno lions.

"They've already penetrated the casino? The Maker didn't stop them?" Shina looked toward the scene with complete shock and despair flooding from her.

Willow shook her head. "Giant mechanical cats appeared to fight them, but the death magi ripped through them. They did buy time for the lions in the casino to retreat, but not much else."

"My daughters?" Shina asked in a whisper.

"Noon's injured, but Sunset and Sunrise managed to drag her back with the retreat." Willow answered, and Shina gave a huff of sheer relief.

"Maker be praised," she said.

"Automatons will never last long against magi who wield entropy and negative energy. If he slowed them down at all, then Jules did what he could. But they have the vault. They knew precisely where it was." Mentally I kicked myself. In our rush to mount our rescue and assault on the Erebus tower, we'd left the defenses entirely open. Hadn't even moved the vault deeper into the Savannah.

Can't do anything about it now. O'Meara's thoughts whirled with a storm of options. *They'll not likely to be able to move it. Stasis planes are generally a Picitrix technique that became popular among the Inquisition.*

"Willow, were you able to relocate anything since we left?" I asked. "Is... Noise still there?"

She nodded. "Naomi and Morie were working on it. Shoved everything she could grab and slammed it into the truck. Including the... werewolf and her children. They're all below, come on. Shina and O'Meara reek of magic, let' s get you behind a damping ward before they notice us."

We circled around the far side of the pillar and spotted the truck. A little camp had been set up, on the far side of a rocky outcrop that sheltered a watering hole. O'Meara and Shina spun together a plane of force which we used to descend down into it, skipping more than a thousand stairs.

Noise, Naomi and Morie greeted us at the bottom of the stairway. Farah and Smiley didn't look up from a casting circle a bit further away. The subtle shimmer of a damping ward surrounded the camp. Naomi gave us a tired smile.

"Got Rudy back. That's a good thing," she said, waving with her remaining hand.

"And I finally got that alabaster bastard!" Rudy chittered back. "Should have thought to bring you back his arm as a present."

"That's alright," Naomi shivered. "That's one less we have to deal with. Wish we didn't have to deal with so many."

My eyes went to Noise. "I don't suppose Weaver's body is finished?"

Her ears flicked and she snorted through her broad nose. "In a way. Come, let me shoooow it to you." With a toss of her head, she gestured for me to follow.

I glanced back at O'Meara and Shina. They nodded, bidding me to take care of this while they gathered more about the situation from the others. Noise led me to the rear of the truck's trailer.

There the wooden spider body for Weaver sat, its legs of twisted wood, its mandibles and pedipalps glued back together so you could scarcely see the cracks. Seven gleaming white eyes reflected the evening light; one socket lay empty. While it lacked the creepy human eyes and the doll-like hands, it bore a stunning resemblance to Weaver herself. The spirit crawled forward through my torso with an eager speed.

"I have finished the woodwork but I have a proposal for Weaver. May I speak to her?"

Weaver scuttled up into my neck, *I listen, cow.*

Noise nervously dug at the dirt, her paw's hard hooflike toes leaving parallel furrows in the earth. "I've been thinking it oooover. When your body is done that will only cleanse the meadow from my children. Not from me."

You broke a pact, child. You must bear the consequences.

"I understand," Noise's heavy head nodded. "The body only requires an eye and two fangs for it to be complete. In exchange for removing the meadow from me I offer my own fangs and one of my eyes."

A sacrifice, Weaver hissed with pleasure. *You do learn, wolf.*

"Isn't that a little extreme?" I hedged into the conversation. "Surely there's no need for Noise to maim herself."

"Thomas, I'mmmoooo." She stamped her front paw in frustration, "-trying to get her out of you. The fangs will grow back." Noise huffed.

"The eye won't!" I growled, "I happen to have a few eyes to spare."

Weaver's laugh bubbled up from my chest. *You cannot sacrifice a gift I have given you back to me. Now hush, my kitty host.* My tail whipped around and its end spun a loop of spider silk around my muzzle and cinched it tight.

"See, you're losing control to her, Thomas. I won't fight a battle for yooooo, but I can moo this," Noise said, her gaze shifting downward. "What do yooo say, Weaver?"

The spirit spoke in a gentle, coaxing voice. *You took the meadow into yourself when you defended your children. You reinforced the connection, and it floods your soul. For your sacrifice I will give you control.*

"No pack will have a cow." Noise growled, ignoring me. "I don't want control; I want it gone, Weaver."

Magi and magic saturate the weave of your soul, woman. Any life you build ignoring that will be woven of brittle lies. You will live in constant fear of a gust of truth. Take control as it is offered, and let us all be free of the knot between the three of us.

Noise bowed her head, pondering. "Doooo it. It's worth the eye to be free of this heaviness oooon my mind."

Excellent. Host of mine, serve as my priest and harvest the sacrifice.

"Mmmph!" I protested but there was no escape from this. I could feel the push of my own debt to Weaver. O'Meara offered no objections, instead helping me weave the planes of force to harvest what Noise offered. Shina offered up a local anesthetic from the medical supplies. Noise endured the plus-sized tooth extraction without complaint, but whimpered as we pulled her eye from its socket. As soon as it left her flesh, it calcified, becoming a shining white orb, and shrank to match the others.

"I'm sorry," I whispered.

"Just give it to her," Noise panted. "Get it oooover with."

And I wish to be free of this cat, Weaver crooned. *Place them in the body.*

I floated them toward the wooden spider and they snapped into place, as if the wood had always waited for them. With a deep breath, I opened my mouth wide. Felt eight legs walk down the length of my tongue and then lift all at once. Green energy rippled through the sculpture of wood. A shiver went through my torso as that hollowness that the spider god had occupied swelled closed.

One wooden leg twitched, then another pressed against the floor of the trailer. Weaver stood smoothly with a soft creak of strained wood. Her mandibles that bore Noise's teeth clicked together experimentally and the white eyes gained their own luminescence. "Yes, this will do nicely. And this Savannah of yours is not in a hurry to push me home. I will find a nice place to spin a web, and see if I cannot snare a snack or two before I return home."

"Not before you fix them." O'Meara said, stepping up beside me.

"The wolfling first, then." Weaver bobbed in a whole-body nod. We stepped back to allow her to creep out of the trailer. Clicking testily, she hovered over Noise, who had sunk down to the ground, breathing heavily through her nose. "An end to your misery, then." Her four front legs reached into Noise's body, grabbed something, magic flared, a pattern of multi colored strands which Weaver looped together and sewed in with several other threads in a motion I couldn't follow, then cinched it closed.

Noise's body spasmed with a bark and dwindled. Her massive muzzle slimming, the rear hooves retracting into single claws as other toes joined it. The powerful bulk of the bovine ceded entirely to the predatory litheness of the wolf. Only small horns remained as Noise picked herself up, gave a wag of her once again fully-fluffed tail, and howled with relief.

To be immediately shushed by O'Meara. "Hey, don't give away our position."

"Oops, sorry," Although Noise couldn't hold back a doggy grin despite the missing fangs. "So much better. I'm me."

Her eyes opened, both of them, one of them the golden amber of a wolf, the other black and featureless. My own eyes widened in surprise and she cocked her head in confusion. "What?" Then she closed her good eye and then switched. "I can see? It's a little blurry but..." She looked up at Weaver, "What did you do?"

"Eye for an eye," Weaver chuckled, "Can't have a lone wolf mother running into trees on her blind side. So what if it looks a little strange?"

Noise looked about to protest, but swallowed it back down. "Thank you. Good hunting to you, but I do hope our territories will not meet again."

"Our threads remain uncut. Should you or your pups call, I shall hear them." Weaver said.

Ears flicked back at that, but Noise bowed doggy style, then looked at me. "Good luck, Thomas." With a huff and a sigh, she trotted off toward the tents where I assumed her pups waited for her.

"Now put Thomas back," O'Meara insisted.

"Certainly," Weaver responded with cheer, reached out with a single leg and tapped the stump of a spider limb that Ratatoskr had broken. With a wet squelch, the damaged segments regrew. "There! Good as new." She laughed, a fuller hiss now.

"Weaver!" O'Meara hissed back, and Shina growled as I experimentally placed weight back on the limb.

The spider didn't bat a single one of her eight unblinking eyes. "Our association is far from over. He trapped me within his body so it's only fair if a bit of me remains."

"I don't need your adjustments, Weaver," I said, "Please undo them."

"In time they will unravel. My mark on your back will re-main as a reminder of-"

"The hospitality we have granted you," Shina interrupted her. "There's no need to rub our nose in it."

"On the contrary: I find that mortals need constant re-minders of their deals with me, or they forget their responsi-bilities. If Thomas falls in this battle, one of you will wear my mark instead. Your home is my home."

"Only so long as you abide by the rules of hospitality." Shina faced down the spider, ears back. "No harming our family, the extended one. You won't touch a single lion, or guest of any of them. That includes attaching your stringlike deals to them. One violation and our sanctuary is revoked."

"I'm aware of the rules. Thank you, God Mother. Thomas, a last piece of advice, that spear you carry is very damaged, you'll need to be quite close to use it on something as hard as that vault. O'Meara, good-bye, but only for now. Watch for webs." She slid herself sideways beneath the reality's rug and skittered off in a direction I couldn't follow.

"Bloody Ashes." O'Meara kicked a rock with a sigh and then turned to Shina and me, rubbing her hands together as if cold. "Spider taken care of. Archmagus in time x'ed out. Just gotta take out, I dunno, half a House of Magi."

A familiar weight dropped onto my back. "Sounds like a party to me!"

I looked back to see Rudy peering at the shredded holes that my extra limbs had ripped through my harness, rendering it useless. His cheek pouches bulged.

"Rudy, we kinda used most of your bombs already. Those we could find. Not sure what you can do. Even if we wanted to unseal your powers, we'd need Weaver to come back," I said.

"Meh, I don't need the powers of an old fossil!" He reached into his mouth and pulled out two tass crystals; we still had quite a bit of that left, fortunately. He banged them together, making a spark, "All I needed to know was..." he sparked the crystals again. "The magic was in me all along!" The third time, the crystals impacted with a flash. When it cleared, Rudy sat on a control saddle in the middle of my back; the harness had been modified to accommodate my extra limbs, with small catapults on either side of him. Behind him a pouch sat bursting with the glow of tass bombs. "Will you look at that! The Wizard Phooey Mark Six is online! It must be a miracle! Praise me!"

I laughed, hard, as Shina and O'Meara stared. "Oh, those Erebus won't know what hit them! The saint of unsafe explosive handling is on our side."

31

AFTER A LITTLE RECON, which consisted of Shina and I peeking around the edge of the pillar we hid behind and squinting at the distant glow of the Erebus magi, O'Meara gathered everyone together. They remained clustered near the cargo yard which contained Death's vault. A ring of black dots guarded them: the undead, lions and otherwise.

I stepped forward. "Alright, everyone. We've learned what House Erebus wants. Inside that vault they're clustered around are their soul keys, particularly the soul key of Michael the 2nd among them. We can't let them have it."

"With Picitrix attacking their mostly empty tower," Shina joined in, "they get those keys and whatever other artifacts are in that vault, they'll take one look at the rest of the Savannah and dig in. With the Maker not allowing any sort of space tunneling here, it's an easily defensible space. Picitrix and then Morganna will follow. The magi war will happen right on our doorstep. The Savannah will become a new front. Even if House Morganna and Picitrix win, we'll never get them to leave."

"But if we can kick them out now, the war will remain in Vegas and they will recognize the Savannah as a place too dangerous for curious magi noses." I finished.

"Can we really take on an entire house?" Willow asked, her green eyes flicking between Shina and me.

A deep-throated chuckle boomed out from the diamond-toothed crocodile next to her. "It ain't the full house.

That would leave all them juicy casinos in Vegas. It's mebbe a third of the House."

"A-And!" Tack entered the conversation with an excited wag of his tail. "They're not good ward makers. Riona and I nearly brought the Tower's wards down on our own!"

"We've used all of our elementals now, though," Riona protested.

"They've only had an hour to dig in." he countered, "We-We can do it."

Farah bounced, "Oooh, and if we hit some hard enough and fast enough, they'll pop panic wards. That will take them out of the fight. If Smiley and I are close, I can totally trap them inside their own wards."

"You won't have to be close with me." Willow took her much shorter wife's hand. "I can't open a portal down here, but a little localized twisting still works."

O'Meara slid between me and Shina. "The plan is simple," O'Meara said to the gathered members of House Khatt. "We punch through their camp. Deliver Thomas, and then we cause enough chaos so they don't see him and the spear until it's too late. Thomas destroys the vault with all the Soul Keys, and the majority of the more powerful magi fall over and die for good. Everyone grab whatever you think you can handle from the trailer and load up."

Rudy jumped up on my head. "If you need bombs, bring me some tass. I can't whip up anything too complicated, but I can rig tass to blow in a jiffy."

"We could use some of those." Naomi stood a little outside our circle of battle planning, Morie at her hip. She looked tired and pale.

O'Meara looked her up and down. "You're wounded, Naomi."

"So is Shina, she's nearly lame." Naomi gestured at the missing arm as Shina snorted. "I don't need my arm to walk.

Give Morie a battle ward; I'll make him a giant eagle and ride. I can make a difference this time."

"Naomi, don't think you need to redeem yourself for getting injured. It's not your fault. Go rest," O'Meara said, dropping her voice to a whisper.

"No." Naomi stared O'Meara down.

Both Shina and I nudged O'Meara. She relented with a sigh. "Fine. Don't try to be a hero this time. Heroes get killed, and I don't want anyone here getting themselves killed." She said as I heard a cold voice inside of her say, *although if our losses are limited to those, that giant bug predicted that it will be a miracle.*

Wouldn't be the first one today, I told her and headed for the truck.

Reentering it felt odd. The same vehicle we had used to run away from this conflict was what we were using to charge back into it. Then, we hadn't known what we were up against. Now, we had an inkling, at least, and some vague outline of a plan solidifying in O'Meara's mind as she oversaw the distribution of tass and weapons.

Shina joined me in the cabin first, and we shared a cheek rub. She hid her pain from our rush healing job well, but it flavored her scent. "We'll get you healed properly as soon as this is over," I promised.

"I will not let this slow me down, Little Lion. We are going to survive. This is the last time any magus will venture into our Savannah without permission. We will bury them here." She growled and subjected the top of my head to a washing.

A tsking sound came from her back, and I peered around her neck to find Midnight crouched on a saddle there. "You former humans cannot even do affection right. Horrible at catting, the both of you." Shina wore the huge Wizard Phooey Mark Five.

"Awww, feeling jealous?" Shina asked, "Here's one for you too, tiny ninja."

"The name is-" he started, but cut off as Shina craned her neck back and licked the small tabby cat from head to tail with a broad lap of her tongue. Midnight shuddered, "Buh, that's almost as bad as Tilly."

She nuzzled my neck. "Now, where were we?"

I opened my mouth, but Rudy's voice got in before I could speak.

"Being mushy," he said, popping up onto the dashboard.

"You bet." I told him and gave my mate a large lick across the side of her face. We ignored our riders for several minutes of purring affection. Then O'Meara climbed up into the cabin and delivered an absolutely savage ear scritching to us both, only relenting when I nearly fell off my seat.

"Time to burn some bones, my kitties!" O'Meara almost sang as she started the engine.

I looked around. The four of us were the only ones in the cab. "Where's everybody else?"

"If you two weren't so intent on distracting each other, you would have noticed me welding handles and casting circles on the rear of the truck. Easier for everyone to bail out when they need to." With an exhalation, O'Meara shifted the gears and the truck rolled out of the cover of the pillar we had hidden behind. Many of the distant dots of magic seemed to stop moving. I could feel many eyes peering at the burning brightness of the battle wards around the truck.

"Peekaboo!" Rudy sang, as my magus and my mate channeled, while I helped shape the spell, directing it outwards using the pile of tass we had set between us.

"Apologies for the mess we are about to create, Maker," Shina prayed in a soft rumble as we poured heat into the ground beneath the truck. The earth moaned and shook as fissures tore through its surface. O'Meara's foot pushed on the gas and we trundled forward, slowly at first but gaining speed with every second. We pushed our heat forward, and the fissures raced alongside and overtook us, where they merged.

The earth yawned open, lava pouring up from its depths. We drove out onto it and the lava surged up under the truck, lifting us high into the air. O'Meara whooped as molten rock surged against the heat ward that surrounded the truck, and tied off the spell as the ground erupted before us, the wave of lava carrying us forward towards the enemy camp.

"Barrier is, like, go!" Farah cried over the radio. The golden-faceted pattern of a panic ward appeared over the windshield as magic lashed out from the House Erebus magi. We ducked back, deeper into the cabin in case of a penetrating spell like Ahimoth's but most of the panicked blasts weren't at us, but at the tsunami of lava we'd conjured. They unleashed a frenzy of beams and bolts into its base, sapping its power. The wave faltered; it began to pitch forward.

"Ready the fleet." O'Meara spoke into the CB and channeled her power into the crystal in the dashboard. A chorus of horns sounded around us. We lifted from the midst of a swarm of duplicate trucks from the wave as it crashed down, sending a blanket of lava hurtling toward the camp. The majority of their magic turned on us and the decoy trucks.

"Willow, ward!" The radio crackled. A great purple-and-gold disk shone in front of the trucks, reflecting the attacks as a mirror.

"Rising Phoenixes!" Naomi shouted, her power lashing down to the spreading lava below us. Dozens of burning wings extended from its surface. With a synchronized flap, a full flock of birds rose below us. More targets, more threats for the invading magi to deal with. We were going to make it. Less than a mile to go.

Shina and I had begun to weave a spell of our own when Rudy shouted with alarm.

"Heads up! I hear anti-magic!"

A gray miasma exploded across our path like a deadly net.

"Bloody ashes!" O'Meara swore, throwing us into a steep dive, trying to thread us beneath the field, but it expanded too fast. We hurtled through. All the illusionary trucks stuttered out and then back into existence within an eye-blink. However, within that moment, House Erebus learned precisely what was and wasn't an illusion. Willow's delicate reflecting ward didn't come back immediately, and a dozen spells struck our front shield at once. It shattered into shards, and without it, the features of the storage yard clarified. Scattered through it were the black auras of the shade lions and other undead. The salvo of spells came from beyond it. A small dome of wards was set against the cliff face, where Shina's vault stood. O'Meara aimed the truck directly for it.

"Meteoro is go." She punched the dash crystal; the doors on either side of the cab blew open a split second before our surroundings lit with the brain-searing brightness of conceptual light. "Everyone, bail, now!"

"Razzle Dazzle Time!" Rudy shouted from my back as I leapt from the passenger seat. I heard the thunderous pop of the Wizard Phooey firing from my back as I stretched out all eight limbs. Blinded by the light, I only perceived the ground when my kinetic ward fired. It felt like getting hit with a cannon loaded with pillows.

As soon as my breath exited my lungs, an explosion thundered over me. The ward tightened over my upper half in time for the earth below me to buck beneath me. "Everyone okay?" I shouted and thought.

Just destroy the vault! O'Meara's voice came back strained.

We got your back, Little Lion! Shina responded as we shook off the daze. Something had knocked the truck off course. Instead of a crater centered on a cluster of magi near the vault, it had impacted the cliff face above it. The wreckage still seethed with the pulsation of the conceptual light, but within it I could just make out O'Meara's wards burning. Worse, we had jumped early, and way too far to use the spear.

Rudy and I had landed in the yard, amid the bones of dozens of lion shades, still smoking from the flare of conceptual light.

Shina and Midnight were ahead of us by fifty feet or so. Riona and her cabal scattered behind us. A panic ward shone around the vault that contained Death's vault. Half of the House Erebus magi were trapped inside, while others struggled with the rubble raining down on them. Less than five hundred feet. Now or never.

Unsheathing the spear! Cover me! I thought to Shina.

As I heard the compressed air of her personal artillery fire, I grabbed hold of the long object inside me and hurled it back into the real world with a, "Hurk!"

The spear fell to the ground, its searing energies whirling within, while my mundane eyes beheld glowing cracks along the shaft.

"Sticky cashew on a bottom of a shoe!" Rudy exclaimed. "That sounds like an explosion contained with spit and bubble gum!"

"It wasn't this bad before you grabbed it out of my stomach!" I shouted back before seizing the shaft with my mouth. My teeth sizzled at its touch as I turned it towards the golden dome.

"Incoming!" Rudy shouted. I dodged to the side as something hit the spear itself, trying to wrench it from my grasp. I gripped it harder but with my magic sight blinded by the spear, all I could see in mundane reality was a slight ripple around the head of the spear.

Slipping sideways revealed the problem, a shadow panther tried to wrestle the spear from my grip. Worse, there were more creatures like him streaking towards me; I'd never seen the sideways space so crowded. "Ruuuddi!" I growled between clenched teeth.

"On it! Boom Kakalaka!" Rudy cried out, flinging a small tass bomb directly into the creature's face. The explosion shredded the shadow cat like fabric, and he let go with a warbling scream, his body dissolving. Spear free, I planted its butt onto the ground as Rudy screamed his best Rambo impression.

Thwang thwang! went the twin catapults, hurling two bombs into the mass of rushing shades. A little one dodged around the blast that claimed so many of his fellows to slam the spear's point back into the ground. This one was the size of Midnight, a shadow with glowing white eyes. Same as the dogs behind the tower, dead familiars. I struck at it with a tass coated spider limb. It yowled as I stabbed through it and flung it from the spear, which had begun to sear my tongue.

Thomas! Hurry before they regroup! O'Meara urged.

Trying! I thought back. Rudy couldn't fling bombs fast enough to deal with all the shadow cats as they surged up through the ground. Nothing for it. I'd have to get close enough that I wouldn't need to aim. I charged, putting all my limbs to the task. They came wailing towards me, more like missiles than animals. Rudy screamed as I flung myself into their midst; twirling my body lengthwise, I lashed out with claws of fire and tass. Their own tass-infused claws shredded my wards as I ripped through their shadow bodies. Their jaws bit at the spear, but none got a solid hold. I landed and Rudy whooped. "You've just been owned by spider-cat! How 'bout that?" Followed swiftly by a pop and an explosion behind me. Sliding back into reality, Shina had fallen behind me, her Wizard Phooey still launching a rain of tass bombs at the dome of the panic ward. Above it, O'Meara had tunneled into the stone for cover as she flung every magic she had available down at the Erebus magi. Caught between the bombs and O'Meara I didn't see any magi casting spells. Through the panic ward I could make out the glistening shine of Death's vault. Close enough, this had to be close enough.

Not stopping, I turned my head to the side and grabbed the end of the shaft with a pincer to steady it. I mumbled the words and bid the spear to destroy. Scorching pain bit through my teeth as power crackled along the spear. Along the spear's blade, white and black flowed up either edge, met at the tip. The energies swirled together, forming a spiraling disk that burned itself into my retina. Just as the energies burst out from the tip, a huge fist exploded from the ground, slamming up into my jaw.

No! I heard both O'Meara and Shina shout, but I was helpless as the blow sent me, Rudy, and the spear arching backwards. The spear carving an arc of nothingness above me. O'Meara burst from the stone face, rocketing toward my attacker before the ground greeted me.

32

I NEVER TOUCHED THE ground. O'Meara caught me, scooped me up, and together we turned to face this new attacker, O'Meara's boots leaving burning skid marks on the ground. A pale giant of a gorilla-like almost-man, oversized arms with fists as large as O'Meara's head resting on the ground. His sloping face grinned with thick, pointed teeth as sparks danced in his empty eye sockets. This was Michael the 2nd, or rather the shadow that puppeted his body made flesh. We'd been too late; he'd opened the vault already. Around his neck hung a small human skull, its jaws holding a black gem. Curling around his left leg, a bobcat with the same pinprick light eyes.

To his side, the spear of Remus lay in sparking pieces. Over his head the void stretched up not even halfway to the ceiling of the Savannah. Useless, all that, and my aim spoiled by a single punch.

"An excellent attack, Mistress O'Meara. That surprise mirror ward slew five magi alone, then the bombardment and your sniping killed the rest that weren't under the panic ward. If tunneling hadn't been at the top of my mind with your escape from Vegas, you might have gotten me, too. But probably not."

Rolling out of O'Meara's arms, I discovered that my right foreleg hung uselessly, forcing the spider leg to compensate. Down to seven legs again.

O'Meara stepped in front of me. "If you have what you want, then we're happy to let you leave. We'll ship your dead home in pine boxes, if you wish." A sword reappeared in her hand.

"Thirty minutes ago, I'd be scared of you. It's been over a hundred years since I've rejuvenated. I was frightened of you when you appeared in my tower. Sixty years under Ghenna and Death's thumb after they stole this from me. And I was scared of so many things." He touched the small skull in a tender fashion. "Now, nothing scares me." His aura lit with power, that black miasma poured out from around his feet. "You cost me the Tower. You have defied me at every turn. Your skulls will decorate the chamber of my new council and sing the tale of your demise." The miasma surged up, lashing out at O'Meara with a thick tentacle.

O'Meara's sword flashed, bisecting the tentacle with white light. "I think you're a little high on your new life, Archmagus, if you think you can take on House Khatt alone. You might be old, but you're no Ahimoth." As she spoke, her body settled into a fighting stance, the spell ripper held out in front of her, the sword held back, ready to strike. Farther down the field the rest of house Khatt were converging on our position. Shina stalked low to the ground; she'd discarded her artillery, maneuvering behind the Archmagus. They were all still here. All standing. All fighting.

Let's do this, I thought at O'Meara, stepping around her legs to stand behind her and extending myself through the link. We shared senses, our minds twisting together, awareness extending to every inch of our bodies.

Shina's confusion lapped at us, but we had no time to address it. We leapt at Michael, our bodies bursting into flame. Our sword slashing at his head and claws, I swiped at the bobcat hiding behind his ankles. The cat shot upwards, riding a geyser of miasma that split into a swarm of tendrils that drove our nearly unwarded cat half back. Meanwhile Michael didn't even bother to dodge the sword, it split his skull ear to ear.

Instead, he opened a giant palm toward our human half and struck with a spike-shaped spell. Human us half dodged, half got flung, back as the white ward, the ward specific against negative energy, rippled and popped like a soap bubble.

We growled. Both the spell ripper and the sword should be able to block his miasma, but we no longer had any room for error.

"Oh, I'm sorry, can you not replace that ward easily?" He laughed, completely unbothered by the missing top third of his head. The pinlights danced in eye sockets half open to the sky. The gem held by the skull amulet whirled with magic and the bone and flesh rapidly regrew while he and the bobcat rapidly wove tight-fitting elemental wards around his body. Clearly, we had to destroy that amulet first.

He wasn't the only one who could break wards, though. We wove a dozen spikes into existence, filling the tips with stasis, the body with fire and launched them in a salvo. He dodged sideways to avoid them, carried by a wave of miasma beneath his feet. The tentacles sprang up in his wake, snatching the darts from the air. As he made to catch the sole remaining dart, we lashed out with the full fury of O'Meara's anchor but not at him. We poured the heat into the ground beneath him. The dirt and rock erupted upwards, propelled by a jet of plasma. His wards shone, but couldn't prevent the blast from hurling him upwards. The bobcat popped from his shoulder with a yowl. Channeling through our feet, we rocketed towards them, cat towards cat, human towards human. We drove our sword at the amulet, but it twisted away from the blade and we skewered only flesh as my tass-laden paw broke the bobcat's back. His hand closed around our forearm. Our paw and arm erupted in pain from the cold burn of his miasma as it burst from them both. Reflexively, our cat body flinched but human muscle memory overruled instinct and drove the buzzing edge of the spell ripper through his wrist.

He screamed as the saw's teeth ripped into bloodless gore and black magic. Human us kicked away, avoiding two tendrils striking for our head.

As we fell back, Shina pounced, snatching the bobcat from the air, her massive jaws crunching down on the front half of the cat. Still clad in the shining white ward of positive energy, the miasma that burst from the body squirted around her teeth. Victory sang through our minds as the familiar's body fell limp onto the ground.

But Michael landed and rolled back up to his feet without so much as a stagger; the light blade fell from his chest. We were not so stable; my left paw pads had been sheared away to the bone, while O'Meara's right arm had nothing but a stick of bone protruding from the elbow.

No familiar, no ward bursting! I'll avenge you, loves. Shina reared up on Michael without bothering to spit out the half cat in her mouth. Claws glowing with tass, she swung paws of stone down towards his head. He ducked away, a flurry of spell work shining in his fist.

Shina, look out! We pulled her awareness to the spell.

At the last moment she flung herself away, as the ward-bursting needle missed her by an inch. She roared with frustration. *I killed his familiar! Crushed it with tass teeth!*

Then I spotted two pinpricks of light hanging over Michael's shoulder. The cat had fled its body entirely. It was hard to see through his armor of wards, but a shadow clung there. *There!*

Damn weasel, Shina growled, springing back at him, swiping at his knees but now more cautious, wary of losing her only protection against the miasma writhing in and out of his body as it desperately defended against the onslaught of magic that O'Meara and I slung towards him. Fire, Earth, and everything else O'Meara had grabbed that we could use without hitting Shina. Most were slapped down by black tentacles, some he dodged, others bounced from his wards. Still, we had him off balance, too busy defending and keeping his amulet out of reach of Shina's claws. Now all he had to do was make one mistake. The others were coming into range. Willow and Farah struck the panic ward with a golden beam and it flared with renewed strength.

Very good!" Michael called out. "Two familiars, very clever. If I only had to deal with you three, I'd be worried." He skated back from Shina and shot off towards the others, zeroing in on Riona with incredible speed. Terror struck us all as the many deaths of Tack rose in our minds.

Oh no, you bloody don't! O'Meara ripped herself from our mind-merge and launched herself as a human rocket, the spell ripper's buzz singing as it cut through the air.

Tack leapt out in front of Riona and let out a thunder clap of a bark, releasing a bolt of whirling yellow and blue. The power of Riona's anchor mixed with something else. The spell exploded, a shockwave that blew away the miasma beneath Michael's feet and coated the ground with green new grass. He tumbled forward, his hands slapped the ground, launching himself into a somersault, and narrowly avoided getting bisected by O'Meara's spell ripper.

O'Meara reversed her thrust and planted her boots, leaving flaming furrows. "Lie down and die, or I will burn out your very heart!" She roared. I felt her pull both her anchor and Shina's knack. Her skin became a rocky gray before heating to the fluorescent red of melted rock. Her exposed bone extending into a sword of magma with it, she became a storm of molten fury that hit Michael without reserve. His miasma lashed out, only to be cut down by her sword. She shoved the spinning saw at his torso. He parried with his arms, sacrificing flesh and wards faster than he could replace either. Still, O'Meara herself diminished as she fended off the slithering miasma, casting off the cooled dead rock.

She's killing herself, I sent at Shina and we rushed into O'Meara's body. We bent her heat to pull fresh material up from the ground as fast as she lost it.

"Give it up!" O'Meara shouted as the buzzing blade scored across his stomach. His tendrils of miasma had thinned as the green of the ground below us sprouted flowers, Riona and Tack's plane of vigor somehow sapping his anchor.

"Not once in over five hundred years have I given up!" he shouted back, erecting a plane of force that we all slammed into before O'Meara shattered it. It bought him a second. "Not while I was under Ghenna's thumb, and you are nothing but a whelp compared to her!" He swept his hand back, as a spell wove inside of him composed of force and darkness. O'Meara thrust the spell ripper out and with his ward shredded, it cut clean through the arm. His attack came from his mouth, a scything tongue sliced through her overextended limb. The spell ripper went arcing from the fight.

"Bastard!" O'Meara swore as she dived around him to re-trieve the spell ripper. Michael turned, bounding in Shina's and my direction toward the border of the green. A new spell already weaving together, this one cave-black as he tore his amulet from his neck. O'Meara leapt, the spell ripper held high over her head of molten stone, pulling as much heat as she could take.

"Be still!" He threw the amulet as he abruptly turned and released the spell. Two waves of blackness exploded out from his body. The first hit O'Meara and ripped her heat away; it froze her body and with second spell her mental scream ended. I lost her. Her body hit Michael's as a thrown statue and it reacted bonelessly, nothing more than meat.

"O'Meara!" I shouted as I realized he'd hit them both with anti-magic. Rendered my magus's body into an unliving statue for half a second, but that been enough. Mr. Bitey reeled back into my head as a void opened up inside of me. "Nooo," I whimpered as my body suddenly filled with stone.

"Not again," Shina whispered beside me and we sagged against each other.

The amulet laughed as pinpricks of light appeared in its eyes, miasma flaring around it. A shadowy arm already extending from it. "Works every time."

Get up, you over grown housecat, O'Meara's voice whispered. *Both of you! Get up.*

O'Meara? I reached for the link, but nothing was there.

Stop looking for me and finish him off. I'm right here with you. We've shared too much of ourselves for me to leave.

A bond ghost, O'Meara was a bond ghost inside of me! I blinked, watching a second arm extend from the gem of the amulet. An incredibly complex spell within it worked as a loom, weaving shadow. A spell. Michael was a spell. That's all.

Listlessly, I pushed at Mr. Bitey. He unwound from my mind and slithered around Shina's neck.

"No, Thomas." She whispered at me. "I'm tired."

"We can't rest yet. O'Meara says get up. Do you hear her?" I asked, inhaling Shina's dusky scent. The rocks in my body lightening. Not alone.

"Yes," she breathed, "And damnit, she's right."

The link opened between us and our souls flowed, heavy with the shock of a sudden absence, but together we bore each other up and stood.

The amulet stopped laughing. His head had appeared and his torso was oozing out of the gem. The seeds of bone appeared in the shadows of his hands. "Oh? You can get up so soon? Go ahead and run. I'll find you."

I slowly limped over to the other side of him. Putting him between myself and Shina. "Not running."

"Heh. Bat at me if you wish. You'll only burn your paws." The miasma surged out of the gem, a protective pyre.

Shina pulled at her knack and redirected it, forming a thin stone casting circle between us. There, in the casting circle together, we saw the shadow of the 4th-dimensional spell that actually was both Michael the 2nd and his familiar. A massive construct of runes that held the threads that composed their minds and the connections they made. The loom part busily worked weaving together the shadow body and fed it the power to create flesh. The whole thing was set up to twitch if threatened, making the amulet dodge in three-dimensional space. The rest of it had no such function. Extending ourselves, we simply began to cut at the most fragile-looking parts.

A shiver went through the shadow of Michael, as we cut the strands of the loom. His extrusion halted. "What? What did you do?"

In the spell, a thick thread, almost a cable, swelled with energy and we quickly tied a knot in it. The miasma died away. "My anchor!" He wailed.

"Can't cut it yet," I said; my own voice sounded cold to my ears.

"It's part of the original soul. It will drift apart once we unlace the supports." Shina responded with an equally clinical tone.

"You can't do that!" He lashed out with his arm and Shina plucked a strand. The arm disappeared, the bones of the hand falling like white Chiclets onto the ground. "You're not magi!"

I chuckled. "Magi, familiars, not much difference. You know how this works, we may lack primal planes to draw from, but you don't need that to take a spell apart."

"No! Not like this!" He groaned as his other arm disappeared. The spell shuddered, some whirling bits stopped and others spun. Shifted gears.

"None of that," Shina said, tearing off a piece, and the spell stilled. "It's a better way to go than to be snuffed out like O'Meara. Make your peace with the world, Michael the 2nd. We're going as fast as we can, but we don't want to get that nasty black flame of yours all over anything." Her voice ended on an almost tender note.

"I can bring her back! It is not too late; the threads can take days to decay sometimes." He pleaded. "She'd be almost back to normal in a few years."

We paused. Our eyes meeting across the circle.

Blood and ashes, you two. Don't you dare. O'Meara's voice rang through our heads.

Together we nodded, then started pulling apart the core of the spell. "Since there is no Council to serve justice, Michael The 2nd of House Erebus, in the name of House Khatt and,"

"The Pride of the Savannah Below."

"We find you guilty of murder,"

"And the attempted murder of hundreds more."

"The sentence is death." I finished and pulled the final thread free. The spell came apart and the tangle at the very center of the immortality spell stood exposed.

Michael made a small sound before the threads of many colors unraveled. The lights of his eyes separated and guttered out.

33

"THE REST OF THEM have surrendered. Farah doesn't trust them and is keeping them trapped in the panic ward for now. She says she can keep it up for a few days if she has to, so long as they don't try cutting out of it." Willow knelt next to me.

My eyes were still on O'Meara's face, trapped in the smooth glassiness of cooled volcanic stone. *I don't suppose asking her to teleport all of them into the middle of a sun is a viable answer?*

Magic gets tricky off planet. Active volcanoes are much more efficient, O'Meara answered.

It's going to be tricky to mourn you with you inside my head, I told her.

In time I'll settle in, drift farther into your subconscious, quiet down. I've been through this more than a couple times, remember? I could almost feel her hand on my back. *Sir Rex still talked to me until you showed up. And well, there's far more of me in here than there ever was of him.*

"Thomas? Farah can't hold the ward forever." Willow asked me again, and I remembered the horrors they created in the basement of that tower. Yet if we cracked the ward open, we'd have another fight on our hands.

"Sorry," I said. "I'm not really in a state for thinking clearly."

"Let me, Love." Shina bent and kissed my shoulder. "We don't have the strength to kill them all at this moment. Tell House Picitrix they're here. They fought what the Erebus released into the city. They might still be fighting it."

Willow nodded, "Okay, with Riona and Tack, we might be able to get the whole jug of them above ground."

Now we don't have to use all that tass to teleport them into a volcaco, Shina thought at me. I leaned against her, feeling like I wanted to sleep for at least a month.

Rudy sat nearby, idly chewing on a peanut, which was a measure of his own mood.

"Rudy... How much tass we got left?" I asked softly.

He shoved the nut into a cheek pouch and his iPhone appeared from thin air. Another new trick. "I dunno. I haven't been here that long, been burning through it like napalm." And yet after pressing a few buttons, he declared. "Bout five hundred groat."

"Gather it all," I said. "As soon as we get the prisoners squared away, I want everyone here and all the fey chains."

Thomas... O'Meara started. *I'm happy with how it turned out. It wasn't in vain. I can rest with that.*

"There's no point to magic if we can't work a miracle every now and again. With time, tass, and knowledge we can do anything. Two out of three ain't bad," I said.

"Little Lion, that was a hideously complex spell. It had connections to over a dozen planes. We can't replicate that." Shina's foreleg slipped around my neck and held me to her chest.

"Not going to do it that way. We're not shooting for immortality. Just one more chance. One more go-around." I purred at her. "But I'll need you. You've made a species before. Doesn't the God Mother have one more miracle in her?"

She rifled through the embryonic plan gestating in my brain. "That's... not... Only if she agrees, Thomas. Even if it works, it's not quite a resurrection."

We waited. I couldn't see O'Meara in my own head, but I could feel her shifting weights in my thoughts as she explored the idea. Stroking its feathers and neck, considering. She reached out and touched the tiny piece of her that lay in

Shina's mind. Compared herself to it before drawing it with her back into me.

I'll do it. From the bloody ashes.

You can do anything with Time, Tass and Knowledge. I'd add to that a good night's sleep and no broken limbs if I could, but then we might run out of time. Time is the one thing you can never get more of, no matter how hard you try. Well, thinking back to Archibald and what burst out of him, maybe I'd simply say the price is too damn high.

Focus. Shina nudged me and I shook my head to clear it of the fog.

Almost there, I lied to myself, as House Khatt solemnly gathered around O'Meara's body. All on the edge of a casting circle. With the four Fey chains, I had bonded Shina, Riona, Willow and Naomi. Through them stood Reynard, Morie and Tack. I held Mr. Bitey in reserve. Seven minds. I kept them all at a distance except for Shina who propped me up, siphoning off exhaustion and pain. I couldn't let her take too much; she had a role to play in this.

When I first met Weaver, I had watched her pull a magus back from death. I replayed that memory over and over. She caught threads of his life and wove them back together while healing the body. The anti-magic that Michael had hit O'Meara with hardens reality, forces matter to obey the rules of our reality. It doesn't destroy the magic, but prevents its action. I don't stop being intelligent when I'm in one, at least not immediately. But he had combined the blast with another dark spell that had cooled O'Meara, frozen her, really. Perhaps moving molten stone is alive enough that O'Meara would have clung on through that brief blast. Magically though, bodies seem to remember being alive. The first thing though, we had to make her whole.

With a nod, Naomi extended her hand into the circle and pushed forth her power. The edges of the stone fluttered. O'Meara's arms, frozen in their dramatic pose began to stretch, and then her legs, which had broken at the knees when she landed, each sprouted their own pair of wings.

No! Naomi pulled back, the stone snapping to its original form. *Not sure this is going to work, Thomas.* Her eyes sought mine. *She's all in separate pieces.*

Try again, I urged, *She's one whole. One whole. One Bird.*

One egg, Shina suggested. *The start of a bird.*

One egg, Naomi echoed, balling up her fist. *One, only one.* Her magic flared. Again wings sprouted, this time from many places, the stone's surface trembling as if to pull itself apart. Morie's will pushed into the circle, pushing the errant wings back into O'Meara's body. *It's like it wants to be many birds. There's a flock inside the stone. I've never tried to control stone birds before, I usually let them become what they want to be.*

As if my body wants to decay. O'Meara's voice echoed through my mind.

I ignored her and growled, *It's not stone, Naomi; it's O'Meara. You force her to be the bird you want her to be,* I thought at her and then joined Morie, pushing wings back into the stone. Others joined in, not allowing any piece to escape and as Naomi strained, the statue began to twist and change. The spell ripper fell from her grip, fingers opening as her index fingers stretched out. The bared teeth yawned open as a curved and sharp beak pushed out. The surface of her clothing rippled into feathers. Limbs to started to twitch.

Not yet! You can't fly yet, Naomi whispered to it. *You're an egg, you have to develop. Rest.* Slowly, O'Meara's figure shifted, curling up into a fetal position.

Shina offered up her knack to me; with it we reached into the earth below and crafted a shell of stone around her, creating an egg. With her encased, we used the pile of tass and crafted spells to sustain the flow of Naomi's energy.

Still she strained, *she's still stone; I can't convince her to turn back to flesh. My anchor's the concept of birds, not biology.*

Then we have to supply that. Riona offered up the plane of life's vigor, directing it into the egg. Nothing happened. *There's something there. A heart, but this magic isn't finding something to latch onto.*

A stone bird. Cold stone. Life for O'Meara, more than her blood, was the fire. I had to find her Anchor plane. No, I corrected myself, we had to find it. We had Earth through Shina, sound through Riona. *Let me see,* I asked of them. A moment of hesitation, and both of them opened themselves wide to me and I extended myself through them. The two threads couldn't be more different, thick steel cabling guided me to Riona's pulse of vibration and sound, while the path to Shina's living stone was ephemeral and not forged of soul at all but memories. Wisps of narratives played as I followed along it, the sensation of skin and bone hardening to stone. Over years of drawing from this plane, instinctually, Shina had found her own path to it. Along them both I scuttled, hunting for the scent of burnt cinnamon. I found fire, all bearing different scents and heats, but not hers. I called to mind the pleasant feeling of my fur bursting into flame, the way it leapt with my anger. How I reached for it.

If memories alone can create a connection, O'Meara stirred in my mind, *then we have all we need.* She reached for her fire; it did not greet her but she kept reaching, calling out to it. Together we remembered its searing heat, how it refused to harm us even as plasma danced over our skins. The memories played like songs as I moved through the planes of magic. And finally I felt a tug, a thread, a thick, severed one, wrap around me and squeeze with the joy of a lost thing suddenly being found. It smelled of burnt cinnamon even as it leaked a searing heat into me, I dragged it back to reality. There, as if suddenly frightened, it fought us. Patches of hair and skin burst into flame as it whirled like a snake. Collectively, we wrestled it to the egg, lashed it there with tass and forced it to warm the chest of the Bird O'Meara within.

We watched the heat eddy there as Naomi and Riona poured magic into it.

Be bird.

Be alive.

Something in the chest squeezed that core of heat and then slowly it began to flow, branching out into vessels and channels, growing into the pattern that speaks of life. A cheer went up among us but there was still so much work to be done. Shina stepped forward, spinning small spells, nudging the magic, helping it balance the transition as we coaxed the stone back to flesh and the lava to blood. Yet there is more to a soul than the anchor and life. Tack howled out a long note, and Riona lifted her voice into a wordless melody. Slowly, the web of silver strands came into focus. One by one Riona and Tack collected the severed, grieving strands that once connected all of us to O'Meara, and tied them to the new life within the egg. Other strands that we had no name for threaded in from the ethers. Components of O'Meara's original soul called back or new threads that all life summoned, we didn't know. As they wove together, a new thing appeared, a mind.

I bonded it and stepped out into a white mindscape. Totally blank, yet it felt familiar all the same, inviting, the fiery anchor settled in the precise way it had before. This new thing still remembered what it was before.

O'Meara stepped into it, carrying an armload of baggage. I saw her for the first time since her death. She wore the mantle of cooling rock. Black skin with iron-hot light shining from her eyes and at her joints. I indulged myself by curling around her legs and rubbing my cheek against her hip. She stared up at the whiteness of the new mind.

Her fingers caressed my ear. "Is this right?" she asked. "This could develop on its own. It doesn't have to become me."

"If I wanted children, I'm pretty sure Shina and I can come up with a much more enjoyable way to do it." I nosed her.

She laughed and hugged me tightly. "Fair. Shina as family is going to be interesting. I haven't had to deal with family beyond a familiar for very long time."

"I don't know the future," I said, "but it's much brighter with you standing with us."

"It will certainly be brighter and hotter." O'Meara wiped away tears.

The merest glimmer of a chair appeared in the whiteness, more of a receptacle, really. "That looks like an invitation to me," I said, nudging her toward it.

With a shaky breath, O'Meara stepped up to the chair and touched its arm. It pulled color from the tips of her fingers, a swirl of black and red. The fingers flinched back and she stuck them in her mouth as if burned. "I'm not going to be the same. I might not even be close. Memories are one thing but bodies matter too. More so for human magi than familiars. I think with my brain and this one is not the same."

"O'Meara," I leaned against her thigh for the last time. While it looked like hot stone it still had the give of well-cushioned muscle. "I love you. That won't change. No matter what happens. Whether you stay with us or fly away."

"And I you. You overgrown housecat. When I get out of this thing, you better be waiting for me." She squeezed my scruff and scratched my neck. I purred for her. Then she flung herself into the seat. Immediately she began to spread into it, her essence swirling into the white canvas around her, taking root. Small pieces of the black stone flaked away, pushed aside by black and red feathers. Her eyes grew distant as she became the landscape around me.

"We'll have a birthday party," I told her and licked her hand. "Goodbye till then."

After a last look I stepped back into my own head and found it rather... spinny. "Wha?" I asked out loud, wobbling before the great egg that contained my magus and friend.

"You're tired," Shina whispered in both my mind and my ear. "It's time for you to rest."

Around us magi slumped with their familiars. Weariness flowed through us all, along with a satisfaction. We'd won, then we'd saved O'Meara. Now, we were all too damn tired to do anything else. The egg radiated a gentle heat that warmed my fur like a sunbeam. "She's okay? We don't have to do any more?"

Shina rolled onto her back and patted her chest in invitation. "Everything's stable. She needs time to grow now. I wonder what sort of bird she'll be?"

"Black and red," I said, giving in and lying down beside her, propping my head on her chest. With a single breath, I fell into a much-needed sleep.

34

THE FIRST GLIMMER OF light pulsed out from the nearest underground sun, and my eyes opened. Arrival day. The thought
made my tail twitch. Couldn't quite muster up the energy
to move immediately, enjoying the warmth of Shina's body
against mine, while the air tasted of a dewy morning's chill.
Also, her foreleg draped across my ribs, which increased the
effort required considerably. Not that it was particularly hard
to remove, I just never wanted to. I licked at her wrist and got
a warning rumble in response.

"It's arrival day," I told her, my tail twitching a little bit more.

"Not this minute. You could let someone else handle it." She
chuckled and groomed the top of my head.

"And miss their adorable expressions when we explain how
they'll actually meet their first familiar candidate? Where's the
fun in that?" I purred. Still, we lay together until I heard the
heavy whoosh and the stained creak of wood outside. Then I
rolled up onto my paws and allowed myself a luxurious head
to tail stretch that made my spine crackle.

Our den wasn't much, a simple oval room, carved out of the
rock. Bookshelves clung to a quarter of the wall space, a few
low tables, lots of dog beds scattered about and a seventy-two
inch TV that also served as a computer monitor. A perfect
space for us to retreat to. Small LED lights mounted on
the ceiling provided the soft illumination of a moonlit night.
Perfect for Shina and me, unless we were reading. Besides the
emergency escape route buried beneath the pillow fort we

called our bedroom, the only entrance was a circular entryway covered by heavy hide curtains.

My doorbell rang sharply, which was literally a chime hanging outside with a small hammer hung nearby on a chain. Although by the tone and loudness of the ring I could tell it had been hit by something considerably larger. "I'm up! Keep your beak on," I called out through curtains, telekinetically grabbing one of several me-sized harnesses by the door, the gaudy one with gold and silver threaded embroidery that I used for official business. The latest emblem for House Khatt, a ring of eight connected circles on its shoulders.

I buckled it on and checked my reflection in a small mirror, making sure I had closed all but two of my eyes. In the years since we vanquished House Erebus, most of Weaver's additions had reverted to normal; the extra legs had fallen off in a few weeks, the spinnerets and fangs after a few months, but after ten years, I still had eight eyes. Everyone's quite used to them now but I try to keep six of them closed for newcomers. Weaver usually leaves the apprentices alone. Usually.

The chime rang twice. "Coming!" I called, licking the back of my paw and slicking a patch of fur back into place. Then I pushed aside the curtain and stepped out onto our front porch. "You should have gotten the early worm without me," I grumbled at O'Meara, who perched on a log as thick as a telephone pole. A titanic cross between a raven and a songbird, even perched she stood four feet tall, the plumage of her wings, crest and long tail feathers the glowing red of embers, while her underside feathers were black as coal, with a diamond of ash gray on her throat.

Bloody Ashes, Thomas, O'Meara said as the mental connection clicked open. *Let's get a move on. I'm wasting away here. See?* She opened wings that could hug an entire basketball team to display her sleek avian body. It looked no more or less skinny than it had yesterday.

Could have gone without me. I nosed her black-scaled feet. One of them lifted from the log to carefully scratch at my ears with one of her long talons. She's only skewered me once.

And let you get there at a sedate pace? You'd miss the meal and then be hangry at me all day, she laughed; it had a note of a hoot to it.

"I'm sure they'd save some food for the Giver," I mumbled unconvincingly; lions weren't the greatest at sharing food. Then I looked out over the Savannah towards Maker Mountain. From this distance, it was a column of rock thick as a finger stretching between the earth and the equally rocky blue-colored sky.

We lived midway up the slope of the underground's second mountain, the bastion. It appeared shortly after Erebus' invasion; it didn't quite touch the ceiling sky. Surrounded by a wide river, it marked a barrier between the Savannah and more temperate forest suitable for cougars. A network of caves, coupled with rock laced with a strange sort of tass that made it highly resistant to both magic and explosives. The Maker had given us a fortress. We kept to the upper chambers; the basement had a rather large spider, and you never knew whether she was home or not.

Regardless of Weaver's plans, it had been a good place to call home. The Cat's Meow Casino remained the main gate entry to this underground wilderness. In another half-decade, it will reach Vegas, and that will be an entirely new can of worms. Sometime beyond then, Shina and I will have to find the right point to use the key I wear around my neck. That's a problem for future me; today I just had to worry about the Arrivals.

Our mountainside apartment had multiple ways off the mountain and down into the forest below. A winding path for a nice stroll, a basket with zip line down into the village, and finally, an extended platform with no railing. Onto this third one I walked, activating a second bracelet-held spell that cut my weight down to that of a burly bobcat.

Shina poked her head out of the den and yawned.

O'Meara's red crest laid back. *Oh, you're up now too, Shina? Does this mean I have to get the harness on?* Her distaste for the feeling of buckles and straps on her feathers shone through the words.

"No, child, I'll take a rover with my daughters." Shina said with her grandmother tone, causing O'Meara's feathers to bristle.

No changing your mind. O'Meara turned, screeching like an eagle and leapt off her perch, diving down the slope of the mountain. Wings spread, she channeled slightly, instantly creating a thermal that sent her soaring upwards.

"You just had to ruffle her feathers, didn't you?" I accused Shina as I edged closer the edge of the diving board. Above, O'Meara climbed to a height where I lost her against the gray of the early morning sky.

"She lets those adolescent hormones go to-"

I missed the rest of it as I spotted the red of O'Meara's feathers streaking down the mountainside and snapped my head to point forward, arched my back and fought the instinct to dig my claws into the wood beneath me. I closed all my eyes but my rear ones to watch her approach, as at the last second her wings flashed open and those terribly sharp talons umbrellaed open. They hooked the handle and plucked me from the platform. Wind tore into my fur as I hurtled toward the tree line and then we pitched up as my heart confused my wind pipe for an escape route.

O'Meara! I protested and heard an echo of Shina's own scolding.

The former fire magus and now young Phoenix laughed as she'd wobbled in a wing wave to Shina. *We missed the trees by a mile. I didn't even have to channel.*

You're going to whack my tail clean off my ass on those treetops one of these days, I told her, forcing my muscles to relax and hang bonelessly in her grip.

I wouldn't let that happen. She tilted and we curved around into the upward spiral of a thermal. We lapsed into silence as we climbed to the point where we could see the individual stones that made up the sky. Breaking from the thermal, we soared effortlessly toward the Maker's Mountain.

See! Without that harness I don't have to channel at all. I'm strong enough now we can just fly. It's soo much better. Don't you agree? she thought at me, but I sensed a bump in the stream of chatter.

What's wrong? I asked her gently. *What's really bothering you? You feeling caged again? Are we asking you do too much?* Carefully I slid memories of her being excited about the harness and the enchantments that allowed her to carry both Shina and myself deeper into my mind, shielding her from them. She had been a fourth of her current size when she had hatched almost a year after we'd sealed her into that egg. She'd been able to fly, but more like a turkey than the graceful predator she'd grown into. Shina had mothered her hard in her bedrock way. O'Meara had taken well to it at first, weakened and wanting comfort. Now they butted heads as O'Meara tried to sort out the instincts of her body and reconcile them with the person she'd been.

The harness makes me feel like a mule. Constrained, it reminds me... Nevermind. Her mind roiled as she stuffed her human-born memories away.

Then we'll take other transport. You'll just have to be patient when it takes us longer to get where we're going, I chuckled.

She cawed unhappily. O'Meara the phoenix made Rudy look patient.

Or take two trips, I suggested.

That earned me a full-on disgusted squawk.

We'll figure it out. Like we always do. I sent her a mental hug as I dangled from her talons. Life with O'Meara and Shina had been one big figuring it out session. In the last two years, she'd moved out of our den, built her own, then moved back and forth twice. She'd left entirely once, breaking our bonds, then returning six weeks later to nestle between us without a word. That had been a happy night. Overall, it's a happy life.

Why are you purring? she asked, pushing lightly into my mind.

Just thinking, you want to see? I opened myself up to her, she fluttered in, prodding at my memories and I sent the purr through the link.

Stop that! Not while I'm flying. She took a breath deep enough to visibly swell her chest. *Not sure what's worse, Shina treating me a like a hatchling or seeing myself complain through your way too many eyes.* She lifted me closer to her body and I lifted my head to press into her soft feathers. Our in-flight hug.

We're willing to make any adjustments you want, I told her as she lowered me back into cruising position.

She paused. *What if instead of making the two of you lighter, you grew your own wings?*

I laughed. *Let's talk to Naomi when we get the chance; should have enough tass after the arrivals.*

The wings flapped hard, *Bloody ashes, of course you'd say that. I could tell you I'm going to rain nuclear fire down on the upper world, and you'd roll over for a belly rub.*

*Only for you, and sometimes Shina. The rest of the world gets to see the teeth of Thomas, the eater of Archmagi. Thinking of...*Maker's Mountain had grown to the point where I could see the bustling village that sprawled out from its base. Low and wide lion-made brick buildings dominated with a minority of human-made trailers and RVs scattered among them. The tall stone pillar of the cargo elevator was slowly descending. *Why don't we give the arrivals a bit of a show this year?*

O'Meara's anchor lit and the ember glow of her feathers brightened to a blazing orange-yellow hue. *Remember you asked for this one, luv.*

I shut all of my eyes as O'Meara did her level best to outrace my stomach.

Acknowledgments

THANK YOU FOR READING. It's been a long and strange road traveling with Thomas and Rudy up to this point and I'm glad you've stuck with me to the end. With this book Thomas's adventure through the magical world has come to an end. He's found/created his place within it. While his struggles are hardly over, others will be doing the journeying. Never fear though, Rudy will always be venturing out, looking for mountains to blow up.

This book was difficult to write as I'd never written one so focused on endings before. It took a very long time for me to decide how to bring all the threads I'd so helpfully scattered niley wiley through the series into a bow that made some sense. Many thanks to my spouse, Amanda, who endured my moaning and griping about how I couldn't get the pieces to fit or how terrible and flat the story was. After 17 years of marriage they're very patient with me.

Many thanks to the people who helped me along the way. Ryu Takemori (WWCO) for doing our sketch-a-thons; Doug Peterson, Dan "Silvermoon Howler" Czarnecki, and Loren Foster for the in-depth beta reading; Andrea Johnson for your always stellar editing. Throughout the process everyone in the Familiar Freehold Discord server was cheering me on, thank you all for that support.

Then, near the end of the journey that was this novel, I got a wild idea to mark the end of the Freelance Familiars with a special slipcover case for all the novels and to use Kickstarter to fund it. Thanks to Russell Nohelty and Monica Leonelle for teaching me how to construct a killer campaign. Thanks also to fellow authors, Jamie Davis, Sarah Biglow, Dyrk Ashton and Tao Wong among others for contributing and promoting the campaign. Over its twenty-two day run we reached just shy of fifteen thousand dollars; bringing the boxset into existence. Thank you everyone who pledged, whether it was a buck or two or you went into the project and became one of my Grand Pumas. I am grateful to have you all as fans and friends. Thank you!

We declare these backers to be

GRAND PUMAS

Dan "Silvermoon Howler" Czarnecki

William Blackwell

Kevin 'sonicthe' Lancaster

Mark (Tger) Grummell

Aria Andrea

Andrea Johnson

Katie Ford

Derek J. Bush

Merv DeGriff

Seth Evans

Scott Pezza

Geo Holms

J. Zachary Pike

Tyler Graham

Cristina

Jacob Sharpsteen

Bryan Haven

George McKinney

Stephanie Shotton

Baylong

Mizuhiro Neko

Josh Emerick

Ryan Hayes

RG Potter

Ryan Scott James

Austin

Xolner

Tommy

Magentawolf

Gabrielle Duncan

BSmithSmithKS

Christine Elliott & Marilyn Sanders

Skogskisse

Marco "Fuwo" Nowak

Duncan Cougar

Steady Prism

Catprog

TOURMENTE Benoit

And a Special Thanks to...

Peter Ford
Rob Martindale
wayne
Robin Hill
Michelle
Michael Brooker
Peggy Kimbell
Chris S.
John E. Rose
Nicholas R. Soika
Robert Barbour
Marcus Merritt
Michael van Dijk
Ooh Cee
Thomas Millesich
Andrew Taylor
Merk
Justin Berger
RecklessPrudence
Eric Altmyer
Hachemalum
lese_terrible
Rhel ná DecVandé
Beth

Gary Phillips
Dread_Priest
Christopher Glen Stritch
Lifeforce
Ian Cummings
Stevie Maxwell
Joe Tuggle
Ryu Takemori
dcp9142
Steven Sledziona
Michael DiCarlo
Chris Gilmer
BirdBrain25
GhostCat
Dodson Brown
Kyle Wilkinson
Deborah Hedges
Snepril
Jim Whaley
Robert Molivas
Bevin Redding
Furrhan
Darryl Malloy
HardWorkLucky

ALSO BY DANIEL POTTER

Freelance Familiars

Off Leash

Marking Territory

High Steaks

Aggressive Behavior

Pride Fall

Apex Familiar

Rudy & the Warren Warriors (a FF short story)

The Full Moon Medic

Emergency Shift

Midnight Triage

Soul Shock

Twilight Run (Book 0 short story)

Rise of the Horned Serpent

Dragon's Price

Dragon's Cage

Dragon's Run

Dragon's Siege

CPSIA information can be obtained
at www.ICGtesting.com
Printed in the USA
JSHW021632080822
29037JS00002B/5